SECRETS DON'T STAY BURIED

J. D. MILLS

This book is for everyone who has ever felt like they couldn't stand
up for themselves. For anyone who struggled to find their voice, or to
feel accepted while the devil on their shoulder whispered
"you aren't enough".

You are deserving of all of the love in the world.
Don't let anyone tell you otherwise.

AUTHOR'S NOTE

This work of fiction features mentions of sexual assault, the non-consensual sharing of nude images, and sexual conduct among minors (which includes both of the above). Please prioritize your mental health, and if this content is not suitable for you at this time—or ever—no one will fault you for putting this book down without reading any further. You can walk away without another thought and know that I, the author, am proud of you for doing what is best for you.

With that being said, I do want to emphasize that none of these things happen *on the page*. Rather, they are recalled through memories as characters talk to one another, or through ruminating on their own thoughts. While these characters are adults now, they may not have been when each of them experiences their own trauma.

We all have different ways of processing our traumas, and—while mine doesn't look *exactly* as it does for any of the characters in this novel—this work is my way of dealing with that trauma and of working through the scars it's left on me.

None of us make it out of this life alive, you know.

If you choose to continue on and read this book, I thoroughly hope that you enjoy it and find something worthwhile within its pages. There are few things better than a book that just 'gets it' and for me it was writing this one (although I truly feel that way about every novel I write—because why would I continue writing it if I didn't feel connected to it, right?).

Anyway...

I have a point, I swear.

Should you turn the page and start the first chapter, know this: I wrote this book as a testament to the strength of survivors.

No one gets to tell your story except for you.

And if you never tell it?

That's perfectly okay.

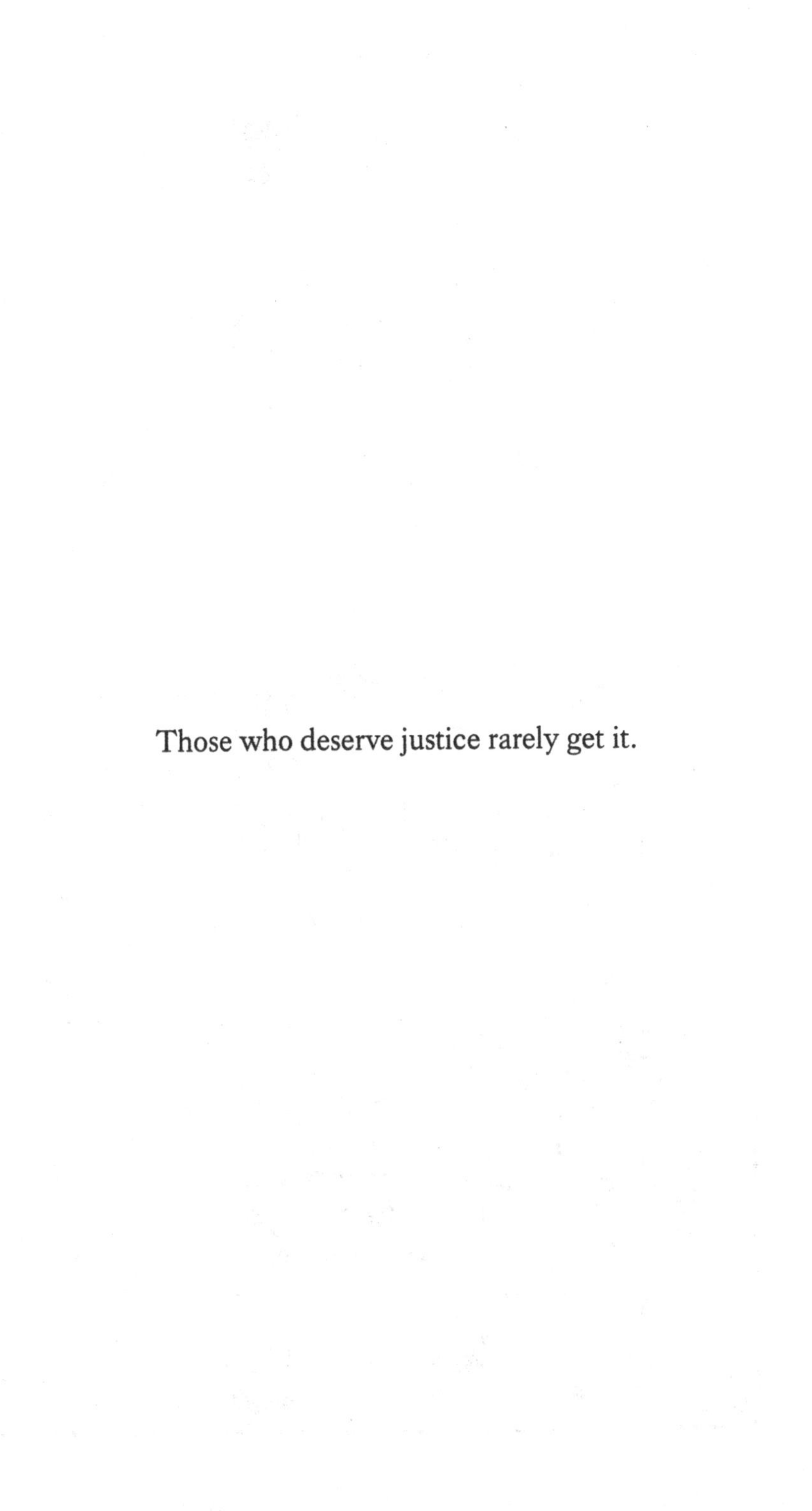

Those who deserve justice rarely get it.

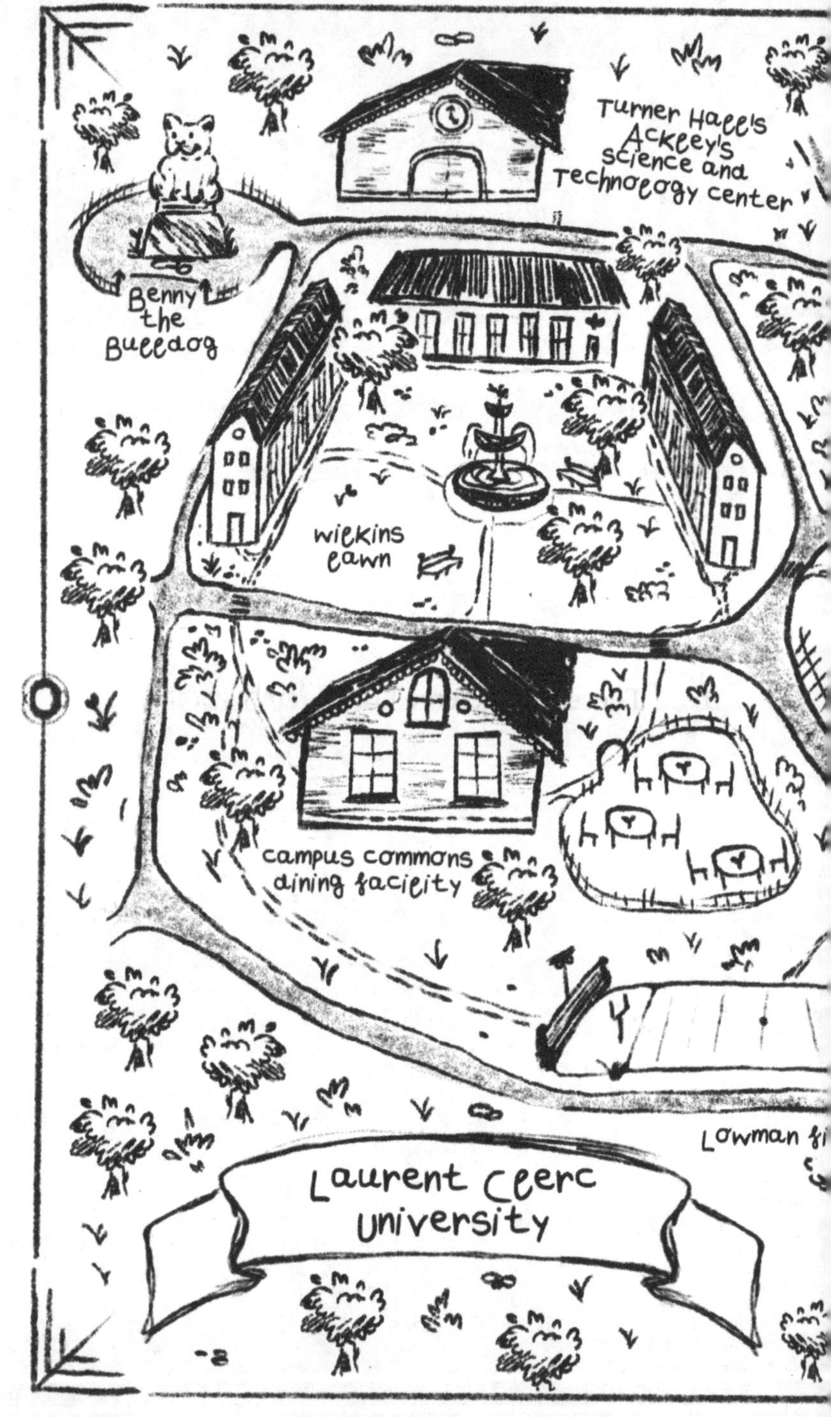

Turner Hall's
Ackley's
science and
Technology center
Benny
the
Bulldog
wickins
lawn
campus commons
dining facility
Lowman fi
Laurent Clerc
University

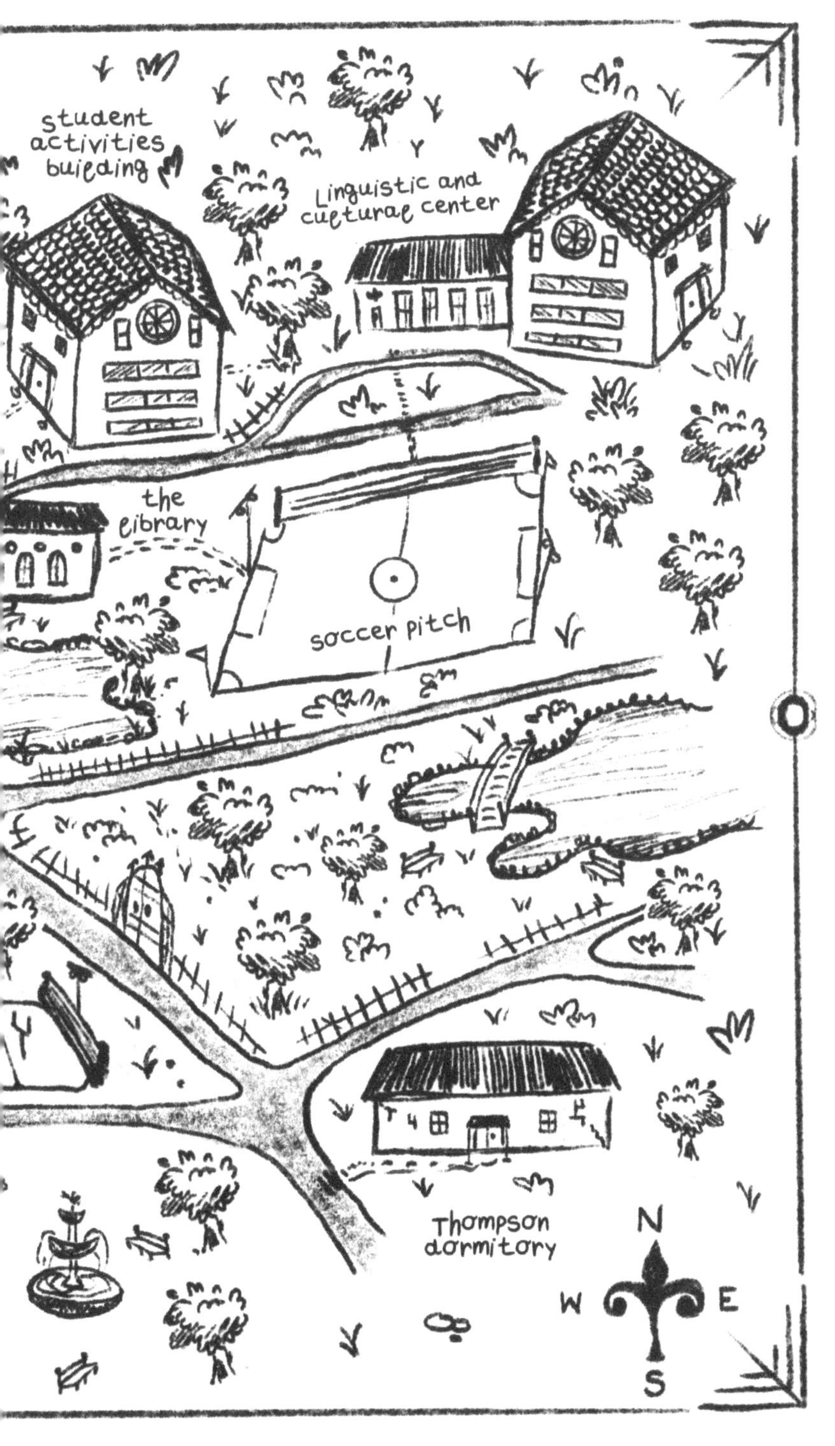

student activities building
Linguistic and cultural center
the library
soccer pitch
Thompson dormitory
N
W
E
S

THE DAY OF THE MURDER

The last thing I expected to see outside my dorm tonight was a dead body.

Blue and red lights dance across the pavement and against the walls of nearby buildings, streaking in through the windows. The lifeless corpse below stares upward with wide eyes that do all but glow in the darkness of the night. Police officers are hurriedly working the scene while attempting to keep everyone in their rooms. My eyes struggle to focus as my field of vision wobbles with the striations of bright light interrupting the darkness. The first officers to arrive set up yellow caution tape barriers to deter onlookers, but a grim crowd gathers outside anyway.

Each breath I take is ragged and jittery. I can't seem to catch it, no matter how deep I crawl into my own chest. Every time I avert my eyes, somehow they drift back and I'm left gazing at the sheet-covered corpse that hasn't yet been lifted from its concrete bed.

This death could've been prevented. If I'd spoken up and told someone what was going on, she might've been spared. This could have ended with me. Instead, her fate was sealed by the unfortunate fact we both chose to attend the same university at the same time. But despite my suffocating guilt, I'm not entirely sure how I got here.

The cool night air hits me in the face the moment I step into the room. Glass litters the floor, sparkles reflecting against the books and pens that are scattered along the carpet. Alarm bells go off in my head and they're louder than my tinnitus has ever been.

There was a struggle.

Bronya's neatly kept bedspread is disheveled and the lampshade has been tilted off-kilter. A few of the photos she'd once taped to her wall have blown onto the floor.

A lone light pole is shining a spotlight onto her body, the contortions of flesh and bone against the blood-blackened cement. Staring down through the shattered glass, all that's left of her is the empty shell of the fashion-obsessed volleyball player I could never seem to connect with. Double-jointed limbs crack and bend in distorted positions as bites of second-hand agony shoot through my legs. The back of her skull is shattered open, leaking a sticky pool of saccharine blood that has already soaked crimson through the once-white ribbon I'd watched her tie into her hair this morning. Color has drained from every inch of Bronya's fair skin, leaving nothing but the artificial rosy tone of blush on the apples of her cheeks.

Falling to my knees, I wretch into the trash can, spewing the contents of my stomach into the plastic liner. The carne asada burrito I had for dinner is barely recognizable, paired with a disgusting scent that turns my stomach a second time. Then a third.

The smell of vomit gets stuck in my nose, from too many minutes spent hovering above the bile-filled trash can. Finley was the one to dial emergency services after she rushed over, beckoned by a panicked FaceTime call. Now, the warmth of her embrace envelops me as we sit on the edge of my bed. She tells me it's okay, but we both know she's lying

Nothing about this is okay.

I'm still for a while, uniforms buzzing and pelting me with questions that I can't quite comprehend. They ushered me out at some point, but mentally I'm still in that room with Bronya and my lingering guilt. By the time I come to, I'm no longer there—I'm at the police station.

Swiveling my head too fast, a wave of dizziness

crashes into me.

I spot the interpreters once the room stops spinning. Detective Melendez is sitting across from me, leaning back in his seat while I search his face for a tell. His brow briefly dips in the center, then relaxes. The American Sign Language interpreter beside him shifts their gaze between us, waiting to find out which of us will speak first. Another interpreter is in a chair a few feet away, their foot gently bouncing beneath the weight of crossed legs.

"Do you want some water?" The interpreter-as-detective asks.

I shake my head, uncertain I could keep it down.

The skin on my arms have turned to gooseflesh beneath the billowy sleeves of my hoodie. It was the only thing I'd thought to grab before being brought here, and wearing it now makes me feel small. Like a child in their parent's sweatshirt, it's four times too big and a poor suit of armor for what I'm about to face.

This room makes me feel like a suspect in Bronya's death. My roommate's death—oh god, my roommate is actually gone. Bronya's gone and I'll never see her again. I won't see her alive again.

My palms are sweating. Shit. That's making me look guilty.

"Do you have any idea who would want to hurt your

roommate?"

The interpreter repeats his words, signing them to me for full linguistic access.

How long was I distracted?

I don't say a word. Instead, my fingers pick at the seams of my jeans which are proving lousy at keeping my body temperature from plummeting.

"Do you know if she had any enemies?"

Again, I say nothing.

I've seen enough true crime to know that when you're in an interrogation room, there is one simple, immutable fact: talking to the police without a lawyer works against you. They'll lie, and twist their words, and tell you things that you want to hear. I could barely understand what was happening myself.

They're wasting time with me. Bronya's killer is still out there, on campus—a shadow, just as they had been these past months.

Detective Melendez sighs and sits up in his chair, fingers interlocking as his forearms rest on top of the file folder in front of him. I squint my eyes at the way his spine stiffens from beneath his ironed button-down. The perfectly coiffed hair and the tie pin and the rolled-up sleeves are indicative of someone who's trying too hard. Obviously he wants to maintain an image, to show me that his experience and his time on the force deserve authority.

Careful to keep my facial expressions in check, I pull my hands into my lap.

The cold air circulating in the room breezes against my neck and sends a chill up through to the crown of my head. Both arms fold across my chest, an attempt to insulate my body heat while concealing any vulnerabilities from Detective Melendez's eye line.

Just then, the door swings open and a woman in a sleek hunter green suit enters. Her escort, another police officer, peers inside for a moment before shutting the door behind her.

I look to the interpreter who signs her words as she takes a seat next to me.

"I hope you aren't talking to my client without her lawyer present," she says, hanging her leather bag on the corner of her chair.

"Hello, Ms. Larkin," she greets. My focus darts between her and the interpreter. "I'm Reagan Throndsen, your parents hired me as counsel. Are you alright?" She asks, resting a gentle hand on the outside of my shoulder.

I nod, mustering a wary smile in her direction.

She's pretty. More so than any lawyer I've ever seen, except for maybe Annalise Keating, but I doubt she counts given she's of the fictional variety. There's a kindness about Reagan, though, that makes me believe she genuinely cares. The smile she returns is gleamingly confident and, for a moment, it makes me feel better. There's a warmth in how she checks on me, but also a hesitation; like there's a question beneath the surface that she doesn't want to outwardly ask.

As she turns her attention to Detective Melendez, Reagan's smile hardens. There's a stoicism to her now, but I'd bet cash money that it's a façade for the benefit of men like him who would otherwise mistake her kindness for weakness.

There's an equal fascination in the way the detective adjusts in his seat as Reagan studies him. Something I'm missing. I'm a third wheel spectating whatever's unfolding here. An unspoken history between the two of them that amps up the palpable discomfort in the room.

"We've just been having a friendly conversation, that's all." The smile he sends my way is chilling.

I'd hate to go to his house for a barbeque if he considered this friendly banter.

"The deceased was your client's roommate," he continues. "So, I find it hard to believe she wouldn't have some sort of insight into what happened." His words are callous and pointed.

Reagan's lips purse slightly.

Then it hits me, and the stupidity of not catching it

earlier wafts over me like rancid garbage.

The history they have is an intimate one.

"Do you have any evidence to support this theory?" She asks.

If he does, it's news to me.

I hope this is the point in the conversation where I'm allowed to go home and forget this has happened. The moment where he walks into the back of the squad room and crosses my name off a suspect list written on a white board like an episode of Law & Order.

"My officers searched the deceased's dorm room—" he begins, but I don't give him time to finish his thought.

"Bronya," I interject, an interpreter voicing for me as I spell out her name nimbly with my fingers. There are two interpreters in the room to ensure communication access is a two-way street at all times. I won't miss a single word said by anyone else, but I also want to make sure my side of the story is crystal clear.

"Excuse me?" He asks, eyes furrowed incredulously like I've stepped out of line.

I lean forward, the speed at which I sign the next words has slowed to a molasses-flavored crawl.

"Her name—it's Bronya. B-R-O-N-Y-A. If you're going to talk about her, call her by her name."

No one deserved to die the way Bronya did, the least they could do was honor who she was. Despite the fact she'd paid more attention to her hair than to her homework assignments, and the choice words she reserved for anyone who dared to think she would ever buy or wear anything secondhand, she's still my friend. She was my friend.

From the outside, I can see how this might have looked like an accident. A fall through a fourth-floor window that was open just a little too wide. A trip over something lying across the floor that sent her reeling over the bed and through the single pane frame that needed to be replaced over a decade ago. A step on the back of a draping maxi dress, or a momentary distraction in the mirror as she changed clothes. There were endless opportunities to mask this as tragedy other than what it was.

I narrow my eyes at the detective, who seems oddly amused that I would care so much about something as frivolous as what he called her. His expression turns to discomfort as my stare intensifies, and I quickly learn that he's not used to anyone other than him weaponizing eye contact.

"Right." He swallows. "Well, we searched the dorm room you and Bronya shared, and we've now ruled her death a homicide." His eyes move back to me and my chest tightens. "It appears she was stabbed before she fell to her death. There's also evidence she was pushed out of her window. So, I'll ask again. Do you have any idea why someone would want to hurt her?"

"No, I don't," I say, keeping my answers short and sweet.

The truth is I know someone who wanted to get to me, who had planned to confront someone entirely different in that room, but Bronya had shown up at the wrong time and screwed up their plan. She was never the intended target.

"Do you know if anyone disliked Ms. Minsky?"

I look at Reagan and she nods encouragingly for me to continue.

"She..." I start, searching for the best words to finish my train of thought. *"She wasn't the easiest person to get along with sometimes, but we were friends. Sort of. Not close, but I didn't want her dead. No one would hate her enough to kill her."*

I bite at the inside of my lip as my brain flips through the possibilities, and then quickly wipe the back of my hand across my mouth and reach up to scratch at my ear.

Without missing a beat, Detective Melendez opens the folder in front of him and looks down at a report.

"You also know Rider Abbot, is that correct?" he asks, the smug smirk returning.

The spelling of his name is enough to make me want

to frown. Of course they're going to ask me about him.

"*Yes,*" I admit, jaw clenching.

"Are you aware that he and the deceased—Bronya— had bad blood between them?"

Yes.

"*I can't speak to the nature of their relationship. She was my roommate, but we didn't tell each other everything.*"

Detective Melendez hasn't taken his eyes off me, and I wonder if he can read me as well as I can read him.

"Was Ms. Minsky involved with anyone?

"*She has a boyfriend,*" I shrug.

"What's her boyfriend's name?" He asked, pen at the ready.

"*Anders Johansen.*"

"And how well do you know Mr. Johansen?"

"*Not very well,*" I start, lifting my shoulders and then letting them drop again under the weight of it all. I feel sick to my stomach. "*But he wouldn't be involved in this.*"

"Involved in what?"

"*All of this. Bronya's death.*"

"What makes you say that?" Detective Melendez asks. I can sense genuine curiosity this time, and wonder if, for the first time in this conversation, he hadn't anticipated what I was going to say.

I shrug again.

"*I just can't see him hurting her.*"

But I know who would.

"And how well do you know Rider Abbot?"

"We went to high school together."

"Are you friends?"

"At one point we were," I answer.

"Just friends?"

If he wants to talk about Rider, the least he could do was give me a trash can to barf into. There was no one I hated more on this planet, and muscles I didn't even know I had were contracting at the thought of being anywhere near him. Not after what happened the last time I let my guard down.

"What are you implying here, Octavio?" Reagan asks, brows furrowing.

"I'm asking a pertinent question about the nature of their relationship, Reagan," he replies, eyes sizing her up before returning back to me.

"Are you asking if we were hooking up or something?" I ask indignantly.

The detective is really starting to piss me off.

"I'm asking if you two were involved beyond the boundaries of a platonic friendship."

"No," I reply with three solemn fingers in a swift movement, my poised deadpan expression once again plastered across my face. I wouldn't have called whatever it was we had a relationship, anyway, even at

its best moments.

"Is there any reason why he'd want to hurt Bronya?"

I know exactly why he would want to hurt Bronya.

And he's coming for me next.

FOURTEEN DAYS BEFORE THE MURDER

I didn't want to be there.

In fact, I wanted to be anywhere else but Rider Abbot's end of summer party.

But it was part of the plan.

I'd caved when Finley told me about the plan she'd cooked up to get revenge on Rider for what he'd done to me, despite my initial disinterest. There were a million things I'd have preferred to do, like organize my vinyl collection, but in the end she swindled me.

We made our way up the familiar driveway, but my pace slowed a step or two behind hers. There was still an unease that kept me from wanting to step inside the concrete castle, some unknown force pulling me back like cattle in a lasso. The weight on my chest was heavy and suffocating, anger clawing up the back of my throat.

The Abbots, always quick to ensure their affluence never went unnoticed. They resided in a four million dollar home—according to the most recent Zillow estimate—that was tucked back in a pocket of Culver City known as Carlson Park. Ballona Creek at its back, it was as if the geography had been fashioned with the sole purpose of guaranteeing only those with trust funds and BMWs could afford to live on that side of the embankment. Their pretentious house, stark and dull and drowned in a muted grey palette, was entirely devoid of anything that could be construed as character.

There had been assumptions running rampant for years regarding Mr. Abbot's rumored infidelity, though such gossip had never been confirmed. It was what one might call a public weak spot, which was hotter gossip among the soccer moms than the Ponzi schemes he'd been involved in. Fodder for the other parents to whisper about in the bleachers of their kids' games, I'm sure. There was no shortage of shady dealings that could be traced back to their family if one were to look closely enough. I'd always wondered how it all affected their children, though the implosion of my friendship with Rider had rendered that train of thought essentially pointless. During the peak of our friendship, Rider had confided in me how much he'd hated his father for tearing at the fabric of their family. Even still, his unending admiration for the man never wavered.

Turning to look back at me, Fin grabbed my hand and pulled me up to the doorway with her. Every inch of my body screamed, urging my legs to move and take off running down the street, to dive into some shrubbery where I could stress out in peace. Instead, I stood beside Finley, facing the impossibly tall front door from my nightmares.

"Trust me," she said again, a reassuring smile radiating warmth.

Famous last words.

The social butterfly to my outcast, and my best friend in the entire world, Finley was my platonic other half. We'd be going off to college together at Laurent Clerc University—the only post-secondary institution on the West Coast for deaf and hard-of-hearing students—next week, where I planned to study communications because of my interest in investigative journalism, while she wanted to dip her toes into the criminal justice pool—an interest I took credit for being that I had first introduced her to the world of true crime.

We hadn't been paired as roommates this coming year despite our request, though it was more than likely a blessing in disguise. From the start, no one thought our friendship would survive a joint living situation. I love the cold and she embraces the heat; I prefer headphones and she loves to play music at full volume on speakers; as an introvert, I relish my alone time while her extroverted self is energized by socializing. Since the first day we'd met in the seventh grade, while attending the same mainstream program for deaf and hard of hearing students at Stone Valley High School, our friendship has always been a delicate dance of compromise. Being two of a few dozen students in the program, the odds were in our favor that we'd end up being best friends. Since then, I've always quietly thanked the universe for her.

But right now, I wanted to strangle her for bringing me here.

Before anything else could be said between us, the door swung open and we were greeted by Theo Osbourne, Rider's best friend. A lanky, six-foot-something with a mop of shaggy copper hair, he stood in the doorway holding a cup full of some mystery liquid that nearly spilled as he reached out to enthusiastically hug Finley. The two of them were friendly, though it was no secret he'd had a massive crush on her since the seventh grade. Theo grew up in one of Culver City's low-income neighborhoods, so he fortunately wasn't cursed with the same entitled attitude that so many of Rider's other friends.

A wave of vibration plowed into me as I crossed the threshold and stepped inside the house, deep bass notes drifting through me in the same way I'd seen ghosts pass through Jennifer Love Hewitt on *Ghost Whisperer*. Bass-heavy songs played through speakers resting on the hardwood floor that vibrated the entire house. Despite the common misconception that deaf people are quieter than hearing people, we're much louder. The stomping of feet against the floor to get attention, shouting, laughing, the blaring of music. Any expectation of a quiet party could be tossed out the window.

"Hey, Lennon, it's good to see you!" Theo declared, signing with his free hand while he held a cup in the other. He used my sign name, his index and thumb in the shape of the letter 'L' as he scratched his finger against the apple of his cheek; an initialized version of the sign for 'suspicious'; a name sign Finley had given me as a callback to my love of true-crime and serial-killer docustories.

A casual smile masked my unease. *"You too, Theo."* I had no interest in exchanging further pleasantries, so I changed the subject. *"What's that?"* I asked, pointing to the cup in his hand.

"This? Uh..." Fighting the booze-fueled fog undoubtedly clouding his mind, his fingers fidgeted in the air. *"Vodka and Hawaiian Punch, maybe? I'm not sure. Do you want some?"*

The cup was held out to me and my brow tightened,

holding up my open hand to indicate my lack of interest. *"No, that's okay. Thanks."* I was playing the part of Designated Driver tonight, ensuring we would have a safe getaway once our plan had been enacted.

Cara Maddox—a girl I knew from school, but who I absolutely was not friends with—ran over hurriedly and pulled Theo away to talk indistinctly near the staircase. Surveying the crowd, I recognized a good number of the kids from school and a larger number from the local school for the deaf. My attention shifted back to Theo as he disappeared with Cara up the stairs and out of sight. Finley dug her elbow into my side and I winced, instinctively reaching up to protect my ribs in case she were to try it again.

"What was that for?" I asked, craning my body away in pain.

Finley turned toward me, her back to the rest of the party. Making sure no one was looking, she lowered her hands to keep the wandering eyes of others out of our business.

"Would it kill you to loosen up? It's a party, Len, it's supposed to be fun!"

"Uh huh," I agreed, mindlessly.

How did Finn ever expect me to have fun in this house ever again?

The party, like an infected wound, was only getting

worse with time. The sporadic pieces of furniture in the living room, no doubt a take on Scandinavian minimalism, caught my eye. So much money and none of it spent on a couch you could curl up on.

Gazing from one piece to the next, the wound throbbed and ached. Rider, sitting in a leather armchair, had his newest flavor of the week perched on his lap. It was disgusting. His eyes flicked toward mine and he contorted his face into the arrogant smile I knew all too well. Jaw set and fists clenched, I was itching to wipe that smug smirk off of his stupid face.

"What will kill me is being here any longer than we have to. I just want to hurry up and do this. Rider keeps looking over at me with that shit-eating grin on his face," I said.

"Ignore him. We've gotta kill some time before everyone is drunk enough that we can sneak off. Don't worry so much. He'll get what's coming to him," Fin replied.

"Yeah, yeah, fine," I conceded, unwilling to spend any more time arguing about it.

"Great! To the kitchen, then." Her hands clapped onto my shoulders and she stepped behind me to steer us toward the back of the house.

If I'd been told there was a time vortex surrounding Rider's house that had somehow caused the night to feel like it would never end, I wouldn't have asked a single follow-up question. It was excruciating to stand in the House of Abbot. After half an hour in that marble mansion, there was an itch inside my brain I just couldn't quite scratch. An hour in, I wanted to brain myself with one of the stupid plaster sculptures laughing at me from the mantel.

I had nothing to say to Rider. In fact, the past two years had flown by without even an inkling of desire to speak to him. Avoiding him had been hard enough at school the past two years, but being in his house? This was a whole other level of hell that even Dante hadn't explored.

Once upon a time, I'd felt something real for Rider. He'd been this good-looking, sweet guy who would stand at my locker and sweet talk me while I collected my books. It wasn't unusual for him to bring me back a milkshake when he'd swing through Jack in the Box with his football buddies, or sit behind me in English and rub my shoulders, or pick me up on weekend nights to drive out to the Baldwin Hills Scenic Overlook and watch the stars. Months were spent with him cozying up to me and lowering my guard, while I waited for him to ask me to make it official.

What I hadn't realized was that he didn't want a girlfriend—he wanted a conquest.

The pot roast my mother had prepared for dinner did backflips in my gut as all of the bitter memories flooded back. Every lie, every brush-off, every mortifying moment of his betrayal. How I believed his care for me was genuine, the words he promised me "I just want to have something of you to keep with me always." The way I'd naively sent him a few photos. How he humiliated me when I'd later they'd not been kept private.

Fingertips tapped against my shoulder, but my head was the only part of my body to react. Some tension released as I realized it was Iris Whitlock. She was a year behind us in school but had always trailed along when it came to parties and social events. Her dad had taken off when she was young—to the astonishment of no one—and her mom had long spent her days wasting away at the bingo hall or drowning her sorrows in Miller Lite. It wasn't exactly the most conducive home-life for fostering an independent, confident kid who could stand up for herself. I heard that her mom had remarried last year, but neither Finley nor I were close enough to Iris anymore to deem it our place to ask questions.

"Hey, Lennon!" Iris greeted, smiling at me with a red cup in hand, her loosely braided hair falling over her shoulder.

She looked so different than I remembered. Happier, although it wasn't hard to imagine why. Two years ago, she'd watched her best friend get pulled out of school and moved states away without so much as a goodbye. It broke her, and we'd all watched it happen. It wasn't long after that before she really cracked. No one would sit with her at lunch, she stopped showing up to anything that wasn't mandatory, and eventually she even deleted all of her social media accounts and took a leave of absence to be homeschooled. According to the rumor mill, she was actually sent to some kind of Christian reformative program meant to help struggling teens. It was a year before any of us saw her in the halls again, and by then she was nothing like her old self.

"Hey, how's it going?" I asked as I sipped on my root beer.

"Can't complain," she replied. *"I have Magliotti for physics this year, so I'm not looking forward to that torture."*

A look of pain twisted my features, remembering how awful it had been to sit through Magliotti's lecture. Finley and I had taken it together, and thankfully we'd both passed, but it was hands-down the most stressful part of the year. Pop quizzes and fifty-plus pages of reading each class had been enough to make me want to pull my hair out, not including the fact he talked to us like kindergarteners.

"Shit, I'm sorry," I said, an unfortunate laugh escaping me.

"Right? Here's to hoping I pass so I don't screw up my GPA and lose my scholarship. It's the only way I'm getting out of here at this point." Iris had never been interested enough in sports to get into college by snagging a spot on a collegiate athletic team. She had, however, earned herself an academic scholarship and early admission to Smith. I'd always assumed distance was a factor in her choice of school, but it felt invasive to ask—so I never did.

"I'm sure you'll do just fine," I attempted to reassure, my attention pulling everywhere other than the conversation Iris was trying to have with me.

Perhaps she sensed my distraction, because she smiled meekly and nodded, offhandedly mentioning something about getting a refill of whatever she'd been drinking. A moment later she was gone, moving her way through the sea of people standing around the large island at the center of the kitchen.

I knew I should've said more—Iris used to be Finley and I's third musketeer—but I just couldn't get the words out. We'd stopped being close shortly after everything happened with Rider, when I'd just wanted the whole world to stop. It wasn't her fault, but I pushed her away like I did everyone else.

Across the room from me, drink in hand, Fin was engaged in her own version of small-talk. Although, I'm not sure anyone could actually consider it small. Even the slightest amount of alcohol buzzing in her veins turned Fin into a ticking time bomb. Sober, she was impulsive and hasty, but drunk, she became reckless and dangerous. Her hands were whizzing through the air exaggeratedly, telling the story of a time she had 'nearly escaped death'. A story I'd seen her tell a thousand times. One that, decidedly, did not include a near death experience.

"So, there I was, dangling just above the fence and holding onto the window ledge with my FINGERTIPS," she continued, keeping her audience in suspense. The emphasis was a nice addition that hadn't been part of the last retelling. The crowd of people gathered around couldn't take their eyes off her, each of them inebriated and entranced by her storytelling.

"I swung my legs out, kicked away from the wall, and managed to land..." Fin paused for dramatic effect, eyes wide as she looked around at the group. *"... in the pool!"* She failed to keep herself from laughing at the sheer idiocy of her own story as the entire group broke out into visual exclamations. A wink fired off in my direction as she finished her tale. As the group began to split off and disperse, my yarn-spinning friend was suddenly at my

side.

"Enjoying the party?" she asked.

"Not as much as you are," I teased, the corner of my mouth turned upward.

"Gotta give the people what they want."

"Wouldn't the people rather have the truth?"

"People never want the truth, Lennon," Finley said, taking a sip of her drink. Entirely unfazed, she looked me dead in the eyes. *"They only think they do."*

"That's not true," I tried to argue, my confidence wavering ever so slightly.

"No?" Her tone was bathed in accusation.

"Don't go there, Finley," I said, signing her sign name with the bent middle finger of my open-palmed hand touching my eyebrow and moving outward twice in a quick motion. It was a nod to a scar that ran through her right eyebrow.

When she was eight, while playing outside in the treehouse built into a large oak tree in her backyard, Fin's haste to climb the ladder led to a missed rung and lost grip. The fall resulted in one broken arm and a sliced-open eyebrow, in addition to a myriad of scrapes and bruises. That was typical Fin, though; impulsive, always caring more about being first than being careful.

"Not right now." I knew where she was going with that train of thought, and I wasn't amused.

"Why not? Afraid Rider's going to see us talk about it? I don't give a shit what he thinks and neither should y—" she rattled off in an alcohol-fueled rant, frustrated as I cut her off.

I turned toward her, shielding my hands from prying eyes and ensuring she didn't misunderstand the seriousness of the point I was about to make.

"Don't, Fin. Neither of us wants you spouting off something you can't take back tomorrow when you're sober. Right?" I paused for dramatic effect, followed by an eyebrow raise and a tilt of my head. I didn't wait for a response, my tone shifting from near-scolding to borderline ominous. *"Exactly. I'm not afraid of Rider, He's the one who should be afraid of me."*

Finley stood there, unwavering, a sinister smile creeping onto her face as glee glinted in her eye.

"Damn right!" She asserted, her excitement uncontainable as her hands clasped onto the sides of my arms. *"Now let's go get our vengeance on and dip out before I have to endure more shameless flirting from Theo."*

The party had reached its peak, with everyone sufficiently drunk enough not to notice the two of us sneaking around. As much as I wanted to feel like James

Bond on a mission, I was without both the slick Aston Martin and the iconic three-piece suit. Not to mention there was a severe lack of confidence broiling at the pit of my stomach.

Nudging my arm as we approached a door at the end of the hall, my mischievous pal tilted her head toward the door as I looked back at her.

'In here,' Finley mouthed.

I followed behind as she twisted the handle and pushed the door open. Once we'd both entered, I shut the door quickly before anyone could see us disappear. Fin flipped a switch on the wall to reveal a massive garage with two vehicles parked inside it: a black, Mercedes-Benz G-Class, and Rider's brand-new, silver, Audi TTS.

"Ready?" Fin asked, the epitome of calm, cool, collected, and slightly inebriated.

"Maybe we should rethink this…" I offered.

"And waste these perfectly good eggs? I think not," Finley said. Her nimble fingers had already removed the plastic bag and revealed a carton of fresh Grade AA eggs, ripe for the throwing.

Of course this was her plan.

This was idiotic and we were going to get caught.

She pulled out the first egg at warp speed and I lunged forward to step in front of her and prevent her from throwing it with all the force she could muster.

"*Wait, stop!*" I said, realizing we had to be smarter about this. Much smarter. I blocked her view of the car, ready to lay out the new plan. "*What if there are cameras?*" I watched Fin's eyebrows raise, clocking her interest in what I was saying.

"*Oh, there are. An obsessive amount, actually.*"

How was she so calm saying that out loud?!

"*Rider shuts them all down before any parties though, just in case his parents ever wake up one day and decide they actually care about the underage drinking and other sorts of teenaged debauchery,*" she added.

"*And how is it you know that?*" I asked, head arched toward my delusional friend.

She shrugged. "*Theo mentioned it once.*"

"*He just casually mentioned the security system at his best friend's house? I don't buy it.*"

Something was fishy.

"*Okay, maybe I asked,*" Finley tossed back, nonchalantly.

"When?"

With a roll of her eyes, she sighed. "*Why does everything have to be a battle, Lennon?*"

Knitting my brows together, frown lines buried into my forehead. "*What are you talking about?*"

"*Seriously?*" she asked. "*Most people would just nod*

and accept the fact they were finally getting revenge on their high school bully, but not you. Not Lennon Larkin, wannabe detective. You just have to dig and dig until you find the bodies."

A catch in my throat developed and I swallowed hard.

"Doubt it all you want, but I'm telling you those cameras are off. Are you going to trust me or not?" Fin asked, eyes boring into me expectantly.

And there I was, cornered.

"Yes, I trust you," I managed. *"But I still don't think throwing eggs at his car is the best plan."*

Fin sighed. *"We can't just walk away and let him think he's off the hook."* She looked down at the cartons she'd tucked against her arm, then back up at me.

"I didn't say anything about letting him off the hook," I assured, a small smile appearing.

There were a lot of things I felt about what had transpired between Rider and I two summers ago, despite how hard I fought to not feel them at all. Anger and resentment were the most palpable. Hating him was easy, mostly because he deserved it. Hating myself was a whole other evil. Part of me resented the naive version of my past self that had let him in. That had waved him across the threshold and allowed even the tiniest sliver of vulnerability to see the light of day.

I hadn't seen him for the monster he truly was—until now.

"How pissed do you think Rider would be if he got into his car tomorrow morning and smelled two dozen rotting eggs?" A smirk pulled at the corner of my lips.

Fin's look of disappointment morphed into one of glee. *"Very."*

"Think the odds are good it's unlocked?" I mused, finishing my question before wandering over to the lustrous sports car.

I tucked my hand under the fabric of my t-shirt and grabbed the door handle, in an attempt not to leave any fingertips. To my surprise, the door opened easily.

"We'd better hurry before anyone notices we've disappeared," I warned.

Fin was already following my lead and opening the trunk hatch. *"There's a ton of people in there and they're all too drunk to walk in a straight line. They won't even remember we were here."*

"Theo would remember. He's in love with you."

Her face dropped, and I watched annoyance overtake her in real time.

She jabbed her index finger pointedly through the air at me. *"That's your fault for encouraging him when you know damn well he irritates the hell out of me."*

I stifled a laugh, shaking my head until she looked

back at me. *"All I did was say you'd broken up with Greer, which was true."*

"Do me a favor. Next time, lie."

We continued on our reverse Easter egg hunt, hiding gems to decompose and rot in the California sun while Rider took his car to campus for pre-season athletic training the next morning, giving the eggs time to really permeate into all the leather surfaces.

You can't run from this, Rider.

I won't let you.

THIRTEEN DAYS BEFORE THE MURDER

I awoke in a cold sweat and sat up so quickly there was static in my vision. The room sparkled as I rubbed at the corners of my eyes before raking clammy fingers through my mess of brown slept-on waves. Clasping the thickness of it at the nape of my neck, I pulled it over my shoulder and hugged my knees into my chest. One arm interlocking the other at the wrist, the center of my forehead rested against my knees.

Breathe.

I hadn't bothered to look at the clock. Judging by the amount of light peeking in through the gaps in the blinds, it was safe to assume it was still early. I wasn't altogether unconvinced I couldn't have fallen back asleep if I tried hard enough, but ultimately decided to get up and face the day. Relaxing my body, feet sliding back out to straighten my legs, I turned to look at the alarm clock on my nightstand.

7:45AM.

I grabbed for my phone, glad that at least I'd remembered to plug the charger cable in before passing out from exhaustion.

I NEW MESSAGE

Finley.

nightmare crocodile salsa dancing?

I think

Often, Finley would wake up in the middle of the night and text me about some wild dream or a thought she was worried she'd forget. Occasionally, they were unintelligible gibberish—those were my favorite ones. Trying to decipher what she'd meant had become a game for me. One made infinitely more entertaining when I could chastise her about it. I selected the new notification coming in now to find the message was, indeed, from my sleep-deprived best friend.

nishhamre cricjjedw salaaa danfing

I have no idea what that's supposed to mean.

nightmare crocodile salsa dancing?

I think

There's no way I would've ever gotten that.

She replied with an emoji of a person shrugging and I rolled my eyes, rolling out of bed and stashing the phone inside the pocket of my sweats. The wooden flooring in my parents' house creaked beneath my bare feet as I shuffled out of the room and down the hall, towards the kitchen, passing my brother's closed bedroom door.

It was like a Where's Waldo puzzle— always something new to be found, tucked between the layers. A homage to all the things Felix held most dear; movie posters for Se7en and Silence of the Lambs, Rolling Stone magazine clippings featuring The Doors and Alice Cooper, among others, and a horde of stickers collected over the years. It was safe to assume he was still asleep, as was his tendency. He liked to blame this inclination as a consequence of having all afternoon and evening classes, but in reality, he was just a chronic over-sleeper who couldn't kick the habit no matter how many times our mother had woken him up by pouring a cup of water over his head.

Mornings were never his thing, but for me there had always been a certain comfort that came with being the only one awake as the sun rose over the horizon. It provided solitary, distraction-free opportunities to think and work and worry about what the future held.

That morning, though, I needed coffee strong enough to wake the dead—or at least shake their caskets a little.

Despite my general irritability when my grasp on the world around me is tenuous at best—apparently this constitutes 'control issues', as I've lovingly been told—I have always been a firm believer that good coffee can turn your entire day around. I was on my second cold brew and the to-do list in the notes app on my phone hadn't gotten any shorter.

What was I going to bring with me? Which clothes did I need to pack? How many trips would I have to take back and forth to campus if my stuff wouldn't fit into the car? When should I email my new roomma—?

"Don—...—ou...t—...b—k?" A voice interrupted my train of thought, its message incoherent. It sounded like it might've been behind me, but I couldn't pinpoint its location. I did a quick half-swivel both ways, trying to decipher where it was coming from, until my eyes fell onto Felix.

My brother shared many of my features, including the mess of dark chestnut waves sprouting from his scalp, a few inches of growth away from hitting his olive-skinned shoulders. There was a lightness to him that drew others in; a charisma permeating his movements and affecting even the smallest of facets down to his posture. The effortless coolness would've made me sick if I didn't also enjoy his company—most of the time. Unfortunately, I was the opposite; aloof, standoffish, and wholeheartedly preferred my own company to anyone else's. People didn't gravitate to me. They avoided me like we were demonstrating reverse polarization.

"Huh?" I asked, brows furrowed, trying to piece together what he might have asked.

"Don't you ever take a *break*?" he asked again, signing the final word as he spoke the sentence back to me. He used the ASL sign that contextually meant 'broken', instead of 'interrupt'. "From the constant overthinking. Should save some brain power for college," he added, tapping his temple with his index finger as a teasing half-smile appeared across his lips.

"Spoken from experience?" I teased in return, remembering how angry our parents had been when they'd found out he failed three classes during the first semester of his freshman year at USC. The constant partying and overall lackadaisical approach to education was one he'd taken on following his graduation from high school. Once upon a time he'd been an A student, but he'd nearly taken a mulligan on his entire first year.

"It's *break*, by the way," I signed it properly to correct him, the side of my right hand cutting in between the middle and ring fingers of my left. "Also, it would be nice if you could sign more often. Y'know, rather than just when it's convenient for you," I said, a tinge of bitterness in my tone.

Felix had never been consistent when it came to signing in his conversations with me. He only did it when he felt like it, or when he wanted to say something secretly in front of other people. I didn't like that. Nor did I like that he still didn't know the difference between the signs for the various meanings of the word 'break'.

Looking away from him, I went back to tending to my coffee, slowly swirling the oat milk, cold brew, and cubes of ice with a metal straw.

Felix stomped twice on the wooden floor to get my attention.

"I know... I just forget, sometimes." His face was draped in sincerity, tone much softer this time.

That was the problem; how easily everyone forgot.

I understood this was a whole new reality he and our parents had only had a handful of years to come to terms with. I got it. Really, I did. But why did they treat it like it was something so painfully easy to forget about? It wasn't an obscure website password, or the name of their first grade teacher, or what they ate for breakfast the previous week. It wasn't any of those things—it was their child.

It was my existence that they were constantly pushing to the bottom of their priorities list.

"I know, it's fine," I replied, masking my disappointment.

Felix walked around me to the pantry, pulling out a box of Captain Crunch cereal and then two bowls from the cabinet next to the fridge. Before I could tell him I wasn't really hungry, there was a full bowl sitting in front of me, with a spoon and everything.

"Thanks." I said as I grabbed the spoon to take a bite.

"So, Len, are you excited to start school?" He slid onto one of the stools that butted-up to the kitchen island and I shared a small smile to acknowledge my appreciation. Facing someone in conversation aided my ability to read lips to support the auditory information—a system that wasn't foolproof, considering only roughly thirty percent of English can be read on the lips.

"I guess," I said, unsure of how I really felt about it all. My emotions were all over the place, and nothing would be quite right until I was actually on campus. "There's only two ways it can go, either I'll hate it or I won't." I shrugged softly and picked up my spoon to nudge some cereal pieces around.

Felix stifled a laugh. "Great odds then."

I'm not sure what I expected to find upon entering campus, but admittedly I was disappointed. It felt too normal, despite being exactly what I was looking forward to. A sense of normalcy, stability, some semblance of balance to right the ship of my life that was in the midst of a hurricane. Droves of other students were moving into their dorm rooms, arms full of bedding and laundry baskets and microwaves. There were temporary paper signs set up in the grassy areas across campus with the names of each building—an effort I appreciated as my eyes scanned each one to find my residence hall.

"Which one is it?" Felix asked, his eyes flicking from one building to another.

"Thompson," I stated, without hesitation. It was the easternmost dormitory on campus and the oldest one still standing.

Felix tapped my arm with the back of his hand and pointed toward a building a little further down the way from where we were, across from a multi-level structure with walls made almost entirely of glass on its uppermost floor. Was the ceiling also glass? I strained my neck to get a better look through the windshield until I felt my brother's hand firmly grip my arm in a panic.

"LEN!"

I jammed my foot on the brake. The car lurched forward and my eyes widened. I'd almost wiped out a pair of kids in bright green t-shirts. We weren't going fast, but it was enough speed to stop us so abruptly our seat belts locked.

The pedestrians in front of the car jumped back and scowled, with the taller of the two looking ready to tear my head off. I shrank in my seat, sheepishly attempting to avoid a confrontation. The taller girl's long, jet-black hair was pulled back into a taut ponytail that hung like strands of silk falling over her shoulder as she turned her head toward her friend to comment on how reckless I was. Red-rimmed, cat-eye glasses had slipped down her nose, but they were quickly pushed back into position as her head spun toward us.

Without another moment wasted on me, the two of them quickly turned and strode off with the names on the backs of their shirts staring back at me. Choi and Jones were clearly no fans of mine. Thankfully they were not going in the direction we were headed.

I let out a sigh of relief, my heart still racing.

Felix and I looked at each other in silent agreement to never speak of this again.

My assigned room was on the fourth floor, telltale signs of its age at every turn—peeling paint revealing color schemes past, scuffed laminate flooring, painfully slow elevators that were far too small and invited claustrophobia to cling to its corners like cobwebs. It was well-worn and lived-in, like an old sweater that's lived a dozen lives in a dozen mothball-riddled closets.

At the front desk, I'd talked with a friendly Resident Assistant who'd introduced himself as Ollie, visible in a bright green t-shirt. As he stepped out from behind the desk, I noted the back read 'Westlake' in a familiar black font. My stomach knotted at the sight. Not even twenty-four hours on campus and I'd already made enemies with a pair of RA's by nearly plowing through them with my car. Ollie was friendly, divulging perkily that he hailed from Minnesota, was studying environmental science, had become vegan over the summer, and lived on my floor. The ivory hallways were spotted with green doors, each of which had a small plaque beside it with the room number and its Braille counterpart. Similar to the keyless entry system at the front of the building, the locks on each door had been retrofitted with new state-of-the-art readers that used our ID cards rather than physical keys. It was all very high-tech and way cooler than using a regular old key that I'd have to carry around with me (and probably lose, if I was being honest with myself).

Like a good tour guide, he showed me where the bathrooms and laundry facilities were, before leaving me alone to get acquainted with the four bare walls of my new room. The room was outfitted with identical pieces of furniture on each side of the room: a bed, a four-drawer dresser, and a desk with a chair. There were two closet doors, one on each side of the room, painted the same shamrock green as the doors in the hallway and sitting open as they waited to be filled with belongings. I plopped down the box I'd been carrying and slid off my backpack to drop it onto the nylon-wrapped foam mattress on the right side of the room.

It wasn't my bed at home, but it would do.

"Who's The Clash?" Bronya asked, walking into the

room, a box in her hand. Her brow furrowed as she watched me tape the final corner to the wall, her finger held in the air as she pointed at the poster I'd just hung above my bed.

I'd ended up with Bronya Minsky as my roommate, and neither of us were thrilled about it. I'd seen her around during our high school years, but we had never hung out in the same social circles. Based on my internet searches, I knew living with Bronya would be a challenge. It took her less than twenty-four hours to start subtly crapping on me and everything I liked, and merely seventy-two for me to notice this happened more often after she'd gotten into a fight with her boyfriend— not that it was the only factor. As it stood, my chances at salvaging a good relationship with her were narrowing with each terse conversation.

"A British rock band from the seventies that revolutionized punk," I replied, wondering whether she actually cared about the response or if she was simply feigning interest in the poster as a way of passive-aggressively dumping on my choice of room decor. Somehow, she had managed to be both confused and judgmental.

Not like her side of the room was any better.

The wall behind Bronya's bed was covered in photos of herself from high school volleyball games, each one a slight variation from another. The same uniform, same ivory ribbon in her tied-up hair, and the same sickly sweet smile plastered across her face as if it had been superimposed there. The entire setup was completely monochromatic, leaving little guesswork had I been asked what her favorite color was. There were bright pink fairy lights cascading down from the top of her window's blinds, across from a lamp on her nightstand sporting a neon pink shade. To top it all off, her bed was covered by a fuchsia comforter bearing an off-white paisley pattern and a pair of matching pillow shams. In contrast to my side of the room, it was jarring.

She was the Paris Hilton to my Joan Jett.

"Never heard of them," Bronya said, shrugging and taking a few steps over to the open door of her closet. Peering through the neatly arranged array of textures and colors, she chose a flowery maxi dress with thin spaghetti straps and held it on its hanger in front of her body. She surveyed her reflection in the full-length mirror attached to the inside of the door, and I waved my arm at her reflection until her focus drifted back to me.

Taking this opportunity to be nice, I complimented her.

"That dress looks nice. Going out with Anders?" I asked, referencing her on-again-off-again boyfriend as I looked

up from my text thread with Finley. According to her social profiles, they'd been together since junior year of high school. The current status of Bronya's relationship was of little concern to me, but if she was leaving, then it meant she'd likely stay over with him and I'd have the room to myself for the night.

She nodded, quickly disappearing to change clothes before vanishing for what would hopefully be the remainder of the evening. A sigh of relief escaped me as I collapsed onto my bed, silently begging the universe for something good to happen.

It didn't.

Not twenty minutes later, the overhead lights flashed—a visual cue to let me know someone had pressed the doorbell for my room. Since this was a campus designed with accessibility in mind, everything that was typically audiocentric had been altered to be visual instead.

Bronya probably forgot her keys.

Or maybe it's Finley, checking up on me.

I'd only given Finley my room number, considerably narrowing the possibilities of who might be on the other side of the door. It was possible, though, that anyone roaming the halls could notice my and Bronya's names handwritten on themed stickers on the door denoting our freshman status. For most people, the first-name-last-initial thing wouldn't be a dead giveaway, but for me and my unique moniker, it might as well have been a spotlight and an inflatable waving clown. As I pulled open the door, taped to it was a folded piece of paper with my name written across it. I peeled it off and retreated back into my room.

Unfolding the paper, my entire body froze. It was a photo of Rider's car, completely trashed. The Audi TT was sitting in exactly the same spot as it had been when Finley and I had been standing in front of it last night. The perspective almost perfectly matched where we'd been standing in that same garage.

Clammy hands trembling, I typed a message to Finley so fast I would've misspelled every word were it not for autocorrect.

DEFCON 3!!!

is that the worst one or the least bad one?

Really not the point

fine fine okay what's up

Someone taped a photo of Rider's car to my door

It's so much worse than when we left it, Fin.

What if someone blames us for this??

show me

Clicking into the camera, another notification pinged across the top of my screen.

Then another.

And another.

Three messages, all from the same unknown number.

Before I could snap a photo for Finley, I clicked into the thread. My eyes scanned the messages—two texts and one image. The image was an exact copy of the one taped to my dorm room door. Holding my phone up next to the printed one I'd pulled from my door, it was clear they were an exact match.

The eggs we'd hidden throughout the inside of Rider's car were now splattered all over its exterior.

The tires were slashed.

The headlights had been smashed in.

And what was in the corner?

I zoomed in, my phone so close to my face that my nose was almost touching the screen.

Oh my god—Fin's backpack.

My heart began to beat erratically in my chest. The palms of my hands were so sweaty and damp my phone nearly slipped out of my hands. I took in a shaky breath and read the pair of texts that accompanied the photo.

IF YOU'RE GOING TO DO SOMETHING, DO IT RIGHT.

DON'T MAKE ME CLEAN UP ANY MORE OF YOUR MESSES, L.

I took a screenshot of the messages and switched back over to my text thread with Finley.

OH SHIT

did you text back?

No.

What was I supposed to say in return, 'Gee, thanks for the help turning my prank into a crime scene'? We were already in over our heads. The second we walked into Rider's house, things had started to go downhill.

Now, with whoever this was watching our every move, we were picking up speed down a black diamond slope.

what are you waiting for?

if they knew it was us then we deserve to know who they are

How was I supposed to respond? How had something as stupid and impulsive as letting a dozen eggs rot in a car turned into this? As I turned the thoughts over in my mind, I knew whoever sent this had been watching us that night. At a minimum, they'd seen us sneak into the garage and must've followed in after we'd left and observed the fallout of our retribution. Someone knew it had been us, out of everyone who'd been at the party. What was even worse was they'd turned up the heat on us. This had to be some sick, sadistic joke. What could they want from us—from me—and what had Fin left in her bag that might've identified us?

Clicking back over to the thread with the unknown number, I strain to think up responses but came up short. Zooming even further in on the photo, I scanned each pixel for clues as to who might have taken it; a reflection, a shoe, a fingernail slipping into the frame. Anything.

The further I zoomed in, the blurrier the image

became. I could almost make out the fuzzy stature of what looked like a person, but the body of the car didn't reflect anything helpful. Its angles mirrored all the wrong corners of the garage, providing cover for our mysterious assailant. The part of me that loved investigations and criminal pathology wanted to call them an UNSUB, an unknown subject, but the more logical side knew this was too personal.

Another text came in from Finley, this time a screenshot from Rider's Instagram. A photo of his car, taken from a different angle than the one I'd been sent, along with text overlaid in the corner that read: **any1 know who the hell did this?** I swallowed hard before texting her back.

Did he post that just now?

30 mins ago

okay, well that's the worst news.

it's on twitter too

with a ton of retweets

The air was thick and suffocating as I gulped down breaths of it, like syrup clogging every inch of my windpipe. The temperature of my skin rose as my mind raced. I stared at the photo, over and over, wondering how I had been so reckless to allow myself to get sucked into Finley's stupid plan. There was a reason I didn't want to be involved in the first place. I knew something would go wrong, even if I couldn't have predicted this would be the outcome. I'd tried so long, spending years distancing myself from everything that reminded me of what had happened with Rider.

I'd moved on, or at least I thought I had.

As much as I wanted to blame Finley, I couldn't. Before we'd even arrived at Rider's, she told me the plan. She acknowledged my pain and offered this as a way of coming to terms with it, of getting closure by making him feel as much hurt as I had. It had been cathartic at the moment, but I suddenly found myself asking whether or not it was worth it.

Now I knew—it wasn't.

After what felt like hours, Finley showed up at my door.

"Someone from the party knows what we did," I said as soon as the door shut behind her.

"Let's not panic," Finley said, walking past me and claiming the desk chair. Taking a seat backward, she leaned forward and rested her arms atop the back. "So walk me through it. This just showed up, out of nowhere?" Her eyebrows scrunched together expectantly, as if some magical beacon would appear telling us who had taken the photo and decided to use it as blackmail.

"Someone hit the doorbell, but no one was there when I opened the door. Just this," I said, holding up the paper copy of the photo. *"Taped to the door with my name on it."*

Fin held out her hand and took the paper, studying it closely before looking back up at me.

"I don't know who put it there," I said, before she had a chance to ask. *"But it has to be connected with who texted me."* I pulled out my phone, navigating to my recent messages and turning the screen toward her so she could see for herself how torturous this game was becoming. *"The photo is exactly the same."*

Fin's eyes landed on the backpack in the corner and her features twisted, landing somewhere between annoyed and frustrated.

"What?" I finally asked, once her gaze had lifted up to meet mine, my brows furrowing.

"Nothing," she said, after a pause clearly indicating there was something she wasn't telling me.

Then the realization hit me.

What else had been in her bag?

"Please," I pleaded, my heart pounding in my chest, *"tell me it was just a bag of corn chips, or toilet paper, or a copy of a Playboy magazine—anything innocuous that won't leave me further regretting agreeing to go with you to that party."*

My friend looked at me with a mixture of pity and apprehension, and I knew whatever she was about to reveal was going to be bad. I willed her to lie, to keep me safe from whatever truth she was about to impart, but deep down, I knew the only thing worse than facing the truth was not knowing it at all. If someone was using this against me, I had to know it all. I needed to know.

I let out a heavy sigh and collapsed onto my bed, letting it gently cradle my body as I grasped at what little comfort my room could provide. She tapped my shoulder and I tried to hide the dread inching up my throat.

"You have to promise not to freak out."

"Just tell me," I replied, fully intent on saying as little as possible until I knew what we were dealing with.

"I borrowed some things from Cam."

"What kinds of things?" I sat up.

It was obvious Finley was uncomfortable in this conversation, though I wasn't sure what she could've brought with her that would make her this visibly uneasy.

"I just want to reiterate... we wanted him to pay for what he did. He DESERVED to pay for what he did. Let's not forget that, okay?"

Was she stalling? Trying to preface her words by doubling down on his culpability?

"Finley, just tell me!" I exploded.

She sighed, rubbing her forehead against the palm of her hand as she searched for the right words. *"I had a crowbar,"* she admitted, her shoulders dropping in defeat.

Sitting in stunned silence, frustration boiled inside

me.

"And—," she started again, her continuation catching me off guard.

"AND??" I could've leapt out of my seat and fainted all at the same time.

"And some corn syrup, in case we really wanted to do some damage. There were definitely some chips in there, too, though! A brand new bag of sour cream and onion," The last words out of her mouth were borderline wistful and I wanted to slap her.

Chips? She was worried about chips while we had a stalker sending threatening messages?

"Oh shit..." she added, all of the color fading from her face.

"What?"

"It's the bag I took to Vermont to visit my grandparents last summer."

I had no idea where she was going. *"I'm not following."*

"My mom wrote my name inside of it, in case it was lost at the airport."

Great. Our stalker hadn't needed to follow us at the party, we'd left them a trail of breadcrumbs. One big embroidered fabric, in fact.

How could she have been so reckless? It was one thing to do something harmless in order to get some kind of vigilante justice. It was an entirely different thing to bring a full-fledged weapon along for the ride. A loud whooshing rang in my head and the room started to spin.

Finley nudged my knee and I blinked her into focus.

"Len?" She asked sheepishly, fully aware of how quickly into an anxiety hole I was falling.

"We're so screwed," I managed.

"At least we're screwed together." She offered me an abashed smile, a metaphorical olive branch I wasn't willing to accept just yet.

"Not funny."

Fin held up her hands. *"Okay, not funny."* She ran one hand through her hair while the other tapped at the wood of the chair. *"Look, all we have to do is find who did this. See what they really want and figure out how to make them go away."*

Easier said than done.

"How do you suppose we do that?" I asked.

"All we've gotta do is figure out who was at the party and who would also be here on campus. We know Rider and Theo were there, for sure."

"Cara, too. She pulled Theo upstairs when we first got there," I added.

"Right. Okay. I remember that, vaguely. Most of Rider's friends also got into LCU, right? That's a good chunk of the JV football team. Doesn't really narrow it down too much,

but it's a decent place to start. One of them has to be The Ghost."

"*The Ghost?*" I asked, wondering if I'd missed something somewhere. "*Did they leave a calling card that I overlooked?*"

Fin rolled her eyes, ignoring my sarcastic comment. "*Yeah, you know, whoever's doing all this. They get around all stealthy-like and we have no clue who they are. It's like they don't even exist, or at least we can't see them. Like a ghost.*"

I nodded. It was as good a sobriquet as any, though perhaps too cool of a by-name for someone who was threatening me. We had a place to start, but there was no telling if we'd make it to the end.

NINE DAYS BEFORE THE MURDER

The next few days were a blur.

Orientation whipped by at a break-neck pace. Mandatory activities, including the numerous and boring workshops kept me busy. I was forced to watch university staff introduce themselves through a variety of presentations for hours at a time, play ice-breaker games, obtain my mailbox key, and listen to an explanation of how easy it was to blow through the entirety of your meal plan before the end of the semester. Finally, after what felt like eternity, it came time to register for classes with my newly-assigned advisor. All of this was a cakewalk when you consider the anvil in the pit of my stomach, a constant reminder of what was lurking around every corner.

By the end of the week, my ass hurt from all the sitting.

During a workshop designed to make sure all incoming freshmen had a basic foundational knowledge of the Student Code of Conduct, Finley and I were put into the same breakout group.

The group consisted of myself, Finley, a girl from Seattle who bore a striking resemblance to Megan Fox during her Jennifer's Body era, and a transfer student from somewhere upstate with a fondness for equines— but the one who stood out to us the most was Marcus Wagner, clad head-to-toe in all-black athleisure and spotless white sneakers. I pictured a nightly ritual of scrubbing and some sort of bleach cleanser in hand just to keep them spotless. He radiated an infectious, goofy energy that sucked us into all his gravitational pull.

We took turns sharing background info on where we were from and what we'd each decided was a 'fun fact' about ourselves, though Finley and I found ourselves doing most of the heavy lifting. Then it came time for Marcus to share, and he was more than happy to oblige.

"I'm Marcus," he started. *"I'm a CODA."* A child of a deaf adult, meaning one or both of his parents were deaf. *"I also have a deaf sister. We're originally from Oklahoma, but my mom moved us out here a few years ago for a teaching job at UCLA in their American Indian Studies department."* His perfectly smooth, russet skin blended into a dark mass of pin-straight hair pulled back

into a tight, perfect braid. *"I guess,"* He continued, *"my fun fact would be that I'm quadrilingual."*

Horse Girl chimed in and asked which languages he knew.

"ASL, English, Choctaw, and Plains Indian Sign Language." Noting our enthralled silence, his deep, bronze eyes smiled at us. *"Mom's Master's degree in linguistics rubbed off on me a little,"* he said with a small chuckle.

We were no longer impressed—we'd flown astronomically past that and went straight to enthralled, past GO and without collecting two hundred dollars.

The three of us got along instantly, with him and Fin diving into conversations about their love of paranormal television shows and arguing about whether the Rams had a decent lineup this year. Unbeknownst to me, the Cowboys-Rams rivalry was as old as time.

"You're a Cowboys fan?" Finley asked, lip tilted and brows concerned. *"I'll try not to hold it against you."*

"Against me?" Marcus scoffed. *"The Cowboys have won the Super Bowl five times. Remind me, how many have the Rams won?"* She leaned forward and grinned in defiance. Marcus' silence was confirmation enough for her. *"That's right. Two. Tell me again how you aren't going to hold my team against me."*

Horse Girl and Seattle fell into their own

conversation, allowing the three of us to continue our conversation more privately. Things flowed fairly smoothly after that, and I realized this conversation was the first time that I'd actually felt relaxed since being on campus.

Ironically, one of my favorite things about Marcus was his intense love of malaphors.

"Do you know what malaphors are?" he asked.

Finley and I looked at each other before shaking our heads.

"They're the only part of the English language I actually like," he joked. *"It's when two idioms are intentionally blended together and it creates something that doesn't really make sense. My favorite one is 'we'll burn that bridge when we get to it.'"*

We laughed awkwardly, prompting a deeper conversation about the differences between ASL and English idioms and the superiority of the former. Neither Finley nor I had spent much time analyzing the English language beyond writing essays or doing reports on famous pieces of literature to appease our high school teachers and satisfy the class requirements. But to know there was something redeeming and even interesting about English? That really was fascinating.

By the time the workshop had ended, we were all chomping at the bit to get some food. The dining hall, officially named the Campus Commons Dining Facility but lovingly referred to as The Commons, sat cozily at the edge of Wilkins Lawn, a stretch of grass acting as the central greenery on campus between the four of the seven dormitories. The building was new and modern, with floor to ceiling windows facing The Lawn. Rows of round tables filled half the large room, opposite a collection of food stations manned by staff in aprons and matching chef jackets. Each station was labeled and included vegetarian/vegan options, make-your-own-pizzas, smoothies, a salad bar, a spot called The Grille serving up burgers and wraps, and a corner station with some questionable-looking sushi.

Growing up, my mom was the chef de cuisine while my dad served as her loyal sous. She would come up with the weekly shopping list and prepare the meals she'd lovingly chosen to cook for us. Requesting something off-menu was a no-go, with the only options being eat or don't. Having these many options all at once was overwhelming, although there was an unquestionable disparity in quality. My mother's homemade meals could outshine anything The Commons offered, without a shadow of a doubt.

Perusing each station, I ultimately decided on a chicken quesadilla from The Grille and a strawberry-banana smoothie. Marcus and Fin were already seated at a table nearest the wall of windows, radiating warm smiles as I took my seat.

"Remind me, what are you two majoring in again?" Marcus asked, swallowing a large bite of his California roll. His eyebrows dug into each other curiously as he glanced between Fin and I. Before either of us could respond, he offered his own response. *"I'm in the interpreting program."*

"Communications," I replied, taking a sip of smoothie as I turned to Fin.

"Forensic science," she added, no doubt coming up with a list of fast facts in her head just in case Marcus was daring enough to ask further questions.

"Interesting," he finally said, grinning. *"Are you one of those girls who watches the gruesome serial killer stuff?"*

"Absolutely." Fin smiled in her usual I'm-awesome-and-you're-right-to-acknowledge-it sort of way. The confidence she exuded could've filled the room if she'd let it. *"I know a dozen ways to bury a body and get away with it."*

But we couldn't get away with a simple prank? Yeah, okay. Go off, Fin.

I kicked her leg under the table with the toe of my shoe in an effort to curb her enthusiasm and get her to back off. I had to chill her out before she ran off the first friend we'd managed to make on campus. Finley didn't have time to react beyond a pained expression as she reached to rub at her shin. Another tray was dropped onto our table and I looked up to find someone new had decided to join us.

"Anyone sitting here?" they asked, sliding into their seat effortlessly as if no one had ever once denied them entry into their lives.

"No, go for it," I said, happy for our little table to grow.

There were a wealth of contributions to my mounting anxiety in the recent days, but making friends had been at the top of the list. Post-Rider-induced-humiliation, I could count on one hand the number of friends I'd made throughout high school, mostly due to the fact I'd spent more time reading in the library than participating in activities, clubs, or social events. To have already made two friends in the first few days was a welcome relief.

"Cool, thanks. I'm Wade. Wade Rivera," they offered, flashing a smile at all of us.

The first thing I noticed about them was the attention to detail they paid to their outfit. Stylish, but not in the avant-garde kind of way that turned heads and seemed out of place. Torn black jeans with an embroidered white patterning sprouted from a pair of black Chelsea boots looking comfortably worn-in from what I suspected were years of wear. A white t-shirt peeked out from beneath a denim jacket while a pair of aviator sunglasses rested neatly at the edge of its neckline. The amber lenses mirrored the warmth of their brown skin, face framed in dark curls falling to their jawline. Everything about their appearance was highly manicured with dedicated precision.

Taking turns surveying each of us, Wade continued as they picked up their fork and prodded at the buffalo cauliflower bites on the plate in front of them. Without missing a beat, Wade smiled at us. "I'm a sophomore. Computer science, although I haven't officially declared yet."

"*You live in Brighton, right?*" Marcus asked Wade. "*I think I've seen you around.*"

"*Yeah, fourth floor. How are you settling in?*"

"*Decent,*" Marcus shrugged. "*Third floor bathroom flooded last night, though. Any tips?*"

"*Get a room off campus your sophomore year.*" Wade chuckled, shaking their head. "*I got hosed in the housing lottery. My neighbors are a bunch of freshmen and one of them is a real prick. He was arguing with some girl in the hallway when I got back from dinner last night. They were yelling at each other and he grabbed her by the arm and pulled her against a wall. Before I could step in, she took off crying. I asked him what the hell was going on, but he just flipped me off and went back into his room.*"

According to the welcome packet I'd memorized,

LCU was on the smaller side. Given it was a private institution with roughly six thousand students enrolled in any given academic year, it was just big enough to offer a variety of majors and extracurriculars but small enough that avoiding people was going to be a challenge. My gaze darted to meet Fin's and I could tell we were both thinking the exact same thing: could they be talking about Rider? His was the only name coming to mind as I listened to Wade's description. Despite the freshman class this year being nearly fifteen hundred, there was only one who would be arrogant and thoughtless enough to treat someone like their own personal rag doll. I knew I had to ask a follow-up question, even if I'd already seen the answer flashing on a giant neon sign.

"Did you catch his name?" I asked, my leg bouncing beneath the cover of the table.

"No, it seemed like he wasn't in much of a talking mood," Wade said, shoveling another bite of cauliflower onto their fork.

The hunger pangs I'd felt earlier had dissipated. As I sat there, trying my best to keep my cool, the only thing on my mind was the fact that Rider was here, on campus, instead of the fancy fancy boarding school his ass should've been shipped off to. Him being here meant that he could have taped that photo to my door and sent me that text.

I cautioned a glance in Fin's direction. The look she shot my way urged me to relax, her eyes wide and pleading as she picked up her fork and took a bite of her scrambled eggs—all without breaking eye contact. How was I supposed to relax when I'd have to spend the next four years with him lingering over my shoulder. This was supposed to be a fresh start. I'd naively told myself, after what had happened between us, Rider would realize the error of his ways without legal action. I'd convinced myself his parents would wake up and see their son for who he was becoming and put a stop to it. But I can't expect them to do anything when they've spent eighteen years enabling his behavior.

"It was great to meet you, Wade," Marcus said as he rose to his feet. *"But I've got to head out. There's a mixer tonight for my cohort. See you guys later?"*

We all nodded as he took off with a wave and a smile that stretched from ear to ear.

The tines at the end of my fork poked at the melted cheese sliding its way out of the warm tortilla. Instead of lifting it to my mouth to take another bite, I nudged at the quesadilla and pushed several loose grapes around my plate mindlessly.

Two thumps wobbled across the table. Finley and Wade were looking at me with quizzical expressions, waiting for me to answer a question I hadn't realized they'd asked. Having neglected our conversation, I tacked on a smile and set my fork down.

I was there physically, but mentally I was somewhere else.

It had been a few days since the photo had shown up on my doorstep, and I had an intense desire to crawl beneath my covers and hide until whoever was tormenting me finally lost interest. I'd more or less written it off as a joke, probably Rider's version of getting me back for what Finley and I had done to his car. A warning that we were even. Maybe we could call a truce and put this all behind us. The further I could distance myself from him, from all of it, the better off I'd be. Besides, in the meantime, I still had a life to live.

"Sorry, what did you say?" I asked, tapping my index finger against my chin.

Fin laughed and resumed eating her omelet, knowing full well this was nothing new. I was a chronic overthinker—incurably so—and, on most occasions, could be found lost in my own thoughts even in the midst of conversation.

Wade shot me a look as they poked a piece of melon with their fork and popped it into their mouth. *"I was saying you seem a little distracted this morning. What's up?"* they asked, brows knitted together in curiosity.

My eyes scanned the room, looking for Rider

lurking in a corner or staring at me from across the room. Instead, that's when I saw her.

She lived on my floor in Thompson Hall, directly across from me. Her long, almost jet-black hair was now tied up in a bun atop her head as she stood at the hot sandwich station, wisps of hair framing her face as she picked out a pair of rye bread slices from a heap on a tray. Of course it was rye. An interesting bread choice for an interesting person.

Wade turned to follow my gaze, a smirk coiled at the corner of their mouth.

"Ahhh, so we've found the distraction," they teased. There was a certain snark to Wade that was both admirable and, at times, frustrating.

"Any idea who that is?" I asked, nodding my head in her direction. She was wearing a green hoodie with the number thirteen printed on the back in large ivory numbers.

"Wish I could help, but I have no idea," Wade replied. *"Judging by her sweatshirt, though, I'd bet she's an athlete."*

Before I could make another comment, or inquire further, Finley had contorted herself in her chair, waving her outstretched arm overhead in Thirteen's direction. She'd been standing there, aimlessly, searching for a place to sit with her tray in her hands. I knew that feeling well, and I sympathized, but my mouth went as dry as the Sahara at the idea of her sitting with us. Admiring this girl from afar and eating a meal with her were two very different things—I was not prepared for the latter. My eyes widened and I banged on the table in a hurried attempt to stop Finley. Swiftly looking back at me with a glare I knew was her way of telling me to chill out, my best friend resumed her beckoning.

Leaning back in my seat, defeat set in. Maybe I could fake a case of early onset food poisoning...

Thirteen noticed Fin and flashed her a tender smile as she headed our way and sat in one of the several available chairs that surrounded the round table.

"Thanks. I think my teammates already ate, so I wasn't sure who to sit with." She reached for her fork and then quickly set it back down, her polite smile melting into a bright momentary laugh. *"I'm Tayen,"* she said. Her sign name, an initialized 'T' tapping against the side of her cheek, which she explained was a reference to the love of sweets she'd had since childhood. The way her eyes glinted when she laughed was infectious, and I instinctively wiped my palms along the thighs of my jeans. Her eyes fell onto me as I chimed in.

"I'm Lennon." A meager half-smile was all I could manage, my mind preoccupied with heightened awareness of every sweat gland on my body.

Tayen grinned before focusing her attention on the

others.

"Wade," they nodded.

"Finley." Fin said, before diving in. *"You said teammates? What sport do you play?"*

Nodding, Tayen leaned back in her seat and stretched out the front of her sweatshirt, which read 'LCU Women's Soccer' across the front in ivory, block lettering. Scooting her chair back up to the table, she clarified. *"I'm on the JV soccer team. Do any of you play sports?"*

"No way." Finley laughed, shaking her head dramatically. *"I'm a watcher, not a player. And Lennon,"* she gestured to me, *"is uncoordinated enough without adding running or any kind of ball into the mix."* Her eyes flicked to me and I was reminded of the week-long badminton circuit in gym class that had been enough to send me to the nurse's office four times.

Frozen, possessed by embarrassment, my eyes flicking between each of my tablemates as I poked at a grape until my fork pressed through it. *"I'm not that bad..."* I tried to defend, hoping she wouldn't ask for a demonstration or a one-on-one display of my non-existent athletic abilities. *"Have you played on the team long?"* I asked, hoping to course correct.

Tayen swallowed another bite of waffle. *"I joined last year as a freshman,"* she replied, indicating the year by tapping the tip of her ring finger against the pad of her thumb as she readied another bite of food on her fork.

"Finally someone in my year," Wade chimed in, before motioning to Finley and I. *"They're freshmen."*

"Oh, cool, my brother's a freshman, too. Are you all going to movie night tonight?" Tayen asked.

I had reviewed the schedule for Orientation Week, but somehow hadn't bothered to actually look at the list of campus events for the weekend now that classes were starting on Monday.

"They're showing The Princess Bride *on a giant, inflatable screen over on Lowman Field,"* Tayen added, *"with popcorn machines and everything."*

"Yeah, we're definitely going." Fin said, without hesitation, nudging me under the table.

I looked at her for visual confirmation, and she shot me a wide-eyed smile that told me to go with it. *"Yeah, absolutely. We'll be there. Should we… go together?"* I asked, realizing mid-sentence that desperation was probably not going to help me make new friends, let alone earn me any points with my cute neighbor. Quickly, I rephrased my proposition. *"Like, all of us… together… as a group."* Finley dug her foot into my leg under the table again, this time harder than before.

Wade stifled a laugh and rubbed the side of their face.

Tayen's relaxed expression was borderline flirty, not that I'd had much experience in the matter, and she nodded swiftly. *"Yeah, let's do it."*

"If you want to sit back and play The Bachelorette, *be my guest,"* Fin snorted.

"What are you talking about?" I queried, snaking two hands up to pull my hair into a taut ponytail. We had both opted to take a nap after lunch, but now it was time to get ready for movie night. *"We've got bigger fish to fry, remember?"*

I waved my phone at her before setting it on top of my dresser, and the screen lit up.

Carefully eyeing Finley, I hesitated to pick it up.

"Len, it's a text. It's not going to bite you."

The inside of my cheek was raw from chewing on it.

As soon as I picked up the phone, there it was: another text from the unknown number.

"Who is it?" Fin chirped.

Clicking into the message, there was a video file waiting for me.

"It's a video," I said.

Finley stepped over to me, neck craning over my shoulder. *"Press play."*

I did, and to our mutual horror it was a clip from the security camera in Rider's garage. It was clearly from the night of the party, with Finley and I in clear view. It was a short clip, and it never showed who entered the garage after we left, but it was enough to make my skin crawl.

"Whoa," Finley murmured. *"Even I wasn't expecting that..."*

"This is Rider, fucking with us," I huff, pacing across the small room. *"I know it is. He's here and he's trying to make us sweat for what happened to his car. That's all this is, right?"*

For once, Finley didn't have an answer.

"He's rubbing our noses in it, that he knows we were the ones in his garage that night," I said, abruptly stopping where I stood. *"You said he turns the cameras off during parties, right?"*

"Yeah. Why?"

"Does anyone else have access to the footage?"

"I don't think so. I doubt it, but there's no real way to know for sure unless you feel like asking Rider—"

"Absolutely not," I interject, frowning as hard as my facial muscles will allow.

"I know that talking to him is your worst nightmare incarnate," Fin started. *"But you might want to consider that talking to him could help us get to the bottom of all of*

this."

I hate it when she uses logic to pad her arguments.

"We're running late," I grumbled, grabbing my crewneck LCU sweatshirt off of the back of my desk chair and heading for the door.

Talking to Rider might eventually become a necessity, but right now I wanted to focus on spending time in Tayen's orbit. Movie night was the perfect opportunity to lay some groundwork, to get to know her and spend time doing something fun.

As the sun set on Lowman Field, the atmosphere began to shift. The smell of buttered popcorn mixed with the crisp evening air as groups of students started to huddle together on scattered blankets, eagerly anticipating the start of The Princess Bride.

Finley and I headed towards the spot Marcus and Wade had staked out near the front, our eyes scanning the crowd for any sign of The Ghost. We were determined to solve this puzzle, starting with identifying our enemy, and movie night presented the perfect opportunity to utilize our sleuthing skills and play detective for the evening. At least, it did for Finley. She was hell-bent on using the next two hours to suss out clues, though I had an inkling she wanted to let me focus my energy on Tayen. Our awkward interaction at The Commons left a lot to be desired, and I needed to make sure our second impression more than made up for it.

As we waited for the movie to begin, we reviewed the plan of action. If I received another message, she would keep an eye out for anyone who seemed to be texting at the same time. Assuming no texts came through, our back up plan was to keep our eyes peeled for anyone paying too close of attention to us or looking around suspiciously. It wasn't the best plan, but we were working with what we had.

Before we could dive too deep into our reconnaissance, Tayen spotted us and turned up at our blanket with a slew of assorted snacks and drinks.

"I wasn't sure what anyone liked, so I brought options," she smiled.

A girl after my own pragmatic heart.

Tayen did a double take as soon as she noticed Marcus.

"What are you doing here?" Her eyes darted from him to me. *"How do you know my brother?"*

"Marcus is your brother?" I asked, remembering that I hadn't asked what her brother's name was when she mentioned him earlier. In fact, he hadn't mentioned his sister's name the other day, either. Seeing them next to one other, I'm not sure how I didn't put two and two together. Their features were so similar, despite hers being softer. Their eyes were the same dark, honeyed

bronze. Tayen's skin was tanner than Marcus', though it wasn't a leap to discern why given all of the time he spent playing video games while she played on the soccer field.

A bewildered expression warped Marcus' features as he gestured between Tayen and I. *"How do you two know each other?"*

"We met at breakfast this morning," Tayen explained, gesturing towards our group. The longer I looked at them the more I noticed they shared oddly coincidental facial features. *"You just can't have any of your own friends, huh?"* Her tone was light and teasing.

Marcus shot her a smug smirk. *"I could say the same thing to you—I met them first."*

As the opening credits of the movie began to roll, we settled in, while keeping a watchful eye on our surroundings. Much to our chagrin, Rider was nowhere to be seen. Every few minutes, I surreptitiously checked my phone, hoping for a text message while also dreading the possibility one might come through.

But the screen remained stubbornly blank.

The movie progressed and the crowd around us grew still, save for the side conversations spouting from the sporadic clusters of students dotted across the lawn. Finley and I kept our focus, scanning the crowd for any potential leads. About halfway through the movie, I felt a tap on my shoulder.

I turned around to find Theo wearing a friendly smile.

"Mind if I join you?"

I wanted to shake my head, make up an excuse, do something to make it clear we didn't want him sitting with us. That he wasn't welcome simply because of his loyalty to Rider. But I couldn't. What reason would we have to be avoiding him? Avoiding Rider's best friend. Someone who had not only seen us at the party but welcomed us at the door like his buddy's personal butler. He was on our suspect list for a reason, and I needed to keep my eyes peeled for any potential clues. No one else would be as willing as he would to make sure his best friend's secrets stayed hidden, and that made him dangerous.

Glancing at Finley, the snarky expression on her face was exactly what I didn't need right now. As if we were sharing a moment of telepathic connection, a silent conversation between us lifted the hairs on my arm.

See?

What?

Thank god one of us is investigating, prime suspect number two just dropped into our lap.

Yeah, yeah, that's enough.

Ignoring something doesn't make it go away.

I wasn't so sure. The more distance I could keep between myself and The Ghost, the better. This was my chance to have the quintessential college experience and I wasn't about to let some masked madman ruin it for me.

To make things worse, Theo seemed fairly harmless. I doubted he was anywhere near underhanded enough to pull this off, and I knew for a fact he'd been upstairs with Cara while Finley and I were busy in the garage. He couldn't have been in two places at once, and that effectively ruled him out as a suspect. Regardless, I couldn't shake the feeling something felt off with him. Something about the way he looked at us and the artificial way his face crinkled when he laid on that thick smile made me uneasy. He'd been spending far too much time around Rider, picking up his traits and the chilling idiosyncrasies I'd spent the past few years trying to wipe from my memory.

I hesitated for a moment, then shrugged. *"Sure, why not."*

As Theo settled in next to us, I silently wondered if I was being paranoid. Maybe I was overthinking this, dragging everyone around me into some fantastical danger of my mind's own conjuring.

"I'm surprised you're not sitting with Rider and your crew," Finley signed, breaking the tension.

"The guys are skipping movie night, but this one's my favorite, so I figured I'd come solo." Theo brushed his hands against his pants and rested folded arms atop his knees.

Finley and I cautioned a glance at one another. The last time we'd all watched this movie together was just at Rider's house. We'd all been at his house for a watch party, eyes glued to the screen as Inigo Montoya said his famous line in the theater room. I was sandwiched between Finley and Iris on a reclining leather sofa while the rest of our group was sprawled out on the other couches. Halfway through the movie, once Iris and Finley had both fallen asleep, Rider invited me upstairs and we went out onto the porch. Wrapped in a single blanket to keep us warm, we talked about the future. Not necessarily a shared one, but what we saw for ourselves beyond the confines of high school. How he wanted to become an architect or a civil engineer or anything other than the businessman that his father wanted him to become, and my own dreams of becoming an investigative journalist.

Theo's presence wasn't inherently bothersome, but spending excess time around anyone close to Rider was feverishly unsettling. Their friendship presented a threat to me, but Finley refused to believe that he could ever do something like that. In a universe where we could reasonably tie his culpability to the movies he liked, his enjoyment of *The Princess Bride* would definitely earn him disarming brownie points.

I returned my attention to the movie and reached toward the feast of snacks nestled comfortably in a pile at the center of our blanket. As I picked up a bag of chips, my hand suddenly felt warm. Tayen's own had crept towards mine, and I discarded the chips haphazardly, feeling the blood rush to my face. Regret sank in, internally scolding myself for jerking my hand away from hers so quickly.

"Sorry," we both offered, awkwardly and simultaneously.

The blood rushed to my face. I was grateful it was dark, the sparse light from the projector screen not enough to cast more than a soft glow across the field. For now, I'd been spared the humiliation of my crush on Tayen being so obvious that I had to wear evidence of it across my cheeks.

The tension mounted in my chest as the movie continued to play, and my mind was running at the pace of an Olympic medalist. Trying hard to keep my focus on the movie, I couldn't help but glance over at Theo every so often.

The movie entered its final act and my phone buzzed in my pocket.

It was an email from the school's student portal, with the subject line: *Are You Ready for a Scavenger Hunt?* I clicked on the notification and opened the message to scan its contents, reaching out to tap Finley's arm and hand her my phone.

"Have you seen this?" I asked. *"Apparently there's a scavenger hunt tomorrow."*

The credits at the end of the movie began to roll and we started to clean up the mess of snacks and fold the blanket we'd been sitting on. Wade and Marcus had taken off in the middle of the movie, having decided to go check out something called the 'gaming lounge', coincidentally giving them an out when it came time for us to clean up and head back to our rooms.

Theo had looked over Finley's shoulder and seen the email, chiming in before she could hand it back to me. *"Are you guys planning to go?"*

I shrugged, looking between Tayen and Finley, who were wearing equally unsure expressions.

"What time is it at?" Tayen asked, tucking the folded blanket over her arm.

"Nine o'clock," he replied. *"I heard there are prizes for the winners and everything."* He flashed a smile at Finley. *"I've still got a spot on my team, if you want to join us?"*

Finley, Tayen, and I exchanged a look, intrigued by

the idea. This could be just what we needed to take our minds off everything and have some fun. Something I'd been incessantly told I was in dire need of.

"I'm gonna have to team up with my friends, but thanks for the offer," Finley added, corralling Tayen and I by draping her arms across our shoulders as she stood between us.

"Too bad." Theo's eyes sparkled with amusement as he eyed Finley. *"I guess I'll see you three in the morning, then."* He waved as he headed off toward Brighton Hall, jogging to catch up with a group of boys he must've recognized.

We made our way off the field and back through Thompson Hall's lobby doors. I said goodnight to Fin and Tayen once we'd exited the elevator on our floor, pushing aside the buzzing thoughts of everything other than the thrill of tomorrow's hunt and another opportunity to learn more about the girl across the hall. Before allowing myself to nod off, I typed out a pair of messages and looped everyone into a group thread.

Scavenger hunt tomorrow.

Everyone in?

Finley was the first to reply, with a simple thumbs up emoji. Typical. Everyone else's responses filed in after that, each person agreeing to join in—even Wade and Tayen, whose sophomore status gave them both an easy out. I sent out one final message coordinating a meet-up at The Commons the following morning and clicked my phone's screen off.

EIGHT DAYS BEFORE THE MURDER

I was up earlier than I should've been, before breakfast was even being served. Several outfits and an unusually exorbitant amount of time in front of the mirror later, I was approaching our table. Finley was half-awake and nursing a coffee beside Marcus and Wade, who were chatting away about some video game I had never heard of. Marcus asked how to pull off a particularly stealthy move he'd failed to master, despite hours spent in front of the console, and Wade warned that he should be careful not to set himself up for failure. Tayen hadn't joined us yet, but she knew to meet us at The Brew.

We discussed our strategy to crush the other teams as we made our way across campus toward the designated starting location. Ever since last night I'd been hyper-vigilantly taking note of anyone who might be staring from across the way or allowing their eyes to linger on me just a little too long. I couldn't help but be wary about who was watching, eavesdropping on our conversations from afar. Was it just my imagination, or did it seem almost too calm since the last message? How much time would pass before the next one would—

The front pocket of my corduroy pants vibrated.

KEEP YOUR FRIENDS CLOSE, LEN.

Along with the text was a photo of the four of us from just a few moments ago. I tried to take note of the vantage point. Towards the side? Behind?

Not everyone was out to get me, but someone definitely was.

How was I supposed to focus now when I just wanted to hide?

Swallowing hard, I entered the Student Activities building. Comprising the first three floors was the Student Union, which housed all of the student organization offices, club rooms, and the campus paper, The Clerc Courier. The two uppermost floors of the five-story building were mostly made up of conference rooms and offices for a variety of campus staff. Sprawling across the entire first and second floors was a student-run coffee shop, known as The Brew. It was a central hangout, a place where students gathered to study, talk, and even enjoy some peaceful alone time with a good book.

Tufted leather couches were tucked cozily between tables with years' worth of scratches and coffee rings, the warmth of the morning's sunlight beaming in through large, multi-pane windows with freshly painted black trim. Round tables with padded chairs provided generous seating throughout the large room, occasionally interrupted by joists supporting the open second floor above. Behind the counter, baristas churned out a variety of drinks while they stood in front of a wall-mounted chalkboard showcasing the menu in mismatched handwritten fonts and colors. Everything smelled like my favorite scent in the world: coffee.

It was clear we weren't the only ones taking the competition seriously, as others had gathered early. There were already several dozen teams present, many of whom were clad in spirited gear and wearing their IDs around their necks on the LCU-branded lanyards every freshman had received during move-in, nursing coffees and gearing up for the competition. We took a seat at a table in the corner, and Wade waved at someone behind the counter. They nodded and confirmed they would be somewhere tomorrow morning at six, but I'd missed the first part of the conversation because I hadn't been paying attention.

"What's happening tomorrow?" I asked.

"I just got a job here, they were hiring for baristas. I start training tomorrow morning."

I raised my brows enthusiastically. *"That's great, congrats!"*

"Thanks, I'm excited about it. It'll give me a break from staring at my computer so much. Can't be any worse than working at my uncle's law office filing papers all summer."

Nodding, my attention was drawn away by Tayen approaching the table we'd commandeered. She smiled warmly at me as she made her way past a few other students.

"Finally," Marcus teased. *"Where were you?"*

"I had some things to take care of," she said, brushing past his question. *"I'm here now, aren't I?"*

The slight defensiveness in her tone was abrasive. Her tardiness was convenient, considering she hadn't been there when The Ghost had taken the photo of the group of us. She'd been the only one missing, and there was no way it was a coincidence.

Then, before any of us could say anything else, our attention was directed toward an older student. Standing atop one of the tables with a stack of papers in his hand, he wore an adhesive name tag stuck to his shirt, 'Gage' scrawled across it in jagged, capitalized letters. He waved his hands above his head, stopping only once everyone's eyes focused on him.

"Hey there, everyone, I'm Gage Harris." He spelled out his name, his agile hands making quick work of the introduction. *"My pronouns are he, him, and his, and I'm a graduate assistant in the Student Activities office. This scavenger hunt is designed to take you all over campus to help you get familiar with the lay of the land, including the library. Don't let today be the only day you set foot in there."* His rehearsed smile was unwavering, despite only a few scattered bouts of laughter. *"This activity is a chance for you to get to know your fellow classmates and learn how to work together toward a common goal. That being said, there are a few prizes to be won, of course!"*

The crowd busted into raucous hollering, like a hive of bees whirring as they worked.

Gage motioned for everyone to settle down. *"The first team back will win a flat screen tv, the runners-up will win a gaming console, and our third-place team will be awarded a tablet and a thirty-dollar gift card to Taco Fiesta."* Excitement among the crowd grew as the prizes were announced. *"This is the list, so don't lose it!"* Gage announced, holding up the stack of papers. *"Each team gets one copy, and you won't be given another one if yours is lost. Understood? At the top of the page, you'll find a link to a folder. For each task you complete, you must upload a photo of all your teammates with the item or area visible. We'll be monitoring your submissions and the first team to upload all the clues and return here wins."*

When Gage stepped down from the table to distribute the lists, Finley bounded up to grab one on our team's behalf before we could begin to strategize. Once they were all dispersed, Gage stamped his feet on the table, sending a slew of vibrations throughout the room. Everyone turned to look up at him, a resolute grin taking over his face.

"Your time starts now!" he announced.

List in hand, we headed out of The Brew as the swell of people flowed through the doors and took off into the crisp morning air. Huddled together, we reviewed the task list. My eyes skimmed the first item: **#1_______ and the Jets.**

It didn't take more than a second for me to figure out the clue.

"Bennie!" I exclaimed.

Everyone looked at me like I'd grown a second head.

"Bennie and the Jets," I said, quickly realizing no one knew what I was talking about. *"It's an Elton John song."*

Blank stares were the only acknowledgment I received.

"Okay, so then that one must be the bulldog statue," Wade said.

Benny the Bulldog, a bronze statue of our mascot, had been standing at the front gates since the inception of the university some eighty-some-odd years ago.

"We should skip further down," Marcus said, pointing down toward the middle of the list. *"Everyone will be rushing to do them in order. If we start down here, we can loop back."*

We all nodded, watching in unison as the entire crowd headed in the same direction.

"If we go with this one," Wade pointed at the fifth item on the list: **#5. 114 ways to kill a mockingbird**. *"We can start at the library. That book is in the library's fiction section. I borrowed it last year and read it for my literature class."* Their observational nature had once again peeked out. Wade was like a pond, its glass veneer shielding vast unfathomable depths.

They led our team across campus to the library. One of the oldest buildings, if not the oldest, its three-story structure mimicked the architecture of the rest of campus. Large windows let in natural light, soaking every surface. Rows of tall bookshelves and circular tables provided ample study space. Each floor was open at the center, from the top floor down through to the lower basement levels. Following our seasoned sophomore, the rest of us trailed behind until we'd found the fiction section, tucked back in a far corner of the uppermost level. Each of us took a shelf and scoured the stacks, but Tayen was the one who found it first.

Her hand brushed the worn cover of Harper Lee's novel and we gathered around her. As we opened the book to page one-hundred-and-fourteen, a sticky note was adhered to the paper. Rough scrawl read: look beneath the shelf. I froze in a panic. Something about this didn't feel right.

"*What the hell?*" Fin asked, her lip arching as her brow creased.

Marcus' hands felt along the length of the shelf and then he paused, eyes wide. "*There's something here,*" he said.

A moment later, he was pulling something down and revealing it to us.

A crowbar.

Finley's crowbar.

Damnit.

Heat rose to my cheek. I knew that had been at the scene of our crime, and the only other person who knew about its existence was Finley and Rider. There was no way it would turn up during a scavenger hunt—unless they wanted it to. They were using it to send a message; to tell us we weren't in control, they were.

"We're missing something, aren't we?" Wade asked.

"No," I answered, a little too quickly. *"I mean… it's complicated."* Lying to my friends, no matter how recently they'd earned the title, was painful. Even the smallest of betrayals made me feel like I was back at Stone Valley, on the verge of losing all of my friends all over again—like they would learn the truth and banish me from their lives without a second thought.

As if called, Rider and his team climbed the stairs into view. I motioned for the others to get down, hoping they wouldn't mind a momentary hiccup in our gameplay so I wouldn't have to face my nemesis this early in the school year. We watched as his team gathered armfuls of books and huddled at a nearby study table, piling everything haphazardly at the center of its circular surface. We all crouched down along the length of the aisle, with Finley playing lookout and peeking around the corner every so often. Tayen and I were sitting shoulder-to-shoulder on the floor nearby, hidden from view behind the tall bookshelf filled with rows of aging literary fiction.

My hand gently tapped against Tayen's knee and then coiled against itself.

"You okay?" she asked, her hands low and slow.

"Yeah, why?" I asked.

The measured gentleness in her movements accompanied sympathetic eyes. This side of Tayen was softer, although it wasn't clear for whose benefit. Either she was trying to put me at ease, or she was working to calm her own nerves; my money was on the latter.

"Just checking."

"I'm okay," I reiterated, her deep eyes reflecting light back into mine like glassy snow globes under the fluorescent light raining down on us.

There was a genuine quality to Tayen, and I adored that she'd chosen to share it with me. Even still, I couldn't shake the feeling she knew I was keeping something just out of reach. As if she could see that there was a skeleton in my closet I didn't want her to know about just yet.

She gave a lighthearted smile, looking to add a bit of levity to the situation. *"Okay."*

Finley flagged us down, tearing my attention away from Tayen. *"They're gone. Let's get out of here,"* she said, the lot of us scrambling to our feet. *"What's next on the list, Marcus?"* she asked, flirtatiously batting her eyes.

Seemingly willing to put the drama aside, for now, Marcus looked at the sheet of paper and rattled off item number six verbatim. *"This deaf person had great chemistry with the Nobel Prize."*

Equally unwilling to let us dwell on the crowbar, Fin shoved it into her backpack and we took a group photo with the library's copy of *To Kill a Mockingbird* before shelving it and heading out the side entrance.

One down, nine to go.

Turning on her heel, Tayen led us toward the west side of campus.

She knew the answer to the next clue and led us to Turner Hall's Ackley Science & Technology Center, home to a state-of-the-art computer lab, multifunctional workspaces, a 3D printing alcove, and a small reference library. It was the hub for all the STEM-majors, and Wade jokingly admitted that most of them spent more time there than in their own dorm rooms. I wondered if their freshman year had been similarly spent, with hours dedicated to coding assignments and reading books on cybersecurity best practices and firewall installations.

Leading the way, after admitting she had poured quite a few hours into her studies here during her introductory science courses, Tayen stopped us in front of the elevator. *"The bust we need to take a photo with is upstairs, on the third floor,"* she said, proudly hitting the call button. *"It's right outside my organic chemistry professor's office."*

The air of confidence and intelligence inhabiting her was beyond attractive. Every time I learned something new, it added to her complexity. It made me want to learn more, to sit her down and ask a million questions, but before I could think of one, a shoulder tap knocked me out of my daze and reminded me we were on a mission.

The team packed into the elevator with childish cackles as we ascended upwards.

Tayen ushered us down a long corridor, past opaque glass office doors, empty meeting rooms, and a slew of classrooms, their desks neatly arranged in functional half-moons creating workable space for visual discussions in ASL. We had traveled not quite twenty feet before we were standing in front of the bust of Sir John W. Cornforth. She rested a hand on the top of the sculpted plaster and turned toward us, as if she'd practiced a monologue to launch into.

"Team, meet Sir John Cornforth. Sir John, meet the team," Tayen said, gesturing toward us for no one's benefit.

It was enough to elicit at least a smile from each of us, Marcus taking the prime opportunity to make a joke. *"Pleasure to meet you, Sir,"* he signed dramatically, bowing before rising back up to his full height.

"Sir John," Tayen continued, glaring at Marcus dangerously, *"was a deaf chemist from Australia who won a Nobel Prize in chemistry in 1975."*

Our clueless expressions conveyed our wild unfamiliarity to Tayen, and she shook her head in mock disapproval. *"Hurry up and take this picture before I give you all a TedTalk on deaf science history."*

I pulled out my phone and snapped a quick photo. Second task, secured.

By the time we managed to circle back to the first four tasks on the list, we knew we weren't going to have a chance at placing in the top three—not that the competition was at the front of our minds anymore. At least, it wasn't in front of mine.

The summer air kissed our skin as we trudged across the lawn and into The Brew, relieved to feel the air-conditioned climate break us from the Mediterranean heat. All we had left to do was upload the final photo of the five of us, looking equal parts exhausted and exhilarated, hugging one of the bright yellow goalposts on the football field, surrounded by sycamore and oak trees, whose branches stretched upward and jutted out to interrupt the bright blue cloudless sky.

A concerned look appeared on Wade's face as we dropped onto a pair of loveseats.

"Um… we have a problem," they said, looking up from their phone screen.

"What now?" Fin complained. *"Tell me there isn't a WiFi problem, again. I fought to connect with it for hours last night."*

"Not an internet problem..." Wade said. *"All of our photos are gone."*

I blinked in disbelief. *"What?"*

"Every photo is gone," they reiterated. *"There's only one in the folder now, but it's not ours."* Tapping away, Wade's lips pressed together as they concentrated. Nostrils flared just slightly, annoyance peppered their collected demeanor.

As I unlocked my phone to have a look for myself, a notification popped onto my screen and my stomach dropped.

SECRETS DON'T STAY BURIED FOR LONG

I handed the phone to Finley so she could read it.

Finley didn't look at it for more than a few microseconds before her eyes met mine.

"We need to go," she said. *"Now."*

The adrenaline had drained from my body at some point during the delirious walk back to Thompson. Today's events were playing on a broken loop in my head like a drive-in movie with a bad projector screen. Thinking about the text I'd received in the chemistry hallway, it was clear Tayen couldn't have sent it while the rest of us were standing right beside her. She also hadn't been at Rider's party that night. The odds were stacking up against her being the one tormenting me. The only person that made sense was Rider, but the back and forth was starting to get to me. I didn't have any solid evidence to prove or disprove Rider's involvement, though. There were so many questions and so few answers.

Tayen's strides unfolded in front of me like a methodically arranged line of dominoes had gingerly been pushed over. They cascaded from one into the next, hypnotically.

We piled into Thompson Hall's lobby and headed straight for the stairs to avoid the long wait for the elevators. They were painfully slow and cramped, creaking and scraping even without any weight on them. Anytime we could take the stairs, it was worth the trek.

Finley tapped her ID against the door lock and swung it open. We filed in behind her, watching as Fin completed her first act of hospitality: lighting her favorite incense. The smell of wildflowers and sandalwood drifted through the room, burning in a tray perched atop her dresser. Incense was on the list of banned items as per the student handbook, but arguing about it with Finley was hardly worth the trouble. I wasn't in the mood to have yet another discussion on the influence of fragrances on the brain and cognitive function, either.

Looking around the room, I realized I didn't really know any of these people. Sure, it had felt like coincidences running into each of them, sitting at our table like a little makeshift family, but these could have all been orchestrated events. What if Rider planned to use those messages to sow discord among us, just as I was finally making friends? My head was swimming with questions and possibilities, on the verge of drowning.

Finley's eyes pierced into me as she looked up from my screen, urging me not to push this aside. I'd been running from it since it began, but there were too few places to hide.

'Tell them,' Finley mouthed.

I shook my head.

I wasn't ready, I couldn't just bare my soul on cue.

Fin's eyes widened and she jutted her chin downward, egging me on.

As it stood, only Fin and I were stuck in the middle of whatever this was. If we told them even the basics of what had led us here, would things get worse for them? Would our innocent friends become targets, too? Maybe it was better to cut them loose, give them a chance to skate past this and avoid whatever trouble they would no doubt encounter because of me.

I shook my head and attempted to step past Finley, no longer interested in telling them what was going on. It wasn't fair to selfishly pull them in when they had no idea what might lie ahead.

Finley sighed and grabbed onto me as I tried to pass her.

"Okay..." She started as she slid a strap off her shoulder and pulled the crowbar out of her backpack. *"I,"* she emphasized, shooting me a daring glance, *"want to explain this."* Her grip tightened as she held it up, her shoulders squared as if she was ready to wield it at any moment. *"Whoever left this in the library, it was a message. For me."*

What did she mean for her?

"What kind of message?" Marcus asked, head turning as his brows met just above the bridge of his nose.

My eyes met his and I passed him my phone. *"That kind."*

Marcus, Wade, and Tayen huddled around the screen to read the messages. Their eyes widened as they took in the seriousness of the situation.

We were all being watched now.

"Who's doing this?" Wade asked, a muddled expression infused within their features.

"We think it's someone we went to high school with," Finley answered, sharing a glance with me. *"This douchey trust-fund kid named Rider."*

I wanted to do more than stand there while Finley spoke for both of us, but my body prohibited anything other than crossed arms and a drifting gaze.

"Why would he have left that as a message?" Tayen asked, eyes flitting between Finley and I.

That was the question I'd wanted to avoid. To answer that meant divulging the details of what we'd done, which would no doubt lead to the inevitable asking of why we'd done it.

"We messed with his car," I explained, hating to admit that I had sunk so low.

"He was a prick, and he deserved more than what he got," Finley was quick to add.

Almost too quick.

I narrowed my eyes at her, trying to read between the lines of what she wasn't saying.

And then I didn't have to.

"Lennon and I did something harmless, like seriously a no-big-deal type thing. We left a bunch of eggs in Rider's car so that it would smell and ruin the interior, but then... it didn't feel like enough. After everything he put her through, I wanted him to pay. So, after she took me home, I went back. Used that crowbar and beat the shit out of his stupid

car. Lennon never even knew about that... until now."

Fin's eyes met mine and I wanted to give her the biggest hug and call her an idiot. She'd done it for me, but that put her in Rider's line of fire.

Marcus was next to chime in. *"And you think that guy is the one sending the messages?"*

Fin nodded. *"Yeah. He has footage of us in his garage, which means he probably knows I'm the one who came back later and finished the job."*

Tayen's expression changed, but it was gone before I could be certain of what I'd caught. Was it the same pity I could read on the faces of the others? Or was it something deeper? Her silence was coated in a shimmering shade of discomfort, that much was obvious. But it was the why of it all I couldn't quite put my finger on.

"Are you getting texts too?" Marcus asked. *"Or is it just Lennon?"*

How had it not occurred to me sooner? I was the only one of us receiving the eerie messages. Part of me wanted to be angry because the prank had been Finley's idea in the first place. I hadn't even wanted to go to the stupid party, yet here I was being the only one punished for it. The other part of me knew I didn't have a right to be frustrated. If I had really fought her on it and stood my ground, refused to go to the party and participate in whatever scheme she'd cooked up, then maybe all of this wouldn't be happening. The situation we were in was as much my responsibility as it was hers.

"Just Lennon," she said, with a hiccup of guilt.

She'd been the perpetrator of the worst part of what had happened, but I was the one paying the price.

"It's too bad we can't pull some crazy FBI move and trace the texts," Marcus joked.

"Actually, maybe we can." Wade's gears were spinning, evidenced by the way they worked their bottom lip between their teeth. *"Even if the phone number isn't registered to anyone, we can at least search it and see if it comes back linked to any addresses or a carrier."* They were used to paying attention to the little things. The ones and zeros everyone else overlooked. *"Text me the number and I'll work on tracking it down."*

"What's the plan in the meantime, then? We just hope everything calms down while we try to trace the phone number?" Marcus asked. *"Whoever this is doesn't seem like the kind of person to respond well to being ignored."*

"Agreed." Fin nodded.

The expression on Tayen's face was worrisome.

It looked like she wanted to be anywhere but here. The words she wasn't saying spoke volumes, half of her face hiding behind impenetrable strands of sable hair. The unintentional shift in her demeanor gnawed at me like a puzzle waiting to be solved. Behavior analysis was a key part of every criminal investigation and interrogation I'd ever seen, but Tayen was no criminal... right? I played back the memories of this morning, only now they stuck out like sore thumbs. Clues in the shape of red flags, flapping in the wind.

Tayen hadn't been walking with us when Rider sent the photo.

Not only had she shown up late, but she'd also shied away from giving any real explanation why.

Walking around me, Fin dropped her backpack, the crowbar falling to the floor. Wade took a backwards seat in Finley's desk chair while she and Marcus let gravity pull them into the squishy center of the oversized bean bag chair living beneath her lofted bed. Fin's roommate was nowhere to be found, so Tayen borrowed the chair from her desk and dragged it across the room. I took a seat on the floor atop Finley's tie-dyed area rug, leaning back on the heels of my hands. The diffused, multicolored LED string lights and desk lamp provided just the right amount of visibility to see one another without the harsh shadows or blinding fluorescence of the standard overhead lights we all abhorred.

"Hey, Wade," Finley said. *"Any chance you want to take a look at that photo that was in our folder? I'm dying to be the cat curiosity killed and find out what our scavenger*

hunt pics were replaced with."

"Hell yeah," Wade agreed, opening up the laptop sitting on the desk.

"Connect it to the projector so we can see everything," I chimed in, pointing to the small device beside the desk lamp. It was great for movies, but would be even better for this.

Wade wasted no time. They set up the projector and angled it against Finley's roommate's side of the room—the only wall in the room left blank. They pulled it up and our jaws collectively hit the floor. It was the same photo that had haunted my nightmares for years, stirring up feelings of resentment and anger and bouts of depression that had dragged me down to my lowest point.

Now, every one of my new friends was seeing the worst moment of my life.

There was tension on Finley's face. Every visible muscle was taut; fists clenched, jaw locked. A faint vein in her neck pulsed with the same seething ire that must've been flowing through her when she'd bashed his car like it was her job.

Tayen's face was sullen, and I imagined the pity she must've been feeling for me.

The pity I didn't want.

"Shut it off, Wade," Finley demanded.

Wade reaches over and turns the projector off without a word.

The silence was heavy and damp, like we were sitting inside of a sauna.

"So..." I say, having turned to face my friends. *"Now that you all have seen it, I guess I might as well explain."* Inhaling deeply, I blew out the huff of air. *"That photo was shared with someone I thought I could trust, and he ended up betraying me in a fucking fantastic fashion."* A small, rage-induced chuckle escaped as I shook my head at my own naiveté. *"And that's why Finley did what she did."* She and I share a moment, our eyes sending waves of appreciation toward the other. *"I completely understand if you three want to walk away from us on this one. This isn't your fight—"*

"We're in," Wade said, speaking up for the three of them.

Marcus nodded, but all Tayen did was share a meek smile.

"I bought the answers to my trig final," Marcus said, looking from one person to the next.

"You did what?" Tayen blinked repeatedly, malfunctioning as she struggled to process what her brother had just admitted.

"I was failing and I needed a boost, or else I wasn't going to graduate." Leaning forward, his elbows rested on his

knees. *"I paid a guy for the answers to the final exam."*

There's another moment of quiet reflection.

"You didn't have to do that," I said, eyes locked onto Marcus'.

Marcus shrugged. *"I wanted to, so you didn't feel alone. We've all done shit we regret, but it doesn't make us bad people. We're just... I don't know, figuring it out."*

I give him a short nod, appreciative for the support.

"Theoretically, I might've remotely accessed the email and/or computer of a corrupt government employee in order to minimize the casualties left in his wake," Wade said. Then, they held up their hands and added to their statement. *"Allegedly, of course. There's no real proof tying me or my name to that particular event or any criminal activity."*

"You're a hacker?" Fin blurted out, wide-eyed and fully invested.

Wade tilted their head to the side and shrugged one shoulder, but she wasn't phased by their non-answer.

"Wow," Fin breathed, dumbfounded and speechless.

"You should be proud, she hasn't clammed up like this in ages," I teased, pointing at Finley. *"Don't expect it to happen again, though."*

Wade laughs. *"I don't know about that, I'm a person of many deep complexities. It'll be a while before I'm out of surprises."*

Eyes shifted to Tayen next, because she was the only one who hadn't spoken up yet.

Her hands were clasped, worming around nervously.

"I, uh… I have to go." Tayen brushed hair behind her ear and quickly stood, not allowing her eyes to linger on anyone as she flew out of the room.

The rest of us were stunned, looking to Marcus for some sort of explanation.

"Hey, don't look at me," he defended, shaking his head and raising his hands in mock surrender. *"She's her own weird person, I can't explain any of that."*

The energy was weird after Tayen left, never really settling after her abrupt exit. It left us all with questions, wondering why she'd leave without telling us why, and whether hers was a secret that would blow the rest of ours out of the water. I couldn't help but wonder what it was, the thing she wasn't willing to reveal. She always seemed so upbeat, but there was a shift today. Maybe she was starting to see me differently and wanted to step away before she got too close.

I would understand that. It would hurt, but I would get it.

Wade tapped my shoulder and I whipped my head around to find them looking at me curiously.

"Everything okay?" they asked, cautiously.

"What? Oh, yeah, everything's cool. Just thinking."

"You do that a lot, huh?" Wade smiled. *"Can you send me the number you've been getting those texts from? I can do some digging tomorrow and see if I can find any information. It's probably a text app number, but you never know."*

"Sure thing," I replied with a quick nod. My hand retrieved the phone from my pocket, moving through the motions while I considered the many possibilities. Whoever it was, they wanted me to know they were close by, watching my every move and following so close behind me they could probably mimic my gait. I didn't know what Rider wanted from me—a confession? It would've taken me years to pay back the damage his car had incurred, but I'd have done it just to make all of this stop.

For the rest of the night, it felt like I was drifting further and further away. The room stretched, adding to the distance between myself and the others as if the ground had opened up to swallow me whole. The lights faded away, my body traveling at warped speed despite me never having moved from my spot. I was there and gone all in the same breath, nodding along as if I was part of the conversations and laughter surrounding me. The room swirled around me, the pressure in my head pounding in step with my heartbeat.

This was not how I wanted to start my first semester

of college.

The last thing I needed was to keep rehashing the greatest mistake of my high school career: trusting Rider Abbott. I'd given him all the ammunition he needed to ruin my life and ostracize me from nearly every friend I had. Except Finley, of course. For two years I'd spent weekends hanging out with my parents and no one from school but her. College was on the verge of becoming a repeat of high school, all that pain flooding back again. I'd already lost all my friends once and I wasn't going to let it happen again.

Over my dead body.

SEVEN DAYS BEFORE THE MURDER

I was falling.

Ten, twenty, thirty feet.

My body dropped limply onto my bed and my system was shocked awake. Wet hair stuck to my face as I gasped, sucking air down into my lungs in massive gulps. Fleeting sensations from my nightmares were all that were left as I regained consciousness. My eyes darted to the dark recesses of the room in search of any menacing shadows that might have followed me out. The hands were mine, but somehow they felt detached from me. They found my face and wiped at the sweat-soaked strands of hair clinging to my skin.

A dusky haze filtered in through the gaps in the window blinds; just enough light to vaguely spot the silhouetted valleys and peaks created by my disheveled bedding. I shifted to the side and tossed my legs over the edge of my bed, hunching and rubbing knuckles into the corners of my eyes. The days were encompassing a strange duality, my concept of time faltering as I struggled to split my mindset between adjusting to college life and fearing what was around the corner.

Every second there was an undercurrent of paranoia. Would the next attack happen in my classroom? In front of my professor? During a shower in the residence hall's community bathroom? There were endless opportunities, and I couldn't exactly always prepare for each of them. The not knowing, paired with the near-constant looking over my shoulder, was making me go prematurely grey.

Not to mention my phone became my worst enemy.

The device was plugged into its charger and resting on my nightstand. That's not where I'd left it. Its flashing red light glowing in the darkness, my entire body was chilled.

COULDN'T LET YOUR PHONE DIE, COULD I?

I lurched forward. The contents of my stomach threatened to double back and play a remix on my taste buds. Dropping the phone onto the bed, I inhaled a few deep breaths to calm myself despite the throes of panic. The muscles in my chest tightened like the skin of a drum. The escalation from creepy, threatening text messages to breaking and entering into my dorm room made me crave a scalding hot shower and scrub every inch of my flesh off. I wanted to seal the room shut and bolt the windows. It could've been Rider, standing right beside me, for who knows how long, in our room while Bronya and I slept, completely unaware.

I needed to get out of there. Fast.

Quickly gathering my backpack and stuffing a change of clothes and my toothbrush inside, I nearly ran out of the room and bee-lined my way to Fin's room. I couldn't spend another second in my own, not while my imagination was running rampant and drawing on every episode of every true crime documentary I'd ever binged to source it for nightmare fuel.

Praying that Finley was awake, my thumb pressed her doorbell over and over until the door swung open and her tired eyes blinked up at me against the blinding fluorescent lights of the hallway.

"This better be an emergency," she warned, stepping aside for me to enter.

"It's whatever is worse than an emergency."

"Huh?" she asked, wiping sleep from her eye.

I let my backpack fall to the floor as I sunk into Fin's bean bag chair. *"I think Rider was in my room last night."*

"Anders have a sleepover with Bronya again?"

"No." I shuffled in and turned back to face her.

Finley sighed. *"I love a good guessing game as much as the next girl, Lennon, but it's way too early for this."*

"Look," I said, pulling out my phone and shoving it into her face.

It took a few moments for her to figure out what she was reading, as evidenced by the changes in her facial expressions. Eyes wide, she handed my phone back and started frantically moving stuff out of the way to make space on the rug beneath her lofted bed.

"Screw that, you're sleeping here tonight," she said.

Finley's words didn't even register to me.

"My phone was in my backpack last night. I know it was. At least, it was until someone broke into my room, rifled through my bag, and then plugged it into the charger," I said, processing out loud.

"The why of it all is the least important part right now, Lennon," Fin insisted.

"At the moment, all I can think about is that I need to shower and get to class. I can't think about this right now."

"Wanna skip? We can go get coffee and feel normal again."

"Normal is relative," I remind her. *"Besides, this is the only class I've been excited about since school started. Let's catch up after. Meet at The Brew at ten?"*

"Deal," she said, tossing me a clean towel.

If If there was one thing that could bring me out of the funk I'd been plunged into, it was my Introduction to Communications class. I'd been looking forward to it since registration, daydreaming about the things I'd learn, how I could hone my craft, the lively discussions I could have with other impassioned classmates who also dreamed of a career in journalism.

Walking into room 203 in Brandis Hall, I noted a few other early arrivals and took a seat at the center of the U-shaped row of desks. Of all my classes, this was the only one in which I was willing to risk being called-on on the first day. The extra attention would be a welcome relief from everything else on my plate. Pulling out my laptop, I opened a document Fin and I had been working on. It detailed all the suspects, the attacks, and potential opportunities. I added this morning's incident to the list. When I thought of who would have had access to my dorm, one name came to mind immediately: Tayen.

Classmates trickled in one after the other until not a single empty chair remained. Our professor, Dr. Sara Martin, was the last to join us.

"Apologies for the late arrival, class," she announced,

setting a stylish shoulder bag atop her desk, draping an olive cardigan over the back of her chair. She stepped around and took a seat against the edge of its front, legs crossing. *"Good morning,"* Dr. Martin greeted, gaze pausing on each of us as she looked around the room. *"I hope you're all ready to dive into the world of communications, but first I'd like to go around the room and let us all introduce ourselves."*

"I graduated from LCU back in the day, then later earned my Master's Degree from the Medill School of Journalism at Northwestern," Dr. Martin continued. *"My career took me all over the country, and I was fortunate to work for several large news outlets, publications, and even had the opportunity to be a foreign correspondent in a few different locations across the globe. I've written articles for* TIME, The Associated Press, *and* The New York Times, *to name a few."*

Dr. Martin was everything I aspired to become. She'd earned her place as one of the most well-accomplished journalists of the twenty-first century through her compelling storytelling. What's better is the fact that she was also deaf, proving to the world how little it impacted her ability to do her job. She was fluent in multiple languages and had been to more than four dozen countries—experiences I'd dreamt of my entire life. By the end of the class period, I had visualized the trajectory of my life; laid out in front of me like never before. I could envision a future that actually intrigued me. One plagued not by fear, but by opportunity.

"My point in saying all of this, is not to brag but to remind you all that each one of you has every opportunity ahead. In this industry, the biggest failure most people run into is sitting around and waiting for the stories to come to them. Whatever you want in this life can be yours, as long as you keep chasing the story."

I slid into the oversized, tufted leather chair beside the one Finley was occupying, tucked back into the corner near a set of bookshelves. There was already an iced latte waiting for me on the cafe table nestled between the seats, identical to the drink in her hand, except I knew hers would have soy milk instead of oat. If I could count on one thing, it was that she'd never order a drink without thinking of ordering me one, too. This alone led to my guessing her love language quiz results on the first try, years ago; quality time with a sprinkling of acts of service.

"You're the best," I said, for what was probably the millionth time throughout the course of our friendship, rushing to pick up my coffee for a little caffeine

recalibration. Two sips later and I felt whole again. The pounding in my skull slowed to a steady beat and I closed my eyes in an attempt to reset. As they opened, the lights in The Brew roared back to life around us in all their overexposed glory.

Finley had been studying me since I walked in, but she was doing it in the same way she always did. Carefully and not all at once. Looking but not long enough to make me feel like a fish in a bowl. Just long enough to make me question what she was seeing and what she might do with that information later.

"*So...*" she started, a caricature of eagerness. Her eyes were peeled, looking ready to dive into a discussion about what I'd alluded to that morning.

I briefly considered a topic change to draw it out, ultimately deciding against such cruelty purely on the grounds that I needed to talk about this with at least one person or I'd explode. Or implode. Whichever was worse.

"*So... I woke up and my phone was charging. But I didn't plug it in last night,*" I said.

"*Maybe you did and you just don't remember?*"

"*I didn't,*" I insisted. I wasn't in the mood to play Devil's Advocate.

"*Nothing else in your room was missing? The door was shut all the way when you woke up? You didn't see anything that might've been left behind?"* She asked, rattling off questions as easily as she would cross off items on her grocery list.

"Nothing looked out of place, but I'm not sure," I said with uncertainty.

The same sickly unease from earlier washed over me again. I hadn't really checked if anything was missing. The moment I realized that there had been an intruder in my room, I high-tailed out of there and booked it over to Fin's. What if they had left something behind? Maybe they'd been sloppy and there were clues left somewhere. The undeniable fact was that the text was the only piece of evidence I had proving someone had been in my room. They wanted me to know they'd been mere inches away from me, and that they could come back any time they wanted. What was going to stop them?

"Then let's go find out."

A cloud of Bronya's sickly sweet Victoria's Secret perfume swirled through the air in a pungent cloud as the door opened to our room.

"Good god," Finley coughed as she swatted the smell away. *"Is this perfume or mustard gas?"*

"Quit complaining and start looking," I fired back, my eyes already scanning every surface of the room. There was little time to search through everything before Bronya came back, and even less of it for witty quips.

The two of us fanned out, lifting up books and blankets, checking in drawers and laundry baskets. It didn't take long for something to stick out to me. Something that not only wasn't where I'd left it, but that wasn't mine in the first place.

"Hey, Fin," I flicked the light switch a few times to grab her attention. *"I found something."*

Her gaze followed my outstretched finger as it pointed to the mirror mounted above my dresser. Tucked inside the bezel, between the glass and the frame, was a photo.

Two people smiling candidly appeared in front of some sort of party happening in the background. A beachside bonfire, maybe. Too dark to tell for certain, but I could rule out that it had been taken the night of the car-defacing-party based on what he was wearing in the photo. I tilted my head to match the angle of the pair in the photo, scanning the figures in the foreground until I realized who I was looking at.

Rider and Tayen.

Together.

The pocket of my jeans vibrated.

BIRDS OF A FEATHER LIE TOGETHER

The constant feeling of being watched never truly went away, but moments like this really brought it to the front of my mind and made my hands shake.

Clearly, I didn't stick this photo to my mirror. Nor had I ever seen it before. Hell, I didn't even know they were familiar with one another's existence, let alone friendly enough to hang onto one another at a party with red cups full of who knows what. Is that why she'd been so weird when I'd mentioned his name during the scavenger hunt? Was she afraid to admit she was friends with him after learning we weren't on good terms? Or is her involvement with Rider—and the text messages— another story?

"Nothing is missing, but... this shouldn't be in here," I said, pinching the corner of the photograph, as if it might bite me. As I turned it toward Finley and the small note stuck to the back became visible. In a rough scrawl, it read: FRIENDS DON'T KEEP SECRETS. Someone had written it hastily, that much was evident. I flipped it over so she could read the back, the two of us exchanging puzzled glances.

"What the fuck?" Finley held her hand in midair, fingers having spelled out W-T-F and remaining frozen on the 'F'. Jaw clenched, her eyes narrowed and then widened again once I spun the photo back around. *"Did you know they knew each other?"*

"Don't you think I would've mentioned that, Fin? Said something like 'oh yeah, isn't it hilarious that the girl I like is friends with the guy I hate most on the planet'?" I asked incredulously while making melodramatic head movements and channeling my inner sarcastic diva. Relaxing back into my usual state, I answered my own question as the rest of me sunk into the chair. *"Of course I didn't know."*

"Okay, relax, it was just a question."

"The better question is who would've put this on my mirror?"

"Well, it's not looking good for the hottie across the hallway."

"Tayen's not involved in this, she wasn't even at Rider's party that night."

"How do we know that? We didn't have the guest list, and we weren't there that long. She could have been there. Maybe we should entertain the possibility that she is part of it somehow." Finley bit at the inside of her lip, her eyes shifting toward the other side of the room and then back to me. *"You said she was acting weird the other day,*

right? What if this is why? Maybe she's secretly straight and dating Rider..."

I picked at the edge of my cup's lid, regretting even coming in here to poke around. What was the point of even trying to make friends, let alone let myself develop feelings for anyone, when anyone on campus could be in cahoots with Rider? I was so sick of him infecting my life.

"Well, if we're adding this to the pile of weird shit with her name on it, then it's probably time to ask her what's going on. If she really is keeping secrets..." Fin nodded her head towards the photo clenched in my palm. *"We need to get to the bottom of it."*

Just then, Bronya walked in with a tote bag hanging on her arm and an iced coffee in her hand. She paused and raised a brow as she looked between Finley and I, then with a scoff she strode into the room and set her things down on top of her bed.

"Why do you two look like you've seen a ghost?" Bronya asked, before unpacking the small canvas bag.

"Just trying to catch our breath after being assaulted with whatever chemical weapon you spritzed in here," Fin said, jumping in.

"I see that college hasn't made you any more clever, Finley," Bronya sneered at us, her lips curling at the corner.

"Or you any smarter," Fin retorted, dramatically flipping her hair. *"Better not lose that volleyball scholarship, or else your ass will be punted out here faster than you can sign 'loser.'"*

Turning on her heel, Fin reached for my hand and led me out the door behind her.

I left dinner early that night while the rest of the gang were still eating, not wanting to risk being late to show up at The Courier's office. Arriving with just minutes to spare, I did a double-take down at the watch on my wrist and paused in front of the large double-doored entryway. A monochrome bulldog in an LCU shirt with a newspaper in its mouth stared back at me. Pulling open the doors, I stepped into a large rectangular room that was abuzz as dozens of people walked around and through the space, visually humming with snippets of conversations lingering in the air.

I spotted framed sepia-tinged front pages of past issues of The Clerc Courier that dotted the walls. Multi-paned windows stretched across the upper half of the back wall from one corner to the other, above a row of computers sitting below a long stretch of mirrored panels pulling double duty to scatter light around the room while also providing a reflection of what might walk up from behind. Large potted plants were parked in the corner, balancing the room and contrasting its brick walls with their organic greenery. The golden light of the setting sun's rays cast a fading glow behind brighter orbs of light shining through the frosted windowpanes.

A group of other interested students had formed and I took it as my cue to join their ranks. As we stood awkwardly in the corner, I checked my watch again. It was five past the hour and our little cohort reeked of nervousness like a cheap perfume. The newspaper staff were hard at work while we gathered, and they probably could've smelled the agitation on us as we shifted and observed their work. The chatter slowed to a dull roar of layered conversations and then ceased altogether as a vaguely familiar face strode toward us. We spread out into a semi-circle and I swallowed hard.

"Hello, everyone." She smiled at us, her dark eyes scanning our faces through red-rimmed, cat-eyed glasses. *"I'm Emery Choi, Editor-in-Chief here at* The Clerc Courier.*"*

Her name... it seemed familiar somehow. It took me a split-second to remember where I'd seen her before, but then it hit me. My near-collision on move-in day. I wanted to slam my head into a wall. Any wall. Repeatedly. If I played it off and acted like I didn't remember, there was a chance she would follow suit and we could forget it had ever happened.

One by one we introduced ourselves. I was one of three freshmen, with the rest of our group made up of upperclassmen and a pair of sophomores. Emery's eyes lingered on me when it was my turn, giving me the distinct impression she'd recognized me as quickly as I had recognized her. The last of the newcomers finished their introduction and our attention shifted back to Emery.

"It's great to meet all of you," she said, her eyes piercing through me. *"As you all know,* The Courier *is looking for a few student journalists to join the paper. All our reporters rotate assignments, so there are always opportunities to propose new stories you're passionate about or interested in pursuing. Each of you will be expected to write a sample article of no more than eight hundred words based on the assignment you're given. Those articles will then be reviewed by our staff and our faculty advisor, Dr. Martine, and we will choose three of you to be invited to join the team as reporters. Are there any questions right now before we dive into those assignments?"*

Everyone glanced around at one another as they shook their heads.

"Alright, let's move on then," she said, grabbing a green file folder off a nearby table. *"These are the assignments.*

When it's your turn, I'll hand you the sheet of paper with the details, due date, and topic. There will be no changes to the assignments—you get what you get."

Emery paused in front of each of us and read the topic aloud before handing the paper to whom it had been assigned. Based on the reactions, it was clear the topics elicited either enthusiasm or disappointment-nothing in between. Finally, it was my turn.

"Pedestrian safety on campus," Emery signed clearly, before handing me the paper. A superior smile tightly pulled at the corners of her mouth as they pursed together.

Clearly, she remembered I'd been the one behind the wheel when she'd been nearly run over on the other side of campus. This article was a shot at winning her over. I could pour all my wit and charm into words on a page and turn this seemingly disenchanting topic into something that would impress the pants off her. Metaphorically, of course.

"Before we dismiss, are there any questions?" Emery asked, looking at each of us for a brief moment.

A tall girl with an assortment of freckles stood beside me with her hand raised, waves of ash blonde hair gathering at her shoulders. Emery nodded and gestured toward her to indicate she was being called upon.

"When are the articles due?" The girl asked.

"You've got one week. Email it to me next Friday before midnight."

The girl nodded and, before I could stop myself, I raised my hand. Emery's attention turned to me and she paused before calling on me.

"Are we allowed to include interviews?" I asked, battling my smile's urge to become a smirk.

"At your own risk."

FIVE DAYS BEFORE THE MURDER

Sitting in the front seat of my car, Finley held a pair of old-school military surplus binoculars up to her face and scanned across campus from where I'd parked near the towering, brick building housing the Linguistics & Cultural Center. Dropping them into her lap and leaning back, Finley sighed deeply. Her head turned toward me and she lowered her sunglasses from atop her head to block the sun from her eyes.

"Are we really just gonna sit here all day waiting for something to happen?" She asked.

"Do you have a better idea?" I asked, raising my brows.

"A few, but most of them are illegal."

"Like what?" I asked, curiously.

Mistake number one.

"So glad you asked." She grinned deviously.

"Hypothetically, he'd get kicked off campus if they found drugs in his room during a search."

"You wanna plant drugs on Rider?"

She had to be joking; even for Finley, it was a bit extreme.

"Just saying it's an option."

"We can come up with something that won't ruin his life."

"Come on, Len. He didn't give a shit about ruining yours. Sometimes you've gotta break a few eggs in order to make a cake."

"First of all, he didn't ruin my life," I corrected. *"Secondly, I'm not trying to break any eggs here, Fin. I just want to figure this shit out and enjoy the college experience like every other person at this school gets to do."*

I reached up to rub my thumb and finger at the space between my eyes.

"It doesn't even matter, okay? Whatever we decide to do, we're going to do it so well we aren't going to get caught." She paused, and then sat up quickly with widened eyes. *"Wait! I've got the perfect plan!"*

"Uh huh," I agreed, sarcastically.

"No, I'm serious!"

"Okay, let's see it then. What's this master plan that won't get us caught?"

"All we've got to do is put a camera in their suite and

we'll catch their conversations. If Theo slips up and says anything to Rider, then we've got him."

"Let's say we do plant a camera without them knowing," I said, deciding to play the part of the devil's advocate. *"How are we going to avoid getting caught when we'd literally have to sneak into their room when they aren't there?"*

Finley sat there quietly for a moment, her wheels spinning as she stared off into the distance to process. Presumably, she was trying to figure out how we could slip through a loophole somehow. Loopholes were her specialty.

"Maybe we don't have to," she finally said, smirking.

"You lost me."

"I know a way I can get into their room without having to sneak in."

"Oh god, you're not going to hook up with Theo, are you?"

"Hell no, get your mind out of the gutter." Finley reached out and shoved me softly. *"My plan doesn't involve anything quite so disgusting."*

"Alright, so what are you scheming then?"

"Theo's in my English class this semester and we've got a project coming up where we have to split into pairs. I can make sure we pair up and I'll suggest we work on it in his room. Say my roommate's hooking up with somebody or

something, it won't be hard to make up a lie on the spot."

"You really think he'll go for it?"

"Yeah," she replied, chuckling. *"Boys are beyond easy to manipulate."*

"Doesn't hurt he's been pining after you for years," I added with a smirk.

"Shut up," she tossed back. *"I'm willing to let him think he's got a shot with me so I can stash a camera in their suite. Y'know, so we can spy on them and see if Rider admits to anything."*

"What happens if he tries to make a move on you?"

Finley sighed. *"Then I guess I'll have to take one for the team."*

My fingers rapped against the steering wheel rhythmically, unable to keep still from the sheer amount of nervousness coursing through my body. The entire situation made me feel uneasy, like we were tempting fate with every legally and morally grey choice we made in pursuit of whatever kind of justice the universe would allow. Part of me, deep down inside, knew this would only end one of two ways: either we'd fight tooth and nail to bring down whoever was behind this or we'd resist just hard enough to call their bluff and topple the entire scheme to the ground.

Fin tapped my arm and I looked up to find her smiling reassuringly at me. *"Don't worry about it, okay? I've got this part in the bag,"* she said, beaming with confidence. *"He'll never see it coming."*

"You were a criminal in a past life, weren't you?" I teased.

"A past life? I'm living that one right now," she replied, laughing as she reached for her phone and navigated to a playlist of songs she'd aptly titled 'mischief loading'. Her fingers twisted the volume knob until the vehicle vibrated with every bass note as the first song blared through its speakers. I recognized the tune as one I'd introduced to her years prior by the artist Greta Van Fleet. It reminded me of Led Zeppelin in the best way, despite my brother's refusal to appreciate them because he considered their lead singer to be a knockoff of Robert Plant. He wasn't necessarily wrong, but I'd never agree that they didn't deserve praise for the nostalgia they'd infused into their bluesy rock-and-roll.

"My apologies, Aileen, I won't overlook your penchant for criminal undertakings ever again," I teased with mock sincerity.

"Who the hell is Aileen?" Fin asked, an eyebrow raised in confusion.

"Aileen Wuornos," I replied.

Finley stared at me blankly.

"The serial killer slash sex worker who murdered a bunch of truckers from 1989 to 1990?" I asked, surprised

she still hadn't picked up what I was putting down.

"*No idea who you're talking about.*"

"*Seriously? You were with me when we watched the documentary about her.*"

"*Lennon, you've forced me to watch a lot of documentaries. You can't expect me to keep them all straight in my head,*" Finley argued as she tilted her head and looked at me out of the corners of her eyes.

"*Forced? Don't even start. You begged me to watch the Dahmer series with you,*" I countered, shaking my head at her.

"*To be fair, it's mostly because that one hot guy is in it.*"

"*Just saying, it's not always me who drags you into watching stuff.*"

"*Agree to disagree.*"

"*Disagree all day, it doesn't change the facts. Besides, you're the one who decided to major in what is effectively criminology,*" I concluded with a laugh. "*Come on, let's get out of here. I gotta go meet up with Marcus.*"

"*Alright,*" Fin agreed, pulling open the passenger door before looking back at me once more. "*Then let's go talk to Cam, I know he's got some cameras we can borrow. But right now, I've got to go meet up with Wade. They said they'd help me with my western civilizations homework, so I'm heading over to The Brew to meet up with them. Meet at my room tonight?*"

I nod and she climbed out, waving me off through the window.

Turning on her heel, Finley marched off toward The Brew and pulled the straps of her corduroy backpack over her shoulders. I shut the driver's side door and reached for the keys dangling from a carabiner secured to my belt loop. The button depressed under my fingertip and the car's lights flashed. The walk from my car to the doors of Thompson Hall felt longer today, stretched out like miles of deserted highway in the dead of summer.

Finding out Tayen had been friends with Rider was a shock, but it didn't mean I was automatically willing to believe she was involved with his mind games. She deserved the chance to explain the photo, her connection with Rider, and why she didn't speak up when we mentioned him in the first place. The problem with that was I hadn't been able to get a hold of her all week. She had basically disappeared since I had info-dumped on everyone, which made her look guilty. Something didn't sit quite right in my gut. Firing off a text to Finley, I crossed my fingers in hopes of picking her brain for some intel.

Have you talked to Tayen lately?

not in a few days, why?

She hasn't replied to any of my texts.

Not a single word all week.

weird

Idk, maybe she's sucking face with Rider somewhere?

Conspiring against me?

Disappearing off the face of the planet to avoid me?

Take your pick.

okay drama queen

THAT'S weird

You said it yourself, she could be involved.

yeah and you fall in love with everyone you meet

you're just freaking out cuz you like her and she's MIA

Pleading the fifth.

either she'll text you back or she won't

or maybe she'll murder us in our sleep

Comforting... thanks.

you're welcome

All I really wanted was to feel safe again. The sanctity of my dorm room had been violated in the dead of night, and I still felt uneasy being in there and knowing that it wasn't a safe haven anymore. I needed a break from everything and we needed to talk to Cameron. Setting up a spy camera was as good a plan as any, and we didn't exactly have any better ideas right now.

done studying so omw to my room

Okay. Still want to go talk to Cam?

yeah let's do it

Is he still pissed at you for taking his stuff?

He may not want to help us lol

yeah but he'll get over it

he always does

Okay. Will you be ready to go soon?

yeah meet me at my room in five

Part of me wondered whether it would be smart to pull Cam in. Her brother had the potential to be a good resource, and he'd always wiped the floor with us when we played strategy-based games like Risk, Catan, and Monopoly during family game nights. But there was the lurking possibility that he'd rat us out to Felix, the guy who couldn't help but treat me with kid gloves regardless of how often I asked him to take them off. Then again, I could've been overthinking it. Once his hard candy shell of overprotectiveness was cracked open, Felix could be understanding. All I had to do was spin it the right way.

The overhead lights on the other side of the door flashed through the gap underneath as I pressed the doorbell, my gaze drawn to the shrieks of light that reflected off the linoleum flooring and onto my shoes. Not more than a minute later, Finley was swinging the door open and grinning at me, her typical casual coolness on full display.

Once we were snuggly in the refuge of my Civic, Fin instinctively grabbed the AUX cable and plugged it into her phone. By the time I was turning past the front gates of campus, she'd already chosen a playlist and cranked the volume up until we could feel our seats quaking with the pounding of the bass line.

A flat, quick wave of her hand got my attention.

"Has Wade found anything yet, about that phone number?" she asked.

"Not yet," I answered, a puzzled look shifting my brow line. *"Why?"*

"I dunno." She shrugged and looked away for a few moments before returning her gaze back to me. *"It's weird that this hacker couldn't trace a single phone number, right?"*

Oh god, I hadn't considered that.

"What makes you think that?" I questioned, a bit stunned at the turn our conversation had taken. *"I'm sure it's not light work."*

"Yeah, but ever since we looked at those photos and found out they're good with tech, I've had this sinking feeling that maybe that's how they know so much about fake phone numbers and everything."

"Come on, there's no way it's Wade. Besides, there are entire FBI teams dedicated to tracking and tracing phones, so it makes sense that they can't crack it in a couple of days," I countered.

"I'm just saying, what if he had it wrong and it's not Rider?"

Fin had a point, as much as I hated to admit it.

"That's a valid point," I said, nodding my head slowly as I processed.

"I could be totally wrong," Fin added, running a hand

through her dirty blonde hair. *"I'm not shooting down the idea that it could be him, because we all know he's a fucking villain. But we should keep an eye out, just in case."*

I dipped my chin in agreement as we turned onto another street. My fingers stretched to reach for the buttons on my door to roll both of our windows down. The summer air was dry and warm, invading every crack and crevice of the car. Finley and I looked at each other, smiling and laughing as our hair whipped across our faces.

We pulled up in front of Finley's house and I watched as she headed up to the front door. Her hands fumbled to check every pocket until she finally found her keys. Typical. Cam wasn't on the porch smoking, like usual. Maybe he wasn't home. Maybe Fin would get lucky and the question of whether or not to bring him into our drama would end up being little more than a moot point. Letting herself in, Finley waved me off. I raised a hand in acknowledgment and threw my car into gear.

The drive from Fin's house to mine was quick. I'd always loved that she lived within spitting distance. Back before either of us had learned to drive, one of us would walk to the other's house so we could get on the bus together to ride to school. Our friendship grew tenfold during those bus rides, through hushed secrets and shared sarcastic glances. I parked in the driveway of my house and shut the car off. I took a moment to lean back in my seat, expelling all the pent-up frustration I'd been storing as a heavy sigh. I'd already decided telling them the truth about the series of terrible events I'd been suffering through wasn't going to happen, but there were other things plaguing me that I was dying to ask for advice on.

Namely, my situation with Tayen.

Despite how much I loved being home, there was still part of me that felt like an outsider, a tinge of resentment always bubbling just below the surface. Conversations like the one I'd had in the kitchen with Felix, where I was the one constantly sacrificing my comfort and mental energy in order to bridge the communication gap.

Fighting through the speedway of racing thoughts in my head, my phone's screen lit up and provided a much-needed distraction. Finley must have left something in my car or forgotten to tell me something before she ran up her front steps. It was a common occurrence. As I pulled the phone out of the cupholder, I realized it wasn't a message from Fin at all.

DO MOMMY AND DADDY KNOW WHAT YOU'VE BEEN UP TO?

The phone dropped into my lap. Everything in me wanted to scream until my lungs gave out. How was I supposed to sit with my parents and act like everything was normal when it was anything but? When there was someone following me and threatening to unravel my life? My chest was tightening again. We weren't any closer to figuring this out, yet here I was wasting time hanging around out at home. Killing time while someone's finger hugged the trigger. Pulling down the visor, I flipped open the mirror and surveyed the face looking back at me. God, I looked awful. I'd managed to cover the dark circles, but my eyes still held a certain weariness to them. A hollowness.

"Get your shit together," I sternly warned my reflection.

I reached into my pocket and pulled out my hearing aids, shutting the battery doors to turn them on as they slipped into place. The familiar powering-up tones played as I climbed out of the driver's seat. One step led into another, shoes scuffing against the walkway toward the front door. My key clicked into the lock and the door pushed open, a fragrant melody floating past me. The house smelled like a fresh batch of my mom's peanut butter cookies had just been pulled out of the oven. The heavenly scent wafted through the foyer and I trapped it inside as I shut the door behind me. The familiarity that came with being home was more comforting than my favorite blanket straight out of the dryer. I craved it deep within my soul, and even being away for just a couple of weeks had made me miss it intensely.

"I'm home!" I called out.

Kicking off my shoes by the stairs, I headed through to the living room. It was empty aside from the presence of our family cat, Freddie Meowcury. The middle-aged tabby was curled up on the far end of the couch in his usual sleeping spot, atop a folded earth-toned quilt my grandmother had made for my parents as a wedding gift. Sunlight streamed in through a nearby window, warming his fur as he slept, his little abdomen rising and falling with calm breaths. I'd missed those little moments of peace; they seemed so out of reach now.

I headed through the kitchen next, welcomed by the familiar euphony of colors and textures I knew like the back of my hand. Vintage geometric tile backsplash lined the walls beneath the hunter green cabinets with their vintage gold hardware. The cream soapstone countertops were speckled with cookbooks and a collection of wine bottle corks. Everything had been carefully chosen and curated over the years, but at a quick glance it was a random assortment of trinkets and decor. My mom called it 'eclectic punk rock modernism' but I'd always just considered it to be the perfect example of her personal, chaotic style.

Behind the dining room table, a pair of French doors opened out onto the covered patio. I peered through the windows to find my parents sitting outside on the couch, enjoying the fresh air as the fan above them circulated. Heading out to join them, I was greeted first by Mom's bright smile.

"Hey, sweetie," Mom called out, holding out an arm and beckoning me to sit in the empty seat beside her.

Dad stood up from his seat in the chair across from her, his usual closed-mouth smile appearing as he leaned in to hug me.

"How are ya, kid?" He asked, one hand squeezing my arm while he held a glass of lemonade in the other.

"I'm alright," I answered.

For years, since everything had gone down with Rider, I'd spent my free time holed up at home with my parents. Game nights with Finley and Cameron, movie marathons with my dad, cooking meals and baking treats with my mom; most of my social interaction had been with my parents, rather than with anyone my own age. Even Felix had found it odd, but whenever he was home I'd find excuses and reasons to keep his suspicions at bay. The last thing that I wanted was to worry anyone more than I already had. What I really wanted was for it all to go away, for the dark cloud above me to dissipate and leave me alone before anyone else could find the skeleton in my closet.

There was a part of me that wanted to break down in front of them, though. A part that ached to ask for help shouldering the weight of everything I'd been through since the texts began. The other part of me—the bigger, more logical part—couldn't bear to say it out loud. Not when I knew how heartbreaking this would be for my parents to discover, how it would shatter their carefully crafted impression of their daughter. Not when I was so close to figuring it out; to coming up with a way to make it all disappear. I'd lost so many people already that the thought of adding my parents to that list was gut-wrenching. Who would I turn to then?

There was too much at stake to tumble the entire Jenga tower over just yet.

The next piece I pulled had to be the right one.

"How's school been?" Mom asked as she sat up and grabbed the pitcher off the coffee table to pour me a glass of the sweetly sour liquid.

"It's been… fine," I said, unable to hide the hesitation.

"Doesn't sound fine. What's been going on?" Dad asked, leaning forward and creasing his brows. He managed to include the sign for 'what's up' with his free hand, a subtlety that pulled at the corner of my mouth and lit a small pile of tinder deep within my chest.

My slight smile transferred to him like an infection and a grin materialized onto his face. Dad had always been good at picking up on the subtle changes in a person's tone. The shifts in body language or eye contact would normally go unnoticed by the average father but seemed to raise a series of alarms with mine. There were times I was appreciative of his observant nature, but other times I wished I could hide from his attentiveness and camouflage myself.

"Just... I don't know." It was time to deflect and steer them off the scent before I caved under the weight of my own stress.

"Uh oh, sounds like something's got those gears going." Dad's features lightened as he quirked a brow, encouraging me to explain.

A small, uncomfortable titter escaped me while I tucked a few loose strands of hair behind my ear. The gears had been spinning all too quickly in recent days, grinding down to almost nothing as I spent all hours of the day and night reviewing each twisted text and rehashing every creepy caper.

"There's just a girl I met during orientation. Well, I guess I met her brother first and then met her later?" I could feel myself veering off toward a tangent. "Anyway, that's not the point. Lately, she's kinda been avoiding me and I can't figure out why. It's weird... We were just starting to get close, but now she's seemingly fallen straight off the face of the planet."

She also had a secret friendship—relationship?—with my nemesis, but I couldn't explain why I was upset without having to explain the reason it bothered me so much.

And that wasn't going to happen.

"Did you two get into an argument?" Mom asked, before she took a sip of her lemonade.

"No, nothing like that. But I found out—," I caught myself before I let too much information slip out. Vomiting the truth was only going to add insult to injury. Non-negotiable. "I found out we're paired up for this class project, so now she's avoiding me and it just makes things a lot more... complicated." It was a plausible enough lie. One they'd probably believe, anyway.

But I hated lying to them. Really, it killed me inside.

Knots formed in the pit of my stomach, mangling and constricting as it threatened my air supply. Repeated mantras in my head were my best attempt at keeping calm, refusing to show discomfort in front of the two people I couldn't bear to let know the truth.

"Well, maybe she just needs some space," Mom offered, gently. "Give her the weekend and then talk to her when you see her in class."

That was going to be challenging, given we didn't

actually have a class together.

"Your mom's right, Len. It's probably got nothing to do with you. She could be going through something she isn't ready to share with you just yet. I'm sure she'll come around and help you finish the project before it's due. Try not to worry about it until you have to, kiddo."

"It'll all work out," Mom soothed, her almond eyes tightening as she smiled warmly at me.

"Yeah... you guys might be right," I conceded, despite the thoughts in the back of my head whirring at a breakneck pace. Thankfully it hadn't culminated in smoke blasting out of my ear canals, so it was safe to assume my brain hadn't melted down yet.

"Are you sure that's the only thing bothering you?" Dad asked. Head slightly tilted, he once again showed off his uncanny ability to read me, even when I didn't want him to. Annoying, yet frustratingly impressive.

"Yeah, no, I'm fine," I dismissed, plastering on my most convincing artificial smile. "Just a lot on my mind with school and everything. Lots of assignments and stuff, that's all. Nothing to worry about. I promise."

I hated lying to my parents, let alone making promises I didn't think I could keep. But it would be better if I didn't tell them. Safer.

After hanging out with my parents for a bit and enjoying a hearty serving of my dad's famous spaghetti bolognese, I met up with Fin and Cam. As I jumped into the driver's seat, I shot a text to let her know I was on my way, to which she simply replied with two emojis: a thumbs up and a face with a finger in front of its mouth, as if it was hushing me like a librarian reprimanding a noisy child.

I assumed that meant good news on the Cameron front, but one could never really tell where Fin's head was at based on her emoji usage. It was a bit like trying to decipher ancient Egyptian hieroglyphics without any training or knowledge in the subject. One time, she sent me a donut and a pair of eyes without any sort of prompt. Turns out, she was asking me if I wanted to go get coffee with her. The fact that a coffee emoji already existed, and hadn't come to mind as a better option, was of no consequence to Finley.

I parked on the street in front of the Teller house, a two-story Craftsman seated smartly behind a precisely trimmed lawn. The roofline was reminiscent of the Gothic era, with rib arched peaks bleeding into barrel vaults. The distinct architectural shift created a stark divide between the upper and lower halves of the structure, and differentiated it from the other houses on their street. The pristine porch wrapped around the front of the house with heavy brick columns contrasting the asymmetrical Revivalist roof, marrying the home in an immaculate combination of form and function.

An architect's wet dream.

As I locked the car from halfway up the walk, I spotted Fin in the upstairs window. Her hands waved frantically at me and told me to go through the gate to the back door. It was possible her parents were home and she didn't want them intercepting me, though I doubted it. Shifting my gaze to the driveway, the only vehicle I could identify was Cameron's 1977 Alfa Romeo Spider, complete with oxidation eating away at its black paint job and a dent in the passenger-side door the size of a grapefruit. Nodding affirmatively to Fin, I headed up to the side of the house and around through the wooden gate that had been left unlocked.

"Took you long enough," Finley teased, waiting for me on the back porch as I came around.

"Couldn't say no to seconds of dad's spaghetti," I replied, tenderly patting my full stomach so as not to jostle its contents too much.

"And you didn't bring me any leftovers?" She shook her head and rose from her perch atop the stairs. *"Criminal."*

Following Fin, we entered through the back doorway and into the house, swung left past the kitchen, and took the stairs two at a time. Her parents weren't home, but

I understood why she hadn't wanted me to go through the front door. The hardwood floors at the front of the house were covered in half-dry streaks and access from the rest of the house was barricaded by a pop-up puppy fence they'd once used to potty train their dachshund, Astro. Evidence it had been recently mopped, more than likely a chore their mother had assigned while she was at work. Giving it no further thought, we ascended to the second floor, hands trailing along the banister.

As we reached the landing, we veered right and Fin opened the door into Cameron's room instead of heading left into her own. Cameron's bedroom was like stepping into an alternate universe. Where the contents of the rest of the house were neatly organized, everything in its place and arranged with a meticulous level of detail, Cam's room was disheveled and stippled with dirty socks and Bic lighters. Half-empty cups and dirty clothes littered the floor alongside stacks of books and CDs. Cameron had no doubt become lazier and more disordered as he'd grown older, my mind contrasting his present state with the days of his parent-pleasing youth.

Where Cameron and Finley wanted nothing more than to escape their father's presence, Dallas—the oldest of the Teller siblings by several years—craved his validation. She'd been the doted-on first child, the guinea pig cosplaying as a third parental figure. Her dedication to following in their father's footsteps was a permanent open wound slicing through Finley's heart. On the other end of that spectrum was Cameron, who struggled the most to follow their father's rules. Cam did just enough to cover his ass while he entertained himself through little acts of rebellion. In addition to secretly smoking cigarettes, he'd gotten a job at the same local music store my brother worked at, and spent a lot of time listening to angry punk artists and curating Spotify playlists—something Fin had developed a love for, too.

Cam was sitting on his unmade bed, with Astro in his lap, leaning against the headboard when we opened the door. His eyes peered over top of the issue of Alternative Press magazine he held in his hands, loud music blaring from an old school two-speaker stereo system sitting atop the dresser in the corner of the room. Astro's head perked up and he excitedly hopped over to wag his tail affectionately in exchange for pats and head scratches.

"Lennon's here," Fin announced, taking a seat at the end of the bed by way of a hearty plop.

Unlike my family, The Tellers had learned ASL after Finley was diagnosed with profound deafness at birth. Cameron was what was known in the Deaf Community as a SODA, meaning he had a deaf sibling. Very few hearing families make the effort to learn to sign, so when I'd first been introduced to hers, I was shocked I'd been able to communicate with them without relying on my voice or lip reading abilities. It was hard to ignore the way it got to me. In moments where I was acutely honest with myself, I had to admit there were shards of resentment below the surface that lived above miles of guilt. Despite my brother's half-assed attempts to become rudimentarily skilled in basic conversational ASL, it still wasn't the same.

"*Hey, Lennon,*" Cam greeted, tossing down the magazine beside him and protruding his chin outward in a slightly skyward nod. "*Fin mentioned that you're having a little problem.*"

"*I'd say it's a pretty big problem,*" Fin quipped.

"*That tends to happen when you leave stolen weapons at the scene of a crime,*" Cam retorted, his tone low and sharp. He roughly nudged Finley in the side with his foot and she swatted him away. To anyone else, it might've looked like he was being serious, but I knew them too well to make that mistake. It was a joke intended to point out that she should've been more careful.

"*First of all, they were borrowed. Not stolen,*" she asserted. "*Secondly, it didn't become a crime scene until after we left.*"

"*What the hell does that mean?*" He asked, his eyes narrowing at his sister.

"*Oh yeah, I forgot to tell you,*" she said, focusing on

me. *"Rider posted something new to his account."*

"Great," I groaned, exasperatedly. *"Do I even want to know?"*

"Depends..." Fin started, pulling out her phone and swiping to his account to view his story.

She turned the phone toward me and my eyes widened.

"How do you feel about a bounty on your head?" she asked.

On Rider's Instagram story was another image of his car with overlaid text informing his followers of a ten thousand dollar reward for information leading to the arrest of whoever was involved in the vandalism.

I rolled my eyes into the back of my head.

Of course Rider was turning this into a money thing. Typical.

Finley pocketed her phone and turned to Cameron. *"We need to borrow cameras. A few of them. The less conspicuous, the better."*

"For what?" He asked, raising a brow in interest.

"That's classified," Fin rebutted.

"That's too bad, because I'm not giving you anything until you explain what you need them for."

Finley and I sighed simultaneously.

"Well, are you going to fill me in or what?" Cameron asked. *"Clearly, you two are way out of your depth here."*

Finley looked at me hesitantly, gauging my reaction.

I bit the inside of my lip in thought. *"We might as well, he already knows about the car."*

As if she was gearing up for a lengthy monologue, Fin took a deep breath and shifted her focus to the puzzled Cameron. It took her a hearty ten minutes to explain everything we'd been through in the past two weeks. She went through every detail, each humiliating moment, and the potential suspects that were on our list. By the time she was done, Cameron could've written a filthy exposé on our exploits.

He nodded thoughtfully, the seconds slowly ticking by as we waited for his response with baited breath.

Without warning, he threw his legs off the side of the bed and stood up.

"Okay, I've got a few that will work for what you need," Cam said. *"All you gotta do is set them up hidden behind something, but don't cover the lens. Catch your suspect saying something incriminating when they think no one's looking or paying attention to them, and their ass is cooked,"* he explained.

It was then, with my eyes darting between her and Cam, I realized Finley's devious smile was a genetic family trait.

"So, we just set them up and wait for somebody to confess?" I asked. *"That could take forever."*

"Depends on how careful they are," Fin added. *"Considering who we're talking about, I don't think we really have to worry about him being cautious."*

"The cameras I have are small and can be hidden discreetly. As long as you don't get caught setting them up like an idiot—" Cam paused for emphasis as he eyed Finley. *"—then you'll be fine."*

Finley rolled her eyes while I laughed, for which she promptly grabbed a pillow and threw it at me. A plan which, ironically, had only made me laugh harder at her expense.

Grinning devilishly, Cameron stepped over to a military-style trunk sitting beneath his bedroom window. The worn olive green footlocker was outfitted with brass hardware and a heavy padlock threaded through the latch at its front. Pulling at a silver ball chain necklace from underneath his shirt, an argent key snaked out at the end of its length. Cam lifted it up and over his head, then clicked it into the lock. Turning toward us as he pulled off the unlocked bolt, his hands gripping the edge of the closure and pulling it open to reveal its contents.

FOUR DAYS BEFORE THE MURDER

"What did you get for number eleven?" Marcus asked.

His hand reached for my notebook and I jokingly slapped it away.

"How about we make a deal? You answer my questions and I'll help you answer yours," I offered, eyes gesturing toward the sheet of lined paper in front of him.

Marcus looked intrigued, a sly smile manifesting at the corner of his mouth as he narrowed his eyes. *"Okay, Larkin, you're on."*

"Alright." I smiled, preparing my first question. *"Have you talked to Tayen lately?"*

"Not sure what you mean." He cocked his head, bewildered.

"I've been trying to reach out all week but haven't been able to get a hold of her." I paused. *"Is she okay?"*

It was hard not to take her radio silence personally. The biggest part of me was worried about her just for the sake of caring about her wellbeing, but I couldn't help but dwell on the uncertainty of how she might be connected to all of this. There was still a chance she was on the wrong side of things. Without giving away what I knew, I needed answers.

"Last time I checked, yeah. Haven't talked to her in a couple days, but that's not really out of the ordinary." Marcus shrugged. Raising a brow, he reached across and tapped my notebook with his pencil.

I managed a smirk and glanced down to check my answers. *"X equals nine."*

"Nine?" He asked, incredulously. *"Shit, I got fourteen."* Erasing his previous answer, Marcus scribbled down the one I'd given him. *"Alright, then what'd you get for number five? I have a feeling it's not eight..."*

"I have a feeling you're not great at algebra," I teased, looking down to confirm my answer. *"I got... seven point five."*

Marcus erased roughly at his paper while he shook his head.

Once he'd looked back up at me, I asked my next question. *"Is Tayen..."* I paused, working out the right way to ask what I wanted to know without coming across like I was trying too hard.

"Seeing anybody? Nah," he replied, smug as all hell. At this point, he could give Finley a run for her money with his quick quips.

"That's not what I was going to ask," I retorted defensively.

"Yeah, it was." The smug confidence was annoying. *"I think she likes you too, for the record. But we aren't gonna get into it, because that's too weird, even for me."*

We both let out a laugh as he finished his thought, but what he'd said continued to linger in the back of my mind. If her brother thought she liked me, maybe she did. The possibility was exciting, but it also made my head spin. Something like feelings shouldn't matter when we had bigger fish to fry. The photo of Tayen and Rider was burning a hole in my pocket, daring me to pull it out and ask Marcus what he knew about their history.

"Speak of the devil," he said, jutting his chin upward and shifting his eyes across the room.

I followed Marcus' gaze to find that Tayen had just walked in, alone, and taken up residence at a table along the far wall.

"I should go talk to her," I said, before realizing he might make an assumption about the reason why. I blurted out the first lie that came to mind. *"We're paired up for a project, so I gotta ask her... about the project."*

Smooth.

"Uh huh, sure you are," Marcus smirked at me, clearly not buying my terrible cover story. *"See you at dinner?"*

"Yeah," I smiled, letting his insinuation roll right off my back. *"Save a seat next to Fin for me."*

Tayen's focus lifted to me as I approached her table. She looked like a deer caught in the headlights, a panicked expression flashing across her face. I interrupted a hurried attempt to pack up her belongings and decided to take advantage of the fact we were the only two people currently occupying this section of the library.

"I was beginning to worry," I began, taking a seat in the chair across from her. *"Thought maybe you'd died."*

Something about her was different. I couldn't put my finger on exactly what it was, but it was palpable. The confidence she used to carry so proudly now seemed tucked away. The boisterous exuberance that used to leak from every pore had been dialed back. There was something holding her hostage, insulating her against some darker force I wasn't able to see.

An uncomfortable smile appeared and then disappeared.

"Yeah... I've just been busy, you know how it is," she deflected.

I set my jaw and sucked a breath of air between my

teeth. *"Marcus said he hasn't seen you much the past few days, either. Is it just me you're steering clear of, or is it a blanket approach you're taking on with everybody?"* There was a coating of sarcasm in my tone, despite my best intentions not to grill her like a beef patty on a barbecue.

The tension between us climbed in the silence, amplified by the fact she seemed to not want to look at me for more than one small moment at a time. Long enough to get what I was saying, but not so long I'd have a chance to see through this façade she seemed to be putting on.

"I'm not sure what you're implying, but—"

She cut herself off as I sat down across from her.

"Look..." I began. *"I really need to talk to you about something. And I need you to be brutally fucking honest here, because I'm on the verge of losing my sanity and I cannot handle any more lies or bullshit. Okay?"*

I nervously picked at the skin around my thumb's cuticle.

Tayen looked up at me, her lips pressed tightly together, but it felt like she was looking straight through me.

"What?" she asked.

"I know you know Rider. I also know that you didn't want me to know that. What I don't know is why, and whether or not you're playing for his fucking team right

now."

"*You don't know what you're talking about, Lennon,*" she said dismissively, closing her laptop and zipping it into one of the compartments in her backpack.

I pulled off my backpack and unzipped the front pocket. Fishing out the photo of Tayen and Rider that had mysteriously been hidden within it, I slid the photo across the table. My eyes remained firmly fixed on Tayen.

"*You can't lie to me,*" I said. "*You know Rider better than I thought you did.*"

Her eyes widened, genuine shock overtaking her features.

"*Where did you get that?*" She asked.

"*You never told me that you knew him,*" I fired back, choosing not to answer her question.

"*It's not what you think it is.*"

"*So this isn't you?*" I asked incredulously, tapping a finger on the photo as it sat atop the table between us. "*Do you have an evil twin? A doppelgänger? Were you body snatched by aliens? I'm failing to understand which part of this isn't exactly what I think it is.*"

Tayen looked at me with glossy eyes. She took a deep breath, her jaw clenching. I knew I was getting closer to the truth, but part of me worried I might be pushing her too hard. If I dared to ask the wrong question, there was nothing keeping her from shutting down and walking away from this conversation entirely.

"*Yes, that's me,*" she finally said, her hands moving cautiously.

"*You think I won't understand something complicated because my life is so simple and easy right now?*" I asked, lowering my brow as a scoff escaped me. This was the worst time for me to be sarcastic. If only I'd realized that moments earlier.

"*It's not about you, Lennon!*" Tayen snapped, glaring at me so hard I was certain I'd burst into flame at any moment.

"*My past with Rider isn't something I like to think about, okay? And this...*" Tayen picked up the photo and held it in the air. "*This is the last thing I want to be talking about with you.*" Angrily, she crumpled up the photo and threw it at me. It bounced and landed on the floor, rolling under the table we'd just been sitting at.

"*So, what, this secret past with him is why you've been so weird?*" I asked, brashly.

"*Lennon, just—*" she started.

Before she could get the words out, I interrupted.

"*Just what, Tayen? Just let it go? I can't do that, because there's obviously something happening here. Everything was perfectly fine until I told you about the messages. I can't just pretend I don't think you avoiding me has something to do with all of this. I told you that I think Rider is torturing me, and you disappear right when I find out that you two know each other. So why the hell didn't you tell me you knew him?"* Angry confusion boiled inside of me and I stood up from my chair. My face contorted in disbelief and frustration as my head tilted toward her. *"Are you part of this whole thing? Are you involved in these weird ass messages? You and me, our friendship,"* I tripped over the word, dying a little bit inside that I'd merely called her a friend. I wanted it to be so much more, despite not knowing whose side of this she was on. *"Has this just been a joke to you? Some kind of game?"*

At this point, nothing else around us registered to me. There could have been a mass of students stampeding through the library and I wouldn't have even noticed. Questions bubbled within me, threatening to boil over and cook my insides.

It was Tayen's turn to be angry now, and she was taking full advantage of the opportunity. Her face ran through the gamut of emotion: surprise, shock, disbelief, and anger. Standing up from her seat, she stepped around the table until she was standing right beside me.

"The fact you would even ask me that is insulting. You really think I'd do something like that? Screw with your emotions?" Tayen retrieved her phone from her pocket, unlocked it, and shoved it into my chest.

My eyes fell to its screen, where I saw several text messages from an unsaved number that looked oddly familiar. The information was still processing and my brain couldn't get there fast enough to wrap itself around this new piece of the puzzle. Brow furrowed, I raised my head to look back up at Tayen. Her anger had dulled and was replaced with a tangible, pricking pain. Thin fingers grasped at the edges of her arms as they enveloped her torso. I finally understood what had seemingly made her feel so fragile, and why she'd fought so hard to put distance between us. She wasn't just avoiding me. It was so much more.

Tayen had been getting texts, too.

Standing there, dumbfounded, I willed my brain to come up with something useful I could say. But all I could manage was a slew of questions I wanted to ask. There had to be a tie between these messages and the strange connection she shared with Rider.

"I—Okay..." I started, stumbling as I articulated my thoughts. *"Honestly, I just don't know what to say here other than the barrage of questions that are floating around in my head."*

"Guess that makes two of us," she replied, grimly.

"Why didn't you tell me? If anyone was going to understand, it would be someone who's also getting these creepy stalker messages." I gestured to myself.

"Because I don't even want to think about it, Lennon. I dread thinking about it. I'd moved past it until you and your friend brought it up again and reopened that wound, because you think you can figure this out. Unlike you, I'd rather ignore it than investigate it. Is that such a wild concept?" Her eyes narrowed at me, daring me to say something in even the slightest attempt to challenge her.

The sarcasm in Tayen's tone wasn't lost on me, and my gut wrenched inward like someone had reached in and tied my intestines into a pretzel. Whatever it was that had happened between them, maybe she hadn't wanted to talk about it for the same reasons as me. I'd spent so much time shoving all of this into the darkest crevices of my mind, I never stopped to think about the fact there might've been others. I'd let myself become so engrossed in my own pain that I didn't consider the ramifications of my silence. The easy choice had been to move past it, choosing to pretend it hadn't happened. That it hadn't happened to me, at least.

Tayen deserved the same chance to wish it all away.

"No, it's not," I conceded. Sighing, I sat back down and leaned against the table. *"You're right. I'm sorry, you really don't owe me an explanation."*

Tayen kept her eyes on me while she took her seat. *"That photo...,"* she slowly began. *"Where did you get it?"*

I reached under the table to pick up the balled-up photo. Unrolling it from itself and flattening it out against the surface of the table, I passed it across the table. *"I found it in my room a few days ago. Someone left it there."*

Tayen leaned forward and craned her neck toward me. Her brows knitted together and her tone was intensely serious. *"Someone broke into the dorms?"*

"Yeah. I woke up to a text confirming it. You know how that feels, obviously."

She nodded.

Violating. Disrespectful. Like my privacy and right to a space that is safe simply didn't matter. I would never know whether they would come back or not and, even if they did, I'd have no protection against them. But worse than that, I hadn't been able to sleep peacefully since. I went online and bought a travel lock that I could place between the door and jamb in order to add an additional layer of security. It wouldn't ease my mind completely, but I knew that it would help once it arrived.

"Do you think it's Rider?" she asked.

"Of course it is. It can't be anyone else, he's the only one who knows everything and had access to the video footage and—god, he's just so fucking arrogant!" The words

explode out of me, a flurry of angry signs and flared nostrils. *"He wanted me to know you were part of this,"* I continued. *"Wanted me to know you two were involved."* For what reason, I wasn't sure, but I was interested in finding out.

Tayen hesitated, visibly uncomfortable as she adjusted in her seat. *"I can explain."*

I didn't want to push her, but I needed to know. Whatever was haunting her played a part in this. Before I could truly trust her, she needed to tell me how her fate was tied to mine. I needed to know why Rider would use this photo to make her a target.

A few moments of stillness passed. Her eyes fell to her hands as she picked at her cuticle. It wasn't until now that I could feel the cool circulated air waft toward us. It brushed against the warm surface of my skin and raised the hairs along my arm, sending a chill straight through me. I straightened in my seat as I waited, giving her my full attention for as long as she needed.

"Okay," Tayen began, inhaling a deep breath. *"Rider and I went to camp together. We've been going to Camp Overland, in Colorado, every summer since I was fifteen and he was fourteen."*

"Wait, Camp Overland?" I repeated, dumbfounded. The pieces were finally starting to come together. The reason Tayen had felt so familiar. How could I have

missed it? *"I was there two summers ago."*

As if I'd uttered the magic words, Tayen tilted her head and scrunched her lips together. Her eyes scanned my face like she was searching for some hidden clue as to who I'd been back then. It was then that I realized she was the same Tayen I'd met back at Camp Overland. The one I never thought I would see again.

"You were in Cabin Eight, right? I was in Eleven, across camp."

"Oh my god—Loser Lenny?" She said, before quickly realizing apologizing. *"No, oh crap, I'm sorry."*

"It's fine," I waved off, ignoring the stinging pains in my chest.

Of course the first thing she remembered was that heinous nickname.

I'd spent that summer with a chip on my shoulder. Camp Overland was a favorite among my classmates and my friend group. Ex-friend group, anyway. I hadn't wanted to go and spend three weeks surrounded by the people who had chosen Rider over me, but my parents weren't taking no for an answer. They were concerned that I was spending far too much time in my bedroom for someone who used to rarely ever be home until curfew. That my once-busy social circle had dwindled down to me and Fin watching true crime marathons every weekend. Despite my excuses, they'd started questioning why none of my friends were coming over anymore, and why I hadn't wanted to celebrate my birthday that year. Eventually, I gave in and agreed to go to camp.

The one bright side was meeting Tayen. She'd looked different back then, or at least she did in my memories. Despite being a year older, she was kind to me. She'd sat with me when she saw me eating alone that first night, talking to me with care rather than concern. The following weeks had been less miserable than I'd expected, with that one interaction acting as a small beacon of hope.

"No, it's not," Tayen corrected. *"Kids are cruel, huh?"*

I scoffed. *"Yeah, you have no idea just how cruel."*

"Well that's the thing..." She started, letting out a slow but heavy sigh. *"The year you were there, I was hanging out with Rider. We'd been friends for a while, but he started flirting with me differently than he had before. Acting like he was interested in something more serious, or at least he made me believe that was the case. We'd had this on-and-off camp romance for a while, but this was the first time it felt like it could become something real. Something serious."*

I remained immovable as she explained, intently glued to her as I watched her brown eyes shift around the room, their golden flakes illuminating as the light reflected in them. She was so effortlessly beautiful, and I wanted so badly to tell her. To hold her hand in mine and reassure her she didn't need to base her worth on the validation of some boy who'd only wanted her attention so he could take advantage of it. But, instead, I remained as stoic as a statue for fear of intruding on her telling of the story.

"It was actually really nice, you know? The attention. Being doted on. It was the best summer... until the end." She swallowed hard, trying not to get caught up in the emotions flooding back as she recalled her memories.

Against my better judgment, I reached across the table and gently rested my hand on top of hers. A soft look of support from me to her seemed to be enough, and I dared not speak as she shared a small smile. I knew what was coming.

"The last night of camp, we had this big bonfire and everyone was hanging out. Rider and I slipped away for a bit, thinking no one would miss us for a little while. We snuck into his cabin and we were making out. He'd pulled my top down and off my shoulders while his lips trailed down my neck. Luckily my pants were still on, but they were unbuttoned and I was exposed. He pulled out his phone and took a few photos of me—the inappropriate kind. I thought he was just playing around. At the time it seemed harmless. I had been so caught up in the moment but I instantly regretted it. The next day, I felt sick to my stomach. I asked

him to delete them, but he refused."

Tayen tucked a few strands of hair behind her ear before continuing.

"I tried to tell myself it was fine. He'd find a new interest and delete them, but when I saw Shawn talking about how hot the black lace on my underwear was, and how he wished it had been him undressing me, I freaked. I told him that I'd report him to the counselors. He just laughed and said they wouldn't believe me, that I couldn't prove I hadn't just sent them to him in the first place. I told him I'd seen Shawn talking about it and knew he'd shown the photos to the other boys in his cabin. But it didn't matter. He said he could show them to the counselors and have them send me home early for misconduct. Threatened to have his father influence the board to rescind every college credit I'd earned since I started going to Camp Overland. He knew it was an empty threat, but it was enough to keep me from fighting him."

I knew how that felt. The helplessness that came with realizing that those in power wouldn't believe you. Especially when they were in your enemy's pocket.

"The only reason I was at that camp is because I was awarded his family's scholarship. My family couldn't afford to send me without financial aid. I never would've had access to the college credits and advanced classes anywhere else. As it is, I'll be able to graduate a year early because of

all the credits I earned there. If I'd lost those, it would've added a whole extra year of housing costs and we wouldn't have been able to swing it."

Camp Overland was the kind of summer camp kids were only allowed to go to if they were connected to the 'right' people. For me, the right people had been some friends of my parents' who were on the camp's Board of Directors. For Tayen, the 'right people' had been the Abbots.

"It didn't feel like I had a choice. His family donated so much money to Camp Overland there was no way the staff would believe my story over his," she continued as the back of her hand wiped away a rogue tear that had welled up in her eye and broken away. *"Not to mention the disrespect to my family, oh my god."* A miserable sigh escaped her as she tried to contain herself. *"My mom's been a single mom ever since my dad passed. She's scraped and saved and done everything imaginable to be able to send us here for college. Even co-signing my student loans. If she knew if I'd let that happen? If she knew I'd gotten myself into that situation and let some boy walk all over me? It would break her heart."*

"Tayen, you didn't let anything happen," I asserted. *"He took advantage of you and that's not your fault. Don't think it's any kind of reflection on you."* I could tell she wasn't quite convinced. *"I'm serious."*

"I know, you're right, it's just…" Tayen sighed, breaking her hand away from mine to tend to the tears that had run down both of her cheeks. She shook her head and tried to regain her composure. *"I just can't shake the fact that I wouldn't be in this situation if I hadn't done what I did. Why the hell did I let him take those photos? I can't believe I trusted him."*

I bit at the inside of my lip while I tried to come up with something insightful to say. Some consolation that might make her feel better. *"Rider has a habit of tricking people into believing he cares about them to get what he wants,"* I offered, hoping the next words out of my hands weren't going to seem narcissistic.

"What do you mean?" She asked.

Part of me knew if I wanted any hope of bridging this gap between us, then I needed to be honest with her. She'd shared her vulnerability and it was my turn to open myself up to her, too.

"He did the same thing to me. Most guys never even looked my way, so I'm the first to admit the attention was kind of nice. At some point, I decided to give in. At the time, I'd just felt all this pressure to be liked, you know? To give him what he'd asked for so those good feelings wouldn't go away. So I wouldn't go back to being the girl everyone overlooked. Ugh, I hate myself everytime I think about it." I physically shook as I finished my thought, the disgust

climbing up my spine like a gibbon ascending a colossal tree.

"Seems like we both owe our younger selves some grace for the mistakes we've made," Tayen noted, reaching across the table. This time, her hand rested on mine.

"No," I replied, the corner of my mouth turning upward. *"We owe them justice."*

Notifications pinged my phone, sending out a pair of vibrations from the back pocket of my jeans. Checking the messages, my blood pressure immediately skyrocketed. The first message was a photo of me, asleep, from the night someone had broken into my room. Seeing myself in such a vulnerable state, knowing they were standing just mere inches from my face, wrenched my insides so violently I couldn't catch my breath.

Being that I was standing in the middle of The Union, the last thing I wanted was to draw attention to myself by having a full-fledged panic attack in front of dozens of students. My eyes darted across the room several times in order to locate the nearest bathroom. Fighting every urge to break out into tears, I scrambled toward the door and shoved myself inside.

The straps of my backpack dropped off my shoulders

as the weight became too heavy to bear. It dropped to the floor as I leaned against the corner of the room and slid down the tile walls. My fingers pulled at the collar of my shirt, neck straining upward as if it would help increase the amount of oxygen I could intake. Pushing the hair from my neck, a few beads of anxious sweat clung to my skin.

Everything was suffocating me.

A few short breaths led to deeper breaths as I closed my eyes and tried to regulate my heart rate. Once I felt like I could handle it, I peered down at my phone again. With the deepest of breaths, I opened my texts once more.

YOU'RE SLEEPING A LITTLE TOO PEACEFULLY THESE DAYS.

IN CASE I HAVEN'T MADE MYSELF CLEAR...

YOU'RE NOT WALKING AWAY FROM THIS

My eyes stung as they welled up with tears, my vision muzzy and unclear. I bent my legs up to my tightened chest and rested my forehead on my knees as tears streamed down my face. The quiet cries turned into sobs and suddenly I couldn't control it anymore. The dam had cracked open and everything was pouring through. Waves and tsunamis of pain and agony and despair, the depths of which were unfathomable. I'm not sure how long I sat there, occupying the bathroom floor, hoping no one would dare walk in.

Unexpectedly, my knee began to feel a warm pressure. Tilting my head, my eyes rose to meet Tayen's. Hints of golden flecks swirled within her amber irises. How had I ever looked at her and not seen them before? It seemed impossible, their magnetic pull greater than any planet could ever dream of. I folded into the infinitesimal dimensions of their deep mahogany hues, begging to stay in their safety.

"What's wrong?" Tayen asked, taking a seat beside me.

The words to explain were nowhere to be found. Instead, I picked up my phone from where it had slid out of my hand and onto the bathroom floor mid-breakdown. Handing it to her, I wiped the wet streaks from my face with a dry section of my tear-stained shirt.

Her jaw tensed as she read the message. Without saying anything, Tayen pulled out her own phone and showed me a message she'd also received this morning.

WAIT UNTIL YOUR FAMILY FINDS OUT WHAT YOU DID

Whoever this was, somehow they'd figured out which buttons to press. Tayen had mentioned how worried she was about her family finding out, and I worried this would add too much pressure. Maybe she'd want to call it quits on our plan and that would be the end of it. Putting her phone away, she returned her hand to my knee and patted it gently.

"What do you want to do?" I asked, wiping away the tear residue from under my eye with my index finger.

"What do you mean?" She asked, creasing her brows together.

"I mean... does that change anything?" I gestured to her pocketed phone. *"Your family finding out that you lied your way onto the team is the whole reason you never said anything in the first place. I'll totally understand if you don't want to keep digging into this."*

"Don't worry about it," she said, fully confident.

I laughed uncomfortably. *"How could I possibly not worry?"*

"I get how that might be difficult given the circumstances." She smiled, returning a small laugh.

"But this changes nothing—I promise. We're getting to the bottom of this, one way or another. I'll deal with my family and the soccer fallout if and when I have to."

Despite how weak and helpless I felt, Tayen's firm conviction made me feel like we could come out the other side victorious. Despite the mounting pressure, and the fact she was now being threatened with one of her greatest fears, she still wanted to keep going. If she had faith in us then I could, too. At the very least, I could put all my faith in her.

"Come on," Tayen said as she tapped her hand against my leg.

She rose to her feet and bent down, holding out a hand for me to grab. She lifted me to my feet and I brushed off my pants. I caught my reflection in a mirror above one of the pedestal sinks that stood in a row along the wall. My face was flushed, the redness in my cheeks and swelling around my eyes indicative of my emotional collapse. I looked haggard, the teenaged-girl equivalent of a bicycle that was left out in the rain for a week.

Once I'd rinsed the soap from my hands, I cupped them under the running water and splashed its coolness into my face. Before I could ask, Tayen was offering me a wad of paper towels and leaning against the sink beside me.

"Thanks." I took the towels and patted my face dry.

"You know…Maybe we should talk to Bronya."

Every muscle in my body tensed.

"Why is that?" I asked.

"She might have seen something, right? Especially since they'd been in your room," she said, holding up my phone before handing it back to me.

"You think she saw Rider sneak in?"

To be fair, I hadn't actually considered it. I'd assumed Bronya would've been asleep, too, or that she would've been around enough to notice anyone being there that shouldn't be.

"The thought has crossed my mind, yeah. I could be wrong, but from a scientific perspective, it's worth interviewing everyone that might have even a remotely important piece of information."

"That's true. Finley brought up the idea of it being Wade the other day, and I can't shake that thought either."

"Really?"

"Yeah, something about it doesn't feel right, though. If I've learned anything from the many hours I've spent watching true crime shows, I know there's got to be a motive. And I can't figure out what theirs could be."

"You can't look at everything like it's an episode of Forensic Files."

"If it looks like a duck and quacks like a duck, it's Forensic Files."

Tayen stared at me blankly for a few moments before bursting into laughter. *"You're ridiculous."*

"Yeah, I know," I admitted before taking her hand and walking out of the bathroom. *"Let's go talk to Bronya."*

We arrived at my room and, surprisingly, Bronya was actually there. Sugary pop music was blaring on a speaker atop her nightstand and she was digging through a pile of shoes and purses at the bottom of her closet. Before the front door shut, Tayen pressed the doorbell a couple of times to signal that we had arrived and wanted her attention.

Bronya looked up at us and gave a short nod, but didn't stop what she was doing. Instead, she looked between the pile and us as I asked her the first question.

"Hey, do you have a minute?"

"Only a few, then I've got to meet Anders. It's our anniversary tonight and he's taking me to dinner." She pulled out a single silver shoe and set it aside, then dug back into the pile.

"Okay, this won't take long." I looked to Tayen for help, unsure how to ask what I needed to know.

Tayen jumped in. *"We're wondering if you've seen anyone strange hanging around your room lately? Someone* who's been here a lot when Lennon wasn't here, or who has been asking for her?"

"What do you mean by strange?" Bronya asked, finding the other silver shoe and putting it beside its mate.

"Anything that sticks out to you as weird. Like, is there anyone that seems to be here a lot?" I asked, still unconvinced that this conversation wouldn't be a total waste of time.

Bronya shrugged. *"Just your friends."*

"Anyone else?" Tayen pushed. *"Really think about it."*

Bronya grabbed a matching silver purse from the heap and hoisted all of the accessories as she stood, tossing them onto her bed.

"I am really thinking about it," she sneered. *"No one weird has been here. Your one little friend is wearing out her welcome, but I'm at Anders' half the time anyway so what do I care."* Bronya unhooks a hanger that's holding a floor-length, flowing, satin dress in a shimmering shade of indigo. *"Now if you'll excuse me, I have a date to prepare for."*

Gathering up her towel and shower caddy, Bronya steps past us and leaves for the bathroom, leaving Tayen and I in the lurch.

"Well, that was helpful," I muttered.

"Your roommate is a real peach," Tayen remarks with palpable sarcasm.

"I knew this would be a waste of time."

"Hey, just because she wasn't all that helpful doesn't mean we didn't learn anything."

"Meaning...?" I asked.

"She said that one of your friends is wearing out their welcome. Did you catch that?"

"Yeah, but she could've meant anyone."

"Which one of your friends would be here if you weren't?" Tayen asked, eyeing me carefully.

"The only person I can think of is Fin, but there's no way she'd be behind this," I defend. *"Absolutely not. Zero chance."*

"Are you willing to bet your life on it?"

I always thought I would be.

We met up with Finley and Marcus at The Commons, ready to scarf down our weight in sushi, pizza, and tofu wraps as the warmth of the day began to retreat into the evening's cool embrace. Deciding it was best not to discuss our recent escapades in a public setting lest we draw too much attention to ourselves, the five of us brought our food back to Finley's room in to-go containers. We spread out across the room and, this time, I snagged the bean bag chair for myself.

"*So, what exactly are we supposed to do with these?*" Marcus asked, picking up and holding one of Cameron's cameras in his hand while he chewed on a bite of pepperoni pizza.

"*Use them to catch Rider revealing himself as the person behind all this shit,*" Finley replied.

"*What if it's not him?*" Wade asked, downing a gulp of their Cherry Coke.

"*Then we're back to the drawing board, I guess,*" I replied.

"*Let's not tempt fate,*" Finley fired back, setting down the chocolate chip cookie she'd been eating. "*We're already playing with fire here, and the last thing we need is to burn our whole suspects list in one go.*"

"*Yeah, the texts are getting dark enough as it is,*" Tayen said.

"*Wait. Wade, what did you mean when you said 'neither'?*" I asked.

"*Well, I've been thinking about what we talked about the other day. Rider seems like a more likely suspect, right? But there's another person I think is even more likely.*"

"*Who?*" Tayen asked, leaning forward with furrowed brows.

"*Theo.*"

We all sat there in stunned silence and my attention fell to Finley. Had the two of them been thinking about this together? Is that why she wanted to plant the cameras, to spy on Theo instead of Rider? If what Bronya said was an actual lead, could this be Finley turning things around to throw the scent off of Rider? It couldn't be here, there was no way that my best friend in the entire universe could betray me—especially when she'd smashed up his car for me.

But a miniscule thought at the back of my head kept thinking: what if?

What if that was part of a long-con and I was falling into the trap?

No. Stop it. It's not her. It can't be.

"He's Rider's best friend. It's not impossible to think he'd know about the photos and what happened since he's close to him and probably has unfettered access to everything in Rider's life," Wade continued. *"If Rider was going to tell someone, it would be one of the people in his inner circle.."*

"Good point," Finley added.

"Guess we've gotta add a new suspect to our list," I stated.

"Even more of a reason to get one of these up and running," Marcus said, holding up one of the cameras.

The rest of the evening devolved into jokes and lighthearted conversations, making me feel like I was back to my normal self, for the first time in weeks. Between questioning my life and the pieces of my past

I'd pushed deep down into the darkest corners, parts of myself were starting to corrode under the weight of everything. Being able to unwind with my friends was a luxury I hadn't been able to enjoy in a while. As I sat back and watched them entertain one another, I wondered how many more of these moments were left before things would go sideways.

Fewer than I'd hoped, as it turned out.

THREE DAYS BEFORE THE MURDER

Fingers coiled around my bicep and pulled me out of the mail room line where I'd been waiting to collect the extra lock I'd ordered the other day. My attention was ripped away from a poster I'd been reading about an upcoming play and I turned to find that the hand tightly gripping my arm belonged to none other than the Worst Person Alive.

Rider Abbot.

"What the hell is this?" he asked, once he'd pulled me aside to a secluded corner of the room where our hands were obscured by a wall of mailboxes.

I yanked my arm away and backed away as he thrust his phone into my face. My eyes adjusted to his screen's brightness and I realized I was looking at a text thread. Specifically, one text:

I'LL BE WAITING FOR MY REWARD

And one image—that of me and Fin sneaking into Rider's garage on the night of the party and holding that suspicious-looking black plastic bag.

What the fuck?

The number didn't look familiar, but that didn't mean anything. They could've created a new number with the same app they'd used to create the ones that texted me and Tayen. The real question was why.

"Looks like a text message to me," I replied, refusing to show my cards.

"Don't play with me, Lennon," Rider sneered. *"Why the hell were you and Finley sneaking around my house?"*

I shrugged. *"We live in an imperfect world, full of people who do all kinds of strange things. I can't stand here all day and debate them with you."*

"Cut the crap. It's no coincidence that you two were in my garage on the same night that someone fucked with my car."

"Sounds like a coincidence to me."

There was no way I was going to give him the satisfaction of admitting to anything. He'd have to pry it out of my cold dead hands.

"You really think I didn't know it was you?" Rider stepped toward me, corralling me into a corner. His gaze dropped, scanning me from head to toe, and his upper lip curled. *"You used to be such a hot piece of ass, Lennon. Naive and misguided, sure, but you were always willing to do whatever it took to be liked. I enjoyed that."*

The hair rose on the back of my neck and a spidery chill crawled up my spine.

"Y'know, before you became..." he said, his hand motioning along the length of my body. *"...whatever this is."*

Instinctively, I slapped his hand away.

"Look, I don't know who sent you that, okay? But Finley and I didn't damage your car." All we did was put a dozen rotten eggs inside of it and leave it to fester. It takes everything in me to keep my poker face while I imagine all the ways I could make him bleed.

Rider's brows furrowed, looking back and forth from me to the image and then back again. *"You two look awfully suspicious. Am I supposed to believe those are snacks in that bag?"* He condescended, zooming in on the photo.

The longer I stood in front of him and that punchable face of his, the more I wanted to cave it in with my clenched fist or dome him with a heavy textbook. God, how badly I wanted to scratch at his eyes or pluck all of his eyelashes out. The possibilities were endless.

"Can we speed this up? As much as you enjoy talking, the rest of us don't enjoy listening to you."

"My point is that you cost me ten-thousand dollars in vehicle damage."

"You mean I cost your daddy ten thousand dollars."

"Do you—" Rider paused as someone walked up to us and dropped a piece of mail into the outgoing box before giving us a concerned look and walking away. *"Do you think this is some kind of joke?"*

"No, I don't. I think whoever sent you those messages knew you'd come and find me."

"So?" he asked, clearly not following my train of thought.

"So you need to consider who would want that to happen," I said, stepping around him. Stopping to look back at him, I clenched my jaw. *"And in the meantime, feel free to stay the hell away from me before I need to get a restraining order."*

Rider's pathetic attempt at intimidating me had ruined any and all interest in retrieving my mail, blinded by fuming rage over the gall he had to try and put his hands on me. I wanted to make him regret it, to smash that phone when he held it up to my face, but I couldn't. Not for fear of Rider, but for what it meant that The Ghost had reached out to him and led him to Finley and

I. They were playing a dangerous game, making it clear that we were merely pawns to their Queen.

As I stalked out the doors of The Union, turning back to ensure that he wasn't following me, my body thudded hard into something. Stumbling back, a hand reached for me and kept me from falling over my own feet. Flitting toward whoever had caught me, my gaze met Tayen's.

"Now I get why you don't play sports," she teased. *"Are you alright?"*

"Very funny," I said. I could feel the heat rising in my cheeks as I considered how to explain the fact that I'd nearly run her over trying to get away from Rider as quickly as humanly possible. *"Sorry, I wasn't looking where I was going."*

"Where are you off to in such a hurry?"

"Away from here," I said. *"We need to find the others, I've got some new information and it's... a lot."*

Just then, Tayen's face dropped and she turned a ghostly white.

Rider was standing in the doorway, staring at us, his jaw tight and eyes glowering.

"You've got to be kidding me," he chided. *"So that's what this is about. You two are fucking with me, aren't you? That's what this is, some sort of crazy ex-girlfriend prank?"* He glanced between us, back and forth as though he

was afraid to allow his eyes to linger on either of us for too long.

"What?" Tayen asked.

"I know what you're doing," Rider asserted, pointing a finger at the two of us. *"And if you think I'm going to go down without a fight, you've got another thing coming."*

Several hours passed and neither Tayen nor myself had received any new texts. We remained cautiously optimistic, but deep down we knew better than to assume the silence meant everything was okay. It was time to come up with a plan of attack, some solid strategy to inch closer and cut them off at the knees before they caused Godzilla-level damage.

In the stillness of late, and the rare chance to catch our breath, we decided to spend some time off-campus and away from the spaces that haunted our dreams. I, of course, jumped at the chance to get to know Tayen. I was dying to dive into her head, to learn more about the things she loved and simply enjoy the comfort of her company. Despite a few side-eyes from Finley, These opportunities were few and far between and it was only right to capitalize on them when they arose.

We took off for Off The Record—one of my favorite

places to relax and drown out whatever I was feeling in music that spoke to my soul. We'd opted to walk and take advantage of the beautiful day, although that reasoning came secondary to the fact that parking spots nearby were few and far between.

"Metered street parking is a menace to society," Wade stated, matter-of-factly.

"Not to mention it's classist as hell," Finley added.

"Damn right it is."

The two of them low fived in agreement as Marcus pulled open the door and held it for the rest of us.

Off the Record was an old-school record store of epic proportions, tucked back off a side street of Ventura Boulevard a few blocks from campus in the heart of Sherman Oaks. The aging brick building stood as a testament to its will to survive both the test of time and the looming threat of a digital takeover. It had been there for decades, the converted event space upstairs serving as a spot for local up-and-coming bands to showcase their skills and debut new tracks. It wasn't quite a club, but still a great place for the under-twenty-one crowd to hang out and enjoy live music.

I'd seen plenty of shows there growing up, including some intimate concerts that older, well-known bands had stopped in to play. The well-connected owner, Geoff Quinn, was a staple in the local scene. Covered in tattoos with a grey-blonde shock of hair atop his head, he was the quintessential aging rockstar with a heart of gold. All the musicians who'd come up in the area would always come back to visit him, citing his support and expertise as a key component to their success. As a family friend of my parents, he'd even done them a solid and hired Felix to work there part-time.

We meandered inside and headed to the back, finding our way to what had long since been dubbed The Listening Pit. Tucked in the far corner, in a separate room with a beaded curtain entrance, it was a section of the store designed for conversation and collective enjoyment, complete with bean bag chairs set up in a wonky circular shape. There was a seventies style shag rug on the floor beneath them, an eclectic addition to the vintage posters and loud paint colors overlapping on the walls. To the untrained eye, it looked as though nothing had changed in the decades since this place had first opened. To those of us in the know, we knew Geoff was always on the hunt for new and unlikely additions he could scrounge up from garage sales and eBay listings. The newest piece was a framed Annie Leibovitz print of John Lennon and Yoko Ono.

I so badly wanted to rummage through the heaps of vinyl organized by genre and arranged in multicolored milk crates, but time was of the essence and we had to use every minute wisely. Growing my vinyl collection was not a priority.

Each of us claimed a bean bag chair, save for Finley who chose to sit cross-legged on the floor between Marcus and I.

"Yo, Wade!" I waved toward them to get their attention as my body sank into the bag.

"What's up?" Wade asked, their focus fixing on me.

"You wanna catch us up on what you were able to find when you looked up that phone number?" I asked.

"Here's the thing... It for sure came from one of those apps where you can create a fake text number. Completely untraceable."

"So then they might not even be in LA?" Marcus asked curiously.

"Technically speaking, they could be anywhere in the world," Wade replied.

"That's not exactly helpful," Fin said.

"Maybe it's better to lay out what we do know. Try to create a profile," I added.

"I've been getting texts, too," Tayen blurted out.

The pounding of my heart grew louder. I was whatever the word is for being stunned a million times over. She'd only opted to share her painful history with me a few days ago, so I hadn't expected her to want to bare such a vulnerable secret in front of everyone just yet.

Marcus' attention hardened and his eyes narrowed in his sister's direction.

"Only... the number isn't the same as the one texting Lennon. It's different."

"That asshole is on campus?" Marcus interjected. *"I thought you said you haven't talked to him since camp last year?"* His fist clenched in his lap.

"I haven't," Tayen defended, her lips pursing together. *"But yeah, he's here. It's no coincidence that both of us drew the short straw when it came to Rider."*

Her gaze drifted to me and I gave a subtle nod in return.

We had the same secret; the same weakness.

"Tayen, when you started getting those texts... did anything happen that might've caused them to target you?" I asked, recalling the way I'd been blackmailed with the photo of Rider's car more destroyed than Finley and I had last left it on the night of the party.

"Yeah, I... I went to the Dean of Student Conduct about Rider. That's why I was late showing up to the scavenger hunt."

"What did you tell the Dean?" Fin asked, one brow arched.

"Seeing Rider was more than I bargained for, so I bit the bullet and went to tell them about what he'd done at camp.

I knew there was probably not much they could do, but I needed them to know what kind of person he is."

We shared a moment of stillness, with no one sure what to say next.

"That explains why you became a target," Fin sighs.

"That and the photos."

"And now that we know Rider's getting the texts, too," I said. *"He's definitely not the one pulling the strings here. The first clue should've been that there's no chance he'd ever willingly damage his own car."*

"Alright," Wade started. They leaned forward, resting their elbows on their knees. *"Given what we know now, it's clear whoever's doing this knows each of your weak points, as well as the history you both have with Rider."* Wade shifted their eyes between Finley and myself. *"They also had to have been at his party to know about the car you guys vandalized."*

Wade was right. There were so many pieces of this and they only fit together if it was someone who had been at the party and who also would've known things I'd previously assumed weren't public knowledge.

"So whoever it is has to know Rider," Fin stated abruptly.

"Right. But who would want to shine such a giant spotlight on what he's done?" Wade questioned.

"Someone that either knows and thinks he's a dumpster

fire of a person, or someone who was also a victim and wants revenge?" Finley asked, thinking out loud.

"You guys didn't tell anyone when it happened, right?" Marcus asked, side-eyeing his sister before he continued. *"If it's someone he told, it could be one of his friends."*

"That would make sense," I said, mostly just working through my own thoughts out loud.

"My money's still on Theo," Finley added. *"I think he harbors some hatred for the guy, deep down. All those years of being his rich friend's lackey can't have been all kittens and rainbows for the guy."*

I nodded. If anyone had a secret vendetta against Rider, as well as access to his private information, it was definitely Theo.

"Okay, let's say it is," Marcus started. *"How do we keep him from throwing you two under the bus just to make sure Rider got what was coming to him?"*

"If we can get Theo to admit that he's blackmailing you guys," Wade said, *"then we can end this whole thing before it gets too far out of hand. We need to catch him on video and use that as leverage."*

"And steal those photos back from Rider's phone," Finley added, smirking in the devious manner to which she was so accustomed.

"You think they're only on his phone?" Tayen asked.

"Hell no, they're probably locked away in a password

protected app or something," Marcus chimed in, a few rogue chuckles accompanying his words. *"One of those photo vaults that cheating husbands use to hide their spank banks."*

"Those aren't impossible to break into," Wade said, raising their brows and tilting their head. *"All I need is his phone."*

"Okay, and how do you suggest we get that?" Fin asked.

"I've got some ideas. I'll test some stuff and, depending on what works, we'll do it on the real thing. Your photos will be history."

Everyone else took off back to campus, but I opted to stay behind and go through the milk crates in case there were any interesting albums I could snag on the cheap. There was still lots of light flooding in from outside, so I had plenty of time before I had to head back to campus to meet back up with the gang for dinner. My fingers nimbly combed through the plastic tabbed dividers jutting out from between the rows of used vinyl. The Smiths. Sonic Youth. Soundgarden. Spinal Tap. Each of the alphabetized tabs were adorned with band names written on crudely stuck-on labels with peeling edges.

"S—oh— Tem— Pi—"

"What?" I raised a brow, my head taking a moment to turn as I finished reading the cover of an album. I looked to my right and found Felix standing beside me, holding an album in front of himself. A proud grin graced his face as his fingers wrapped around the edges. It looked like an original pressing of their 1992 album, Core, complete with a tattered paper sleeve inside of a plastic cover.

Felix and I have long since shared an affinity for both horror films and old school rock-and-roll, the latter of which was infused into our bloodstreams directly through our parents' unending encouragement. As children of the sixties, they grew up listening to the kinds of music that defined not only a decade but a cultural movement. The Rolling Stones, The Who, Led Zeppelin, Aerosmith, AC/DC, The Clash, Queen, and Lynyrd Skynyrd to name a few. That their children had developed a love for that same music was an overflowing wellspring of nostalgia for them.

My dad, a studio musician, had played guitar on tracks for a laundry list of artists across all genres while my mom, once upon a time the lead singer of an all-girl punk band back in Brooklyn called The Lost Girls, now gave vocal lessons out of our home. A career that afforded her the kind of flexibility that made her the envy of every other PTA mom in our district.

Music had always connected our family in a way words never could. Whenever we failed to find the vocabulary to adequately convey our thoughts or feelings, there was always a song we could play to explain it better than our words ever could. Some lyrical melody to perfectly capture what hung in the air between us. I'd always had a knack for being able to swipe through my mental discography and choose the one that felt just right.

It's in your blood, our parents always told us, paired with quiet smiles and loving glances.

Maybe they were right.

It would've been a dream to pursue music like my brother and my parents had, but it was never in the cards for me. Even before I started to lose my hearing, I had an insufferable singing voice and hand-eye coordination so bad I couldn't even get through a round of Rock Band. It's funny how the universe doesn't always let things play out in the ways we expect. It chooses, instead, to operate by its own rules and in its own time. A cyclical pattern, like watching at dusk as the moon dips below the earth's surface before rising again and warming the soil at dawn with its bright golden rays.

That's all well and good, sure, but my Type-A self has always desperately wanted to understand the madness so I can find my place within it. The universe's unwillingness to give me full control will never cease to irk me.

"Oh, hi, stalker. Nice, Stone Temple Pilots. I don't think I have that one," I said.

Somehow, he'd always managed to keep track of which bands and albums I liked, even when I couldn't remember what I already owned. At one point, I'd considered creating an Excel sheet to track my inventory, but Finley had relentlessly teased me about it so hard I'd abandoned the idea just to shut her up.

"I literally just said that," he shot back, handing the album over to me. "And how am I the one stalking you when you're showing up at my place of employment?" Felix raised a brow at me, which was a cue for my eyes to roll to the back of my head.

"How was I supposed to know if you were working today?" I threw out casually. The variances in his schedule from week-to-week were unpredictable at best.

"You could've asked," Felix said, matter-of-factly, as he returned to sorting a heap of albums to their rightful homes along the row of rock bands with 'T' names.

"If you want me to avoid you while you're on the clock, you might as well send me your schedule every week. Otherwise, deal with the consequences of seeing my face," I concluded with a smirk. I flipped through more albums, quickly skipping over the names of bands I wasn't interested in. I felt his eyes on me as I stood there, his retinas boring holes into the side of my head, so I decided to find out what was running through his. "Is there something else you wanted to say?" I asked, meeting his gaze under an arched brow as my chin angled downward toward the floor.

"Yeah, actually." Felix clenched his jaw and a muscle tensed along the side of his neck. "I saw you earlier," he continued, before looking away briefly and gesturing for me to follow him back to the far corner of the room where I'd been talking with my friends. Attention back on me, a familiar look of confusion and frustration plastered itself across Felix's face. "What the hell was all that about, Lennon?"

"You're going to have to be specific, because I have no idea what you're talking about," I said, unsure of what exactly he was referring to.

"You know exactly what I'm talking about, don't play dumb."

"Oh, so now I'm dumb? Real nice." Not the best strategy, but I'd hoped it would be enough to get him started on a tangent and drift away from whatever this was altogether.

"No—what?" Felix sighed heavily as his index finger and thumb reached up and pinched the bridge of his nose. Then his arm flung outward and he shook his head. "Look, I saw what you said earlier about the... the *texts*." Felix signed the final word as he trailed off his sentence. The movement of his hands hung in midair like an unspoken truth I wished I could rewind. Part of me knew Felix would find out one way or another, but I'd hoped I could buy myself some time before I had to spill my guts. I waited for Felix to continue, but instead he was silent. Waiting expectantly for me to answer some unasked question.

I stood frozen, appearing calm, cool, and collected.

"Okay." I replied, signing the letters 'O' and 'K' as I spoke. "What do you want me to say?"

"What do I want you to say?" Eyes widened as he blinked several times. Disbelief colored Felix's face following the reiteration of my question, his sentence punctuated by the touching of his pointer finger to his chin. "I want you to explain why I'm only just now finding out some creep is threatening you."

Taken aback, I blinked a few times and let it sink in that he'd been watching us—watching me—and actually understood what we'd said. Some of it, anyway.

"Wait, how—" I started to ask, unsure of his ability to understand that much signing at once.

Felix cut me off, signing his next thought as he spoke. *"I've been taking classes."*

"Why didn't you say anything?"

"You first."

"Okay, okay, just..." I glanced around us to find that the few loitering customers had peered over in our direction. The blood rushed to my cheeks and I lowered my head, instinctively grabbing Felix's arm and tugging him through a doorway into Geoff's closet-sized office. "Relax, okay? I'm handling the whole texting thing. It's under control."

He started to laugh but caught himself and cleared his throat. "Not that I don't think you can handle yourself, but get real, Len. If someone is sending you threatening messages, then it's very obviously not under control."

"See? This is exactly why I didn't want to say anything to you, because you always assume I can't handle myself," I shot back, doing my best to keep my voice low.

The ambient noise of the record store added to my struggle to regulate my speaking volume. Felix had always treated me with kid gloves. My parents, too. They were all so worried about what they perceived to be my shortcomings they were overlooking my abilities.

"Oh yeah? Let's see then." Felix nodded toward his newly outstretched hand that marred the space between us.

"No," I argued. My gut recoiled at the thought of handing over my phone, anxious our whole plan of attack would implode at the hands of my brother's unwarranted intervention.

"Give me your phone," he demanded. That time he switched back to ASL, emphasizing the point he was trying to make. His hand flexed several times, beckoning me to hand it over.

There were only two ways this could go: either I continued to refuse and let it potentially get back to our parents that this was going on, or I could let him in on the situation and pray for the slightest chance he could actually be of some help to us. Neither option was particularly great, but only one could give me the fighting chance at getting to the bottom of this myself.

"Fine," I surrendered, reluctantly, before rolling my eyes.

Unlocking the phone, I dropped it into Felix's hand. He read through the messages I'd received from the unknown number, glancing up at me every so often. Finally, he handed it back, his face distorted into a grimace.

"Happy?" I asked, mustering up as much sarcasm and snark as I could. Given that he hadn't threatened to tell our parents—or worse, the police—gave me hope he might be willing to let me handle this one with only a sprinkling of interference.

Felix scowled, his arms crossing over his chest indignantly. "Alright, so what do you know? About whoever sent you those." A finger pointed at the pocket where I'd holstered the phone as he dipped his chin.

"Not a lot, but I'm working on it."

"Well, what's their angle?" His eyes narrowed at me, indirectly prodding at the secret I was harboring.

"They want me to dig up a past I don't really want to revisit." My gaze didn't meet Felix's until after I'd spoken. "And I'm not particularly interested in talking about it with you either, so don't start."

He threw up his hands defensively and then crossed his arms again. "I can't help you if you don't tell me what's going on."

"Did it ever occur to you that I might not actually want your help with this?" I asked, frustrated that I'd been resisting his help this entire time and yet the possibility hadn't seemed to have even crossed his mind. Then again, maybe he simply didn't care.

"Too bad," he signed back to me, a stupidly smug grin painted across his face.

"Even if I did tell you, you'd just go straight to mom and dad, and they'd lose it. I'm handling this my way, because I don't want the attention, or the pity, or the sad eyes staring at me like I'm this fragile thing that's going to shatter into a million pieces. I just..." I paused. A deep breath fueled a heavy sigh that fled my chest. "I don't want people looking at me and only seeing this one thing that happened like it's tattooed across my forehead. I don't want to be 'Poor Lennon the Victim' any more than you want to be known as 'Felix Who Puked on the Bus Driver in Tenth Grade'."

"Hey, I had food poisoning that day. It wasn't my fault," he interjected.

"That's so not the point I'm making."

Felix waved me off. "Yeah, yeah, I know. But I'm not gonna make some weird judgment call because of something that happened however long ago."

"This isn't about a judgment call, Felix. It's just really personal and I don't need everybody knowing my business."

"So now I'm everybody?"

"I didn't say that."

"Well it sounds like you're saying you can't tell me personal things."

"Yeah, well... sometimes I can't."

As soon as I said the words, I hesitated. Part of me wished I could take them back, but another part of me knew it was a long-overdue truth.

Felix's eyes softened and he turned his head away from me. Biting at the inside of his cheek, his eyes shifted down toward his feet. A few still moments were all it took for me to feel the pang of regret that something I'd said had actually hurt his feelings.

"I get it," he finally said, before looking up and meeting my gaze. "I know I haven't always been the easiest person to talk to, but I want to help with this. Whatever it is. Seriously."

I wanted to keep this close to my chest. So many of my friends had already been burdened by dragging them into this mess. The last thing I wanted to do was involve my family. The best possible outcome was to keep them shielded from this; prevent their involvement in order to protect them from the nasty truth. Ensure they continued to look at me like they were proud of me instead of worried for my future. Then again, maybe Felix could help.

"Okay," I finally agreed. "But not here."

TWO DAYS BEFORE THE MURDER

"I don't understand," Marcus said, leaning forward with his elbows resting on his knees and a confused expression coloring his features.

"The Ghost wanted Rider to get in on the action," Finley replied.

"But why? What do they stand to gain from it? It doesn't make any sense."

"My best guess?" Wade chimed in, the fingers of one hand curled around a sweating bottle of Diet Coke while their forearms rested on the back of the desk chair they were seated backwards in. *"They want to force our hand."*

Wade's attention turned to me.

"Meaning what?" I asked.

"Think of it like you're in a room where the walls are slowly closing in. Everything The Ghost has done has been

in an effort to push those walls closer together, to crush us between them until what they're offering is the only way out."

"Telling Rider what you two did puts you directly in his line of fire," Tayen added. *"Not to mention that now he knows we know what he did to both of us. Even worse for him, we're friends."*

Hopefully not just friends, but that was a conversation for another time.

"But then why drag you two into this, too?" I asked, my eyes shifting from Marcus to Wade. *"The rest of us have a history with Rider. But you two are what, casualties of war?"*

"Leverage," Wade answered, calmly.

"They know that by hurting us, they hurt you even more," Marcus said.

Great.

That meant that whoever The Ghost was, they knew my weakness. They know I'd do anything for the people I care about, even at the risk of sacrificing myself. It was incredibly violating, the sense that they knew me so well while I was completely in the dark about who they were. Like being naked in a room full of strangers. Or worse, having a private photo of yourself shared with half of your class by someone that you erroneously thought liked you as much as you liked them.

One would think I'd be used to the humiliation by now.

We had upped our number of suspects from zero to two—four if we were counting our secret suspicions of Wade and Finley—and that meant that our list consisted of Wade, Finley, and Theo. Now all we had to figure out was which one of them was most likely to be The Ghost. The best way to do that was to collect as much information as we could in order to determine which of our suspects was the one responsible. Rider had also been receiving the texts, so we had even more of a reason to go through his phone. Whoever was contacting him knew which thread would unravel everything.

Since Rider was on the football team this year, we knew we had a shot at getting into his phone during practice. I'd done a little research and figured out the team hit the field every day of the week, usually from three to five. This meant we'd have to get in and out as quickly as possible in case of any irregularities, because getting caught was not an option.

"To get to the locker rooms, we have to go through the fitness center, right?" Marcus asked.

"Right," Finley agreed.

"That's where you two come in," I said, gesturing toward Marcus and Finley. *"You're the lookouts. Keep the front desk person busy while we sneak back into the locker room and get Rider's phone."*

"How are we supposed to do that?" Marcus asked.

"You know how you have a tendency to ramble when it comes to talking about sports? Do that," Tayen replied, smirking in his direction.

Marcus made a face at her and shook his head. He leaned and rested his forearm on Finley's shoulder, highlighting their immense height difference.

"Got everything you need?" I asked Wade.

"Yep, we're good to go," they said, clasping the buckle at the top of their shoulder bag.

"Alright, everybody stay in contact over text. Code word is the skull emoji in case anything happens, alright? If you see anyone coming, or any reason for us to get the hell out of there, send a skull."

Everyone nodded in agreement and we headed out, splitting into our two groups.

Marcus and Finley headed out a few minutes before us to trek out to the fitness center from my dorm room. By the time Wade, Tayen, and I had caught up to them, the pair had successfully distracted the front desk attendant in conversation.

Phase one was complete and as long as they held

their position, phase two would go off without a hitch.

"—*like that, right?*" Marcus asked as we snuck in.

My eyes had only caught a glimpse of the end of his question, but it had seemed like he was asking something rhetorical. While he and Finley were deep in conversation with the curly-haired girl at the front, they attempted to block the entrance from her view. Fin's eyes darted to the door as we approached, taking the opportunity to ask a question and point at a piece of paper on the desk to give us a quick second to dash inside and down the hallway while the attendant was distracted.

We took a collective sigh of relief once we were safely out of sight. Moving quickly down the green-painted cinder block hallway, vibrations from our footsteps echoed against the concrete flooring followed us as we snaked around turns and wound through the maze of branching halls. It was a strange cacophony of sounds through my hearing aids, like robotic clapping fizzling as it faded away.

Approaching the football team's locker room, Tayen turned to us.

"*I'll stand watch. You guys go on ahead,*" she said.

I nodded. "*Any sign of trouble—*"

"*Send a skull,*" she smiled, holding up her phone. "*I got it.*"

Wade pushed open the door and held it for me as they stepped inside. Following their lead, I turned back in time for Tayen to smile and nod confidently at me as the door shut.

Motion-sensing lights were triggered as we stepped past the doorway of a large, tiled bathroom and into the center of the locker room. The far wall was covered by a whiteboard with some sort of game play scrawled on it. Lockers lined opposite walls with each player's last name and number above it. Each space had a metallic, mesh door beside a pair of stacked shelves and a mesh metal drawer beneath a cushioned seat. Helmets with illustrated bulldogs ont the side of them rested atop a few of the lockers, signs that some players were not at practice today.

"Which one is Rider's?" Wade asked.

Scanning the room, I pointed at a cubby on the left side of the room.

"Right there. Abbot, number seventeen."

We stepped over to it and Wade began to dig through the backpack sitting on the cushioned seat of Rider's locker.

"Got it," they said, showing me the phone.

"Great, how do we get into it?"

Wade grinned and sat down, pulling their backpack off.

"With this," they said, unzipping the bag and lifting out a laptop. *"Give me a few minutes, I'll get all his files downloaded onto my laptop and he'll be none the wiser."*

"Let's just take the phone, or the memory card, and just put it back later."

"Too risky. We need to clone the phone if we want access to everything," they said. *"At this point, we don't even know where he's keeping those photos. He's probably not stupid enough to keep them in his photo gallery, but if he's got them locked away in a password-protected app I'll be able to find them. It's safer to take a copy of the whole phone and comb through it later."*

I nodded and pulled out my phone, shooting a text off to Tayen. She quickly replied back.

Everything still good out there?

Coast is clear!

How's it going?

It's going.

Should I be worried?

> No, it's just taking some time.

> okay, well hurry if you can

> You got it, captain.

It took about twenty minutes, but Wade managed to finish cloning the phone in what they proudly announced as 'record time'. Oddly, they'd finished at exactly the same moment my phone vibrated in my pocket. Cautioning a glance at the screen, I saw the singular skull emoji I had hoped wouldn't make an appearance at all.

Urgently, I tapped Wade's shoulder and turned my phone's screen toward them.

"*We gotta go—now!*" I urged, through speedy and exaggerated signing.

"*Shit!*" Wade cursed, quickly stowing away their laptop.

I dropped Rider's phone back into his bag where we'd found it. The two of us looked at each other, but behind Wade the door was starting to open. I shoved them forward as they grabbed their backpack, rushing the both of us through the secondary doorway that curved into the bathroom. We hid inside one of the showers behind a curtain, my eyes peeking out through the gap between the curtain and the wall. All we had to do was find our moment and slip out without anyone noticing us which, admittedly, sounded easier than it was going to be.

All the football players filed into the locker room and started chattering and laughing as they peeled off their gear and kicked off their cleats. The overwhelming stench of sweat and dirty uniforms was suffocating, and for a moment I thought about how dreadfully embarassing of a death this would be. To have 'died of jockstrap fumes' as my epitaph would be worse than leaked nudes, that's for sure.

"How are we going to get out of here without them seeing us?" Wade asked, leaning against the tiled wall of the shower.

"Hold on," I replied, sneaking another peek past the curtain.

No one else had entered the bathroom yet, which meant we had a straight shot to the door if we could get there without being made. Then the coach entered the locker room and gathered their attention, corralling them into a semicircle around him facing the whiteboard on the back wall. It was impossible to see what he was saying past the players' heads, but I knew this was our best chance.

"Okay. As soon as I make a break for it, follow me," I instructed.

Wade nodded and I pulled back the edge of the curtain to peer into the rest of the room.

The coach turned toward the board to begin writing something and I carefully stepped out of the shower, booking it to the door as quietly as I could manage. There was no telling how much residual hearing any of the players had, and we couldn't risk that any of them would turn toward us at the exact wrong moment. Pulling the door open, we tiptoed out and let it close softly behind us to avoid raising any alarms.

We ran past Tayen in our urgency and she followed after us until we were safely two turns down the hallway and out of visible range of the locker rooms.

"Please tell me you two were able to finish so we don't have to go through that again," Tayen said, eyes wary.

"We got it, don't worry," Wade tossed back, catching their breath from the quick sprint.

"Little outta shape, huh?" Tayen grinned, elbowing Wade in the ribs while being seemingly unbothered by the quick bout of cardiovascular exercise.

"In case it hasn't been painfully obvious, I'm more of a 'sit in front of a computer and play video games for hours on end' type of person," they retorted, gesturing at their

physique and overall lack of ultra-defined muscles.

"Valid," she replied with a soft laugh.

"Not all of us can be as athletically inclined as you are, Tayen," I added, shooting a flirty smile her way.

"What a shame," she countered, with a flip of her hair and a flirtatious grin.

The wood of my desk was warm where my forehead rested against it. The late afternoon breeze wafted in through my open window, blowing tenderly through my hair. The brightness of the day had dimmed while my eyes were shut, and the glow of the sunset was losing its edge as the minutes ticked on.

I'd been waiting for inspiration to strike for a little over two hours. Sitting in front of a blank page was torturous. Not a single word had come to mind, let alone a string of them that could be put together to create a cohesive sentence for my Courier audition article. My best bet was to wait until the sun had fully set and the moon was rising into the crisp air of the night sky.

BRRRRRRRRRT

BRRR—

I lifted my head and reached up to quickly snatch my vibrating phone up off the desk mid-ring. By the time the third vibration in the series began, my eyes had blinked enough times to focus on the caller ID and realize who was calling me.

"Yes?" I asked as I answered the FaceTime, a bit gravelly and grumpily, and leaned the phone against a pile of textbooks.

"—ere you —sl—p?," Felix asked, the words unintelligible.

"Huh?" I asked, my vision clearing as I focused on him.

"Were you asleep? It's like four o'clock in the afternoon."

His phone appeared to be propped up against something, his face and torso filling most of the screen of the video call. Sat on a black leather couch, he was leaning forward with his elbows resting on his knees. The wall behind him was a bright candy apple red, contrasting the dark brown tufts of his hair that gently brushed the top of his textured polo shirt collar.

"Oh, um, sort of. Been trying to write this article but my head's kinda all over the place," I replied, shaking my head and pushing it to the back of my mind. "What's up? Wait, where are you?" My eyes squinted as I analyzed the background, looking for clues.

"My buddy, Max, scored us some studio time at his cousin's spot in Van Nuys," Felix said.

"Max, the drummer in the band you were trying to start?"

"Did start," he corrected. "But yeah, that Max."

"Ah, the hot one," I countered teasingly.

"Anyway," he emphasized, changing the topic. "I've got a favor to ask."

"Should I be afraid?" I asked, glancing at him skeptically.

"Oh, shut up," he tossed back, eyes rolling. "I want to record a track I've been working on for a while, but I have this idea to overlay it on top of a sample from an old Lynyrd Skynyrd album. Can I borrow your copy of the vinyl to sample it? It sounds so much more alive than the MP3 version."

"Uh, yeah, sure. Go ahead. It's on the shelf in my room at home with the rest of my collection."

Smiling, Felix reached out of frame. Then, without a word, my copy of the album he'd been asking about was already in his hands and he was smugly beaming at me. "Awesome. Don't worry, I found it."

It was my turn to roll my eyes. "So you just took it without asking and hoped I'd say yes?"

"No, I took it and then asked because I knew you'd say yes. Entirely different."

"Uh huh," I replied. "Just be careful, it's an original pressing."

Felix waved me off and set it down beside him, once again changing the subject. "So, how's school been?"

"That's... a complicated question these days," I said, reaching up and tucking a few loose hairs behind my ear.

"Complicated, how?" He asked as he raised a brow.

"I don't know, lately it feels like I'm drowning but somehow I still can't stop adding shit onto my plate."

"Uh oh, what are you taking on now?"

"Writing an article—or trying to, at least—for the paper. But the head bitch in charge is definitely not my biggest fan."

"Already? Damn, what did you do to her?"

"She's the one we almost sort of ran over on move-in day," I said, grimacing.

"You really aren't doing yourself any favors these days, huh? Pissing people off left and right. Maybe she's the one sending you those texts, trying to get in your head." He tapped his temple with his middle finger, using the ASL sign for 'mindfuck' to drive his point home.

I scowled.

"Oh, come on, it was a joke!" Felix said, stifling his laughter.

"You know jokes are supposed to be funny, right?"

"It was hilarious, you just don't appreciate

sophisticated humor. But speaking of those texts, have you gotten any more of 'em?"

My fingers picked at the hemline of my striped t-shirt and I bit at the inside of my lip.

"Yeah," I admitted solemnly.

"And?" He asked, his face full of concern.

"I'm handling it."

"Lennon—" he started.

"Felix, I've got this," I interrupted. "I need to handle this for myself. I know you wanna help, and I love you for it, but I can't just sit back and let other people solve problems for me anymore."

"There's a difference between other people solving your problems and letting them help you when you need it," he countered. "You need all the help you can get if we're gonna find out who's messing with you and beat them to the punch."

"We, huh?" I asked.

"Yeah. We. I'm in this with you one hundred percent, Len. Just tell me what you need."

A small, proud smile manifested in the corner of my mouth. "Well, right now, I just need this damn article to write itself."

"What's it about?" He asked.

"Pedestrian safety on campus."

Felix burst into laughter. "I take back what I said

before. That's way funnier than my crappy joke," he said. "You must've done something in a past life, because clearly the universe wants you to suffer."

"So helpful, thank you. Okay, I gotta get back to writing my article now," I said, ready to hang up on him.

"Okay, okay, relax," he said, his hands outstretched defensively in front of him. "You always manage to pull it together the night before, so don't sweat it."

All my best ideas came to me in the middle of the night, like preternatural visitors basking in the glow of my laptop's screen. If there was one thing I could count on, it was that procrastination would ultimately turn into a well-crafted article and earn me a spot as a staff writer. This was the part of my future I preferred to dwell on.

"Yeah, I guess you're right," I half-heartedly agreed.

"Always am," he beamed.

He wasn't, but for now I'd let him have it. Looking past his phone, I could tell something was happening in the background.

Felix's expression shifted from surprised, to concerned, to frustrated and then his attention focused back onto me. "Hey, I gotta run, Len—Max is gonna be the death of me today, I swear. Good luck with your article!"

The call ended and I clicked my screen off.

It was a little past one in the morning and Bronya was staying at Anders', so I'd taken the opportunity to pull an all-nighter and finish my article. I wrote and rewrote paragraph after paragraph, ultimately scrapping everything thrice over because I hated it. Every word felt forced, like the side of a fist hammering in a puzzle piece that didn't quite fit. There were so many things I wanted to say, but the perfect words just wouldn't come out of me.

Finally, a groan strained out of me as I closed my laptop and coarsely raked a hand through my hair. The longer I stared at what I'd written, the more it disappointed me. If I was ever going to finish it, I had to step away and give myself a chance to marinate on the ideas circling around in my head. I swung my legs over the side of my bed and they carried me to the door.

As I pulled it open, my eyes widened and every organ inside me did a double axel. Fliers covered every surface; the walls, tables, doors, and even the backs of the chairs. Each flier had the same photo of me I'd tried to wipe from my memory. The vulnerable photo I'd sent to the callous boy whom I'd thought cared about me. The boy who'd treated me like I was an old toy to be thrown away when he was done playing with me. My face had been crudely crossed out to the point my features could no longer be made out. Capitalized text scrawled across the photo read 'No WALKING AWAY'.

That phrase rang in my head while my cheeks flushed. I wanted to throw up. Violently. Every muscle in my body tensed and I held my breath until my vision feathered at the edges. My lungs no longer knew how to function. Given the circumstances, I paused and weighed my options before allowing oxygen the chance to flow through me again. Breathing out of spite was better than dying in vain. I couldn't give The Ghost the satisfaction, after all—no matter who they turned out to be.

How long had these fliers been here? How many people had walked by and seen them? Has anyone taken a photo of it and posted it online somewhere, where it would live on for all of time? Or worse, has Tayen seen them? My stomach lurched and I felt sick again, hands clammy and heat bubbling under the surface of my skin.

Looking across the hall at her door, I knew it would be easy to ring her doorbell and pull her out of bed for this. She'd help me take them down, or burn them, or do whatever it is that we needed to do to ensure that no one else saw them. But if I did, it would mean that she would see them. She'd already seen the photo the day of the scavenger hunt, but her seeing a hundred copies staring at us like macabre portraits of my worst moment? That was worse, hands down.

Before I could process and make a logical choice on what to do next, I was ripping down the first of the fliers—one that had been crudely stuck to my dorm room door. Balling it up between curled fingers, I darted to the next one and tore it free from the wall. And the next one. And the one after that. Dozens and dozens filled every trash can I could find. After all but one had been taken down, I ripped the final one down and brought it back into my room with me while I fought the urge to crawl beneath my bed and hide there forever.

Instead, I collapsed onto my bed and curled my legs into my chest as tightly as I could. The final flier still in my hand, I stared at it until the air stung my eyes and held-back tears blurred my vision. The anger welled up inside of me, clawing at my viscera and threatening to tear me asunder like the iconic chest-bursting scene in the movie Alien. Turning over onto my side, I grabbed my phone off the desk and began typing out a text to Fin. Realizing she'd definitely be asleep—and being unwilling to wake her for a situation I'd already mostly dealt with—I deleted the message and backed out to my list of text threads. My thumb clicked on Tayen's name, instead, despite every reason not to bubbling in my gut.

Are you awake?

I hadn't expected a reply, but one came in moments later nonetheless. Then another.

Yeah. Is everything okay?

Not at all, actually.

??

I took a photo of the flier I'd kept and sent it to her, showing it off like some sick and twisted souvenir. So many of the events in the weeks since this ordeal had begun had felt surreal and phantasmagorical. Every day, when I woke up, I questioned how many of my memories from the day before had been hyper-realistic illusions meant to make me question my own sanity. Keeping proof was the only way to ensure the Lennon of tomorrow would know just how real this was.

My phone buzzed again.

Holy crap

My thoughts exactly.

Nice of them to scribble out your face

oh yeah, they're a real saint.

What do you think it means?

Idk. Nothing good.

Agreed. Is there anything I can do?

Can you come over?

Kinda freaked out to be alone.

On my way

ONE DAY BEFORE THE MURDER

Warmth radiated along the side of my face as light poured in through the window. The foam mattress sunk beneath the weight of my body. It cradled me, lulling me back to the solace of sleep every time I stirred awake. The memory of my dreams from the night before were fading fast, slipping through my grasp as I scrambled to hold onto them. I exhaled a deep sigh, not yet ready to open my eyes and face another day. Another chance for The Ghost to make me question who was on my side and who was waiting in the wings to strike.

As I laid there, an arm reached over and rested across my torso.

A surge of panic coursed through my body and I slowly turned over. Eyes falling onto the face of the sleeping angel beside me, the panic dissipated as quickly as it had materialized. Tayen's body was coiled beside mine, our legs entwined beneath the comforter. The smell of fresh coconut danced through the air. It soaked into my sheets and enveloped me in a delightful cocoon.

I watched her lay there peacefully at my side, hoping this moment wasn't some Inception-style dream within a dream situation that would inevitably turn out to be nothing more than a figment of my subconscious. That I wouldn't wake up in a cold sweat alone—or worse, beside whatever creep had been sending those weird texts and inching way too close for comfort.

Tayen's eyes slowly blinked open and I melted into her dark mahogany irises.

"Good morning," she greeted, gently rubbing the sleep from her eyes.

"Good morning, sunshine," I said.

She offered a soft smile; the one I liked to think she was always saving just for me. At least, I hoped that was the case. Even if it wasn't, I was willing to live in a state of delusion. Being close to her lent itself to a familiarity I didn't think could coexist with the distrust that had grown inside me since I'd erroneously gotten involved with Rider in the first place.

The only bright spot in all of this had been Tayen. As soon as she knew how distraught I was last night, she'd rushed right over. The moment she arrived, a wave of peace washed over me. Her presence brought a sense of calm to the chaos we were living in. Nothing happened between us, but somehow we'd ended up tangled up in my bed together. This was the closest I'd ever come to sleeping with anyone in the carnal sense, and I was glad that she was the person I was waking up beside.

"How'd you sleep?" She asked.

"Decent, I guess," I replied. *"You?"*

It wasn't a lie, but being too truthful had a way of ruining things.

"Convincing," she teased.

A smile crept onto my face as I indulged in her sarcasm. She was catching on quickly and it was impressive.

"It helped that you were here," I admitted. *"Not sure I would've been able to sleep last night if you hadn't come over."*

"Really?" She looked at me with the warm, inviting gaze I hadn't been able to stop thinking about since I'd seen it the first day we'd met.

"Really. Thank you."

Tayen nudged the hair out of my face, her fingers grazing my cheek and vibrating electric. It breathed life into me in a way I didn't know was even possible. I closed my eyes and a deep breath inflated my lungs as I inhaled her. The scents of freshly washed cotton and ocean-borne sea salt crashed into me in waves as I laid there beside her. That moment could've lasted forever and it still wouldn't have been long enough.

As I opened my eyes, their bolts of azure met the burnt ochre of her gaze.

"What are you thinking about?" Tayen asked.

"The truth?" I asked in return, answering her question with my own.

"Always."

"I'm thinking about how much I don't want this to end."

I was also secretly hoping she hadn't decided to come over out of pity, babysitting me while I sorted out my frantic state. Despite my panic at the sight of those posters covering every inch of my dormitory floor, Tayen coming over was an opportunity for us to commiserate together. I wanted her to be there because she cared in the way that lacked judgment. There was nothing more I wanted in the moment because the only thing worse than feeling sorry for myself, was having someone else feel sorry for me.

She giggled. *"Why are you worried about it ending? Live in the moment, Larkin."*

A raspy laugh escaped me. *"I think I'm just used to things not lasting as long as I want them to. And... I really want this moment to last."*

"Me too," she said. *"Is that the only thing you're*

thinking about?"

Damn, she was good.

I tilted my head from one side to the other. *"Mostly."*

"Oh, come on, tell me," She eagerly smiled and I crumbled.

"I don't know how to explain the way my brain works without coming across like I'm having one of those Charlie-Day-Pepe-Silvia moments with the string on the bulletin board," I said, a slightly embarrassed laugh clipping on to the end of my sentence. *"It feels straight-up unhinged."*

"Then consider me Mac, because I live for the Charlie Day moments."

Our laughs twist in and out of one another and the bed quakes beneath us in its creaky wooden frame. Everything seemed so much brighter in the room with her around—and safe, for the first time since waking up to proof that some creeper had broken in while I was sleeping. A sigh spilled from my lips and I propped up onto my elbow to face Tayen with my back against the window.

"It all feels like the calm before a storm, you know?" I started, looking around the room and then back to Tayen as she nodded. *"I know all of this is probably going to get a lot worse before it gets better, but..."* My thoughts trailed off as I got lost in my own head, dreaming up every way this could go horribly, nightmarishly wrong.

Thinking about the worst-case scenario and every way The Ghost could make our lives even more of a hellish nightmare than it already had become.

"*But?*" She asked.

"*I don't know what it's going to look like at the end, after all of this shakes out.*"

"*What do you mean?*"

"*Well, it's not like things can just magically go back to the way they used to be. Whatever version of normal we were living in is over now,*" I said.

Tayen's soft, aureate eyes pierced into my soul.

"*That doesn't mean we won't like the version we get in the end,*" she said. "*Granted, I don't think there is such a thing as normal. We're all weird as shit, you especially.*" A cheeky smirk was tossed my way, along with a gentle poke of her index finger into my ribcage.

"*Oh, me especially? Weirdos must be your type, then,*" I teased, without a second thought.

Internally, there was panic to the nth degree. Sweat began to build at the back of my neck and the blood drained from my cheeks. How could I have said that when I had no clue if this was going to wreck our budding friendship? I've been so careful, watching the words threatening to jumble out of my mouth, because I was afraid of saying the wrong thing at the wrong time. Every moment I'd allowed my mind to wander curiously and drift through the possibilities of what could happen between us, worry settled in the pit of my stomach that whatever was developing here might end before it even began.

"Yeah, I guess they are," she replied, a glint of what could only be described as magic in her eyes.

Every inch of my body was screaming like ten thousand raucous fans at a rock concert in full swing, fists pounding into the air alongside heads banging back and forth. The sweat glands in my hands were working overtime. Niagara Falls might as well have been pouring out of my palms, though it certainly would have dampened the mood. Perhaps Marcus had been right, maybe Tayen was interested in me beyond the platonic lines of our blossoming friendship.

If there was ever a time to play fast and loose and fake-it-til-I-make-it, it was now. As I searched her eyes, something in my gut told me to test the waters.

"A variety of weirdos or is there one particular weirdo you've got your eye on?" I asked, scolding myself for phrasing it that way.

"Oh, I've got a whole roster full," Tayen stated matter-of-factly. Seeing my face fall for a moment as I was caught off guard, she broke out into a teasing grin. *"I'm just kidding!"*

I shook my head and rolled my eyes.

"There's only one, but I don't know if I'm their type," she continued.

Raising a brow, I calculated the chances it was me she was talking about. Fifty-fifty, I figured. Maybe sixty-forty if I was lucky. Of course, the fact she was cuddled up against me in my bed sat firmly at the top of the 'pros' column. As for the cons? My complete inability to pick up on flirtatious behavior had led me to resolutely believe she wasn't interested because she hadn't outright said the words.

Her fingers lightly tapped against my temple.

"Getting lost in there, Charlie?" She asked.

"A little," I admitted.

"I think I know a way to help."

"Yeah?"

Tayen's tongue swiped across her bottom lip before her upper teeth softly bit into its rosy flesh. The few moments of tension-filled stillness between us were endless and all-consuming. I wanted so badly to make a move and do something—anything—but instead I just laid there beside her, paralyzed by the fear of uncertain rejection.

The downward spiral drove me deeper into my anxious thoughts, until it was abruptly halted by the gentle grip of her fingers along my jaw. The warmth of her skin against mine weakened my breathing. Hairs on the back of my neck raised as a tingling bolt of electricity traveled the length of my spine and down to my toes. Her thumb brushed my cheekbone and my eyes closed, mind reeling with possibilities. What was going to happen next? Was it my turn to put a hand against her cheek? Should I open my eyes or leave them closed? One wrong move and I might ruin everything.

Then, every thought and worry dissipated all at once.

I looked into her deep cedar irises, admiring the auriferous glints reflecting back at me. Tayen's hand gripped my torso and pulled me in close, to which I leaned in the rest of the way. Inches became centimeters until our noses nudged against one another and her parted lips met mine. She smiled into the kiss and my hands found her waist and I wrapped my arm around her to draw her body against mine. Fingers curled at the hem of the shirt she'd borrowed from me last night, and I lifted it to reveal the skin underneath.

Butterflies the size of chinchillas pranced through my guts. A flurry of movement and peeled off clothing against the backdrop of the morning sun and pure ecstatic joy—I had never experienced anything like it.

After what felt like forever, our lips broke apart and we settled back. Side-by-side, our heads rested on the king-sized pillow I'd brought from home.

Lightheadedness swooped in as I struggled to find the words humming at the edge of my fingers. I wanted to say everything and nothing, scream into the void yet lay there soundlessly, stare into her eyes and close my own under the weight of heavy eyelids. It took everything within me not to drift off to sleep and relive that moment over and over in a dreamscape.

If only I could've had a chance to relax with her for just five more minutes.

Tayen shifted beside me to check her phone, one hand reaching back to tap my arm hurriedly. I raised my head from the pillow to discover what she was looking at. Her face was ghostly white, my phone in one hand and a single slender finger pointing at its screen. It was lit up, showing a message from the same unsaved number that I recognized. I cautioned a wary glance back at Tayen, who retracted her finger and took a deep breath. The beat of my heart was getting louder, its pulsing drowning out my tinnitus.

I gingerly took the device from her, treating it like a bomb ready to go off if it was jostled.

ENJOY IT WHILE IT LASTS...

BEFORE SHE GETS TO KNOW THE REAL YOU.

The slow-flashing cursor in my open word document had been mocking me, judging me for the lack of motivation to work on my communications essay. It was assigned over a week ago, yet I'd hardly found time to work on it given my preoccupation with everything else going on. All I could think about was the looming threat that my dirty laundry would become public—again.

This essay was the least of my worries.

As I sat in my desk chair, searching for some kind of inspiration to get down to business, I felt the dorm room door rattle against the walls as it slammed shut. Leaning back on the rear legs of my chair—risking the possibility of a near-death experience—my head whirled around as Bronya stormed into the room. Dropping her belongings onto the floor, she threw herself onto her bed and began to cry into her ugly, paisley comforter.

For a moment, I weighed my options.

If I tried to comfort her, I might get sucked into whatever the problem was, which had a high probability of being related to her boyfriend. On the other hand, if I kept my eyes on my screen and pretended I hadn't seen her come in upset, she might've taken it to mean I didn't care. Either way, I had to prepare myself for some sort of emotional conversation.

Standing from my chair, I stepped over into Bronya's side of the room, careful not to sneak up on her. My hand reached out and tapped her leg, waiting for some sort of acknowledgment that she was interested in talking to me about whatever plagued her.

Bronya rolled over, eyes a swollen crimson with rivers leaking down her face. Her legs recoiled towards her and she pushed herself up until she was leaning against the wall at the head of her bed with a pillow gripped tightly to her chest.

"Are you okay?" I asked.

Clearly she wasn't okay, but the why of it all was eating at me.

"You can sit if you want," she offered, her legs folding inward as she avoided my initial question.

"Okay," I agreed, as I sat gingerly at the foot of her bed.

Bronya wiped the tears from her face with the back of her hand, and she seemed so small and frail. I was so used to her being a force to be reckoned with, a strong personality who was unabashedly straightforward about her dislike of everything I held dear. A shell of her former self, it was obvious whatever was going on was deeper than a spat with a significant other.

Pinched between her leg and the mattress, Bronya's

phone began to violently vibrate. In a panicked whirlwind, her grip around it tightened and she launched it off the bed and out of her sight. The crying resumed, her forehead resting against her arms as they hugged her knees.

I considered reaching out, an attempt to offer some form of awkward comfort, but didn't want to overstep. If she was hurting, the last thing I wanted to do was make it worse. In truth, I'd never been very good at dealing with upset people, especially if they were crying. I'd never figured out what to say when someone was upset, or how to approach their emotions in a way that would validate them or make them feel better. The complexity of my own emotions was usually too much for me to handle, so the thought of trying to tackle anyone else's emotions was wholly overwhelming.

Tapping her leg softly to get her attention again, Bronya looked up and met my gaze.

"Did something happen with Anders?" I asked, thinking she'd thrown the phone to escape talking to him or avoid listening to a barrage of desperate pleas to talk it out. Between the two of them, he was most certainly the one who would be doing the groveling.

"No," Bronya answered, shaking her head.

"Are you sure?"

The question only seemed to make her cry harder.

We sat like that for a while, me sitting beside her and hoping that she'd stop crying. She eventually did, but as I stood to try to walk away, her hand took hold of mine and she looked up at me.

"Please stay?" she asked.

A bit taken aback, I did.

"I know we've always been really different," she said. *"Plus all that stuff that went down with Rider... I should've stuck up for you with him."* Pulling her sleeve over her hand, she wiped away the tears that were cascading down her cheeks. *"I'm sorry for not believing your side of the story."*

Where was this coming from? Never once had Bronya been the type to apologize, let alone admit that she was in the wrong two whole years after the fact.

"Not that I don't appreciate the gesture," I said. *"But why are you apologizing all these years later?"*

"Because I feel guilty about it every day, especially in this room." Bronya looked around, her eyes touching the walls and scanning the furniture. *"It's like the universe wanted to punish me, so it made us roommates to force me to look you in the eyes every day."*

I looked down at the floor, trying to figure out what to say next. Forgiving her felt like the right thing to do, but it also flew in the face of what I'd been through. The pain of losing every single friend, including

Bronya's tertiary 'friendship' as far as group hangouts went, never truly left me. I couldn't just waive her of the responsibility for that.

But maybe it wasn't about her. Maybe it was for me.

"Okay," I finally said. *"It's okay. Really."*

"What do you mean?" Bronya asked, through the tears.

"I mean... I forgive you." Even if I didn't think she deserved it, it might be what I needed to move beyond the trauma of the past and stop looking at her like she was a physical manifestation of that anguish.

"Oh, Lennon, thank you!" Bronya lurched across the bed and hugged me, her arms wrapping around my neck so tight that I could feel every muscle in her bicep constrict. She let go and smiled through the tears still streaming down her face. *"Really, I don't know what to say."*

"Say you'll give The Clash a chance," I tossed out.

It accomplished my goal of deflection, lightening the mood and giving us both the chance to breathe, but I wished I would've come up with something better to say. Something that wouldn't have left me feeling like I handed over forgiveness to someone who didn't recognize its worth.

THE DAY AFTER THE MURDER

The moment I'm back on campus, I send a text to the group chat as fast as my fingers will allow me to type.

The Brew. 10 mins.

Outside of the dorm is a memorial to Bronya, with flowers and photos and cards left as tokens of affection from mourners who have stopped to remember her. Even those that didn't really know her have made the effort to take a pause where she died and sit with her death. It was a shock for the entire campus, but it's nice to see how well she was liked—even if not by me. It wasn't anyone's fault that we didn't get along, but now I regret not making more of an effort. I should've tried to find common ground between us before time ran out. It's hard to look at this spot now, after having seen her body bent, broken, and bleeding out.

Struggling to catch my breath as I run inside, I spot my group waiting on the upper level, leaning against the railing and waving me up. Taking the stairs two at a time, I follow them back to a secluded corner table that affords a decent amount of privacy. It's empty, thankfully, but my paranoia forces me to look all around us to make sure no one is watching. All it takes is one wrong word spoken in the wrong place.

"The police think Rider is connected to Bronya's murder," I blurt out, skipping right along before anyone could ask me about the details of my interview with Detective Melendez.

"Why would they think that?" Marcus asks, eyebrows tilting down skeptically.

"The detective mentioned something. He asked me if I thought Bronya and Rider could've been in a relationship," I reply, remembering how strange the interaction had been. *"Or, I guess, involved somehow. I'm not sure why, though."*

At this point we know there are three of us receiving the texts—myself, Tayen, and Rider—but who knows how many others might be out there. We also don't know how Bronya's death was connected, which means that any of the others could also be in danger.

My mind fades back to a conversation I'd had with Bronya, the last time I'd seen her alive. She'd planned to be out all night with Anders and had even taken a bag full of makeup and clothes along with her.

Finley smacks a hand on the table and it knocks me out of my trance. *"Len?"*

"What? Sorry, I missed what you said," I reply, my brain fog starting to lift.

"Do you think Bronya was The Ghost's intended target?"

"I don't—" I start, then abruptly pause.

"What?" Wade asks.

"She wasn't planning to be in the room at all," I try to recall the specifics of what she'd said to me that afternoon. *"I watched her pack a duffel full of too many clothes and a makeup bag the size of Texas. She said she was staying with her boyfriend, that she wouldn't be back until... today."*

If she had just gone to Anders she'd be alive and well. Instead, our room is cordoned off while the crime scene is investigated.

"Oh my god," Tayen says, leaning her crossed forearms onto the table we were gathering around. *"Oh my fucking god."*

"What?" I ask.

"It was supposed to be me."

We all stare at her, the expression on her face colorless and pale.

Tayen pulls out her phone, frantic, her hands shaking.

"Did you send this text?" she asks. *"You showed up at my door before I could respond, so I didn't think about it. But now..."* She navigates to her messages before handing it across the table to me.

> Meet me in my room tonight, around midnight?

My stomach drops. Tayen could've been the one bleeding out on the concrete instead, staring up at me with sorrowful eyes.

"So Bronya was, what? Caught in the wrong place at the wrong time?" I think aloud, my mind swirling with every worst-case scenario I can think of. *"If The Ghost had expected to find Tayen and instead found Bronya... maybe they panicked and decided to cover their ass."*

It would explain the fact that they'd stabbed her and pushed her out a window, as if one or the other wouldn't have been sufficient on its own.

"Or maybe Bronya saw The Ghost's real face," I think

aloud. *"They couldn't let her go after that, could they? They probably panicked and had to improvise, so they killed her."*

"Okay, so if we assume Bronya's death was accidental," Marcus chimes in, *"Are we saying we think The Ghost wants to,"* Glancing around, he lowers his hands. *"...kill Tayen?"*

"We're saying they tried to meet up with her. They could've wanted to hurt her, and she's likely not the only one on their hit list, but we also have to consider that it might have been more innocent than that." Finley's eyes dart around our group. *"But why would they want to get Tayen alone?"*

"We're missing something." Tayen's face twists, and it looks like she's trying to figure out some kind of complicated mathematical gymnastics. *"Only the two of us have received these texts, right? Aside from Rider, I mean."*

"That we know of," Marcus adds, tilting his head toward his sister with his eyebrows raised in an attempt to emphasize his point.

"The main thing that ties us together is the fact that we were cornered into compromising situations by Rider," Tayen says. *"But why does someone want us to talk about it? Shouldn't he want it to stay swept under the rug? Keep himself out of trouble? Why would they be bringing it up now, when by all accounts it went away?"*

"Tayen's right," I say, leaning back in my seat. This

feels defeating, like we're taking three steps back for every step forward we manage to stumble through. *"If they wanted us to keep quiet or intimidate us into burying these secrets even further, it would make sense, but this doesn't make any sense at all."*

Wade leans forward then. *"What if it's someone who wants Rider to be held responsible? What if this person is trying to make you admit what happened, to call him out publicly and hold him accountable for what he did?"*

"Then it would have to be someone who knows what happened to both of us," I add.

"That considerably narrows the pool of prospects," Tayen says.

"Whoever it was had to have been at the party. We know that for certain right?" Finley chimes in.

I nod. *"Definitely."*

"Okay so we start there." Wade decides.

"That's everyone I can remember," Finley says, combing fingers through her hair. The strands tuck neatly behind her ear, her tense jawline sharper than the edge of a broken mirror.

There's almost ten names on the list, most of whom are Rider's friends.

"How do we even begin to eliminate people?"

"The same way that we eliminated Rider. He started receiving the texts, and the way he confronted Tayen and I tells me he's not involved. We have to find the one aspect that doesn't fit, and then that unravels their potential to be The Ghost," I say.

"Think back, did anyone seem like they were behaving strangely at Rider's party?" Marcus asks, leans forward to position his chin atop his fist while his elbow rests on the table.

My eyes scan the list of names as my finger scrolls down the page of notes on the screen of my phone. I go through the list again, starting at the top. Revisiting the party in my mind's eye, I review everything in chronological order. Theo's name is the first one on the list.

"Theo was the one who opened the door for us when we first got there," I say, repeating my thoughts for everyone seated around me. *"He'd already been drinking,"* I muse, then look right up at Fin with a sly smile. *"And he was flirting real hard with you."*

"What's new," Finley groans, dramatically, rolling her eyes so hard they threaten to fall right out of her head. She's leaning back in her chair, balancing precariously on its rear legs while her foot provides leverage against the underside of the table.

"Then we went inside and Theo went upstairs with..."

Her name escapes me, but I can still visualize her face in my mind. Caitlin, Courtney, Christine... I'm pretty sure it starts with a 'C'. She's more or less been what I would call a groupie, for lack of a better word. A hanger-on who trailed after Rider's crowd of narcissists and nepo-babies. The exception to the rule was her infatuation with Theo, though he was wealthy-adjacent by association rather than birth.

Finley knocks on the top of the table until we all look over at her. She says, *"Cara,"* and it fits into my train of thought like the final piece of a puzzle.

"Right, Cara, thank you," I responded, before continuing with the walk-through of my memory. *"Cara and Theo went upstairs, and I don't remember seeing them for most of the party."*

"Me either," Fin adds.

Now she's incorporating little rhythmic bounces to her balancing act while she continues to challenge the forces of gravity. Marcus glances around the table and winks at us just before he takes the opportunity to poke at Fin's ribs. The combination of the unexpected force and a giggle of ticklish laughter causes her to shift in her seat just enough to disrupt the carefully crafted balance.

It unfolds slowly in front of us, happening in slow motion.

Finley's body topples over the side of the chair as

it buckles beneath her, and she lands onto the wooden floor with a thud which sends a rolling vibration across the floor. She rubs at her back instinctively, then throws her head back and breaks out into a fit of laughter.

"You okay?" Marcus asks, laughing as he offers a hand to help her up.

"You just wait until it's your turn," Finley tosses back, slapping his hand out of the way as she rises to her feet on her own.

"Alright, kids, quit messing around," Wade chastises, attempting to settle us all back down as Finley picks up her chair and regains her composure. *"Keep going, Lennon. What happened after?"*

"I watched this one," I point to Finley and smirk. *"Tell a story about the time she climbed out of a second-story window and jumped into a pool in order to avoid being caught by—"*

"Hey, hey, hey, we don't need to go into those details," Finley interrupts, shaking her head at me profusely.

"Why not? You seemed super into telling this story at the party. Had a whole crowd and everything, if I recall," I continued, teasing her mercilessly.

"You don't recall."

"What's this story? I'm super interested," Tayen chimes in, leaning into her elbows and resting her head in her hands.

"God, I hope it's embarrassing," Marcus laughs, wearing a proud grin.

We all break out into howling convulsions, taking a second to appreciate the moment of levity since they've been so few and far between lately.

Finley raises a middle finger to Marcus and then gestures across her neck, indicating her wholehearted unwillingness to tell the story.

"Guess we'll just have to wait until you get drunk enough to tell it again," I tease, beaming from ear to ear. *"But anyway, Rider was in the living room with some girl on his lap and a group of idiots flocking around him. Everybody else was just lingering, drinking, dancing, chatting. I talked to Iris for a little while. Nothing out of the ordinary. Once we knew for sure no one was looking in our direction, Fin and I snuck off down the hall and into the garage."*

"There were at least a hundred people there, if not more," Finley adds.

"Doesn't exactly narrow it down," Wade says as they scratch behind their ear.

"Of the names that we have, which one is our top contender?" Fin asks.

"Um..." My fingers twitch as I go down the list. *"Theo."*

I'd already crossed Theo off my list days ago, purely because his connection to Rider wasn't substantial enough, but maybe it was a mistake on my part. After all, what better cover was there than to be the best friend of the person you're plotting against?

For all the shit Rider did, I had to believe that there was no way Theo didn't know all of his little secrets. Which meant that he must've been aware of the exact kind of shit he pulled on girls like me and Tayen. Theo always struck me as a genuinely kind guy, and I can't imagine Rider's antics would've sat well with him. If that was the case, it meant there was a motive for why he'd want to hold his best friend accountable. It would've been a matter of time before it all spilled out one way or another. After all, I was certain Theo saw the photo of me circulating after Rider got his way. That very well could've been the catalyst, but that didn't explain why he would've waited two years to enact this whole revenge ploy.

"So are we saying we think it's Theo?" Tayen asks, raising her eyebrows as she looks around the table.

"Yeah, I think It's time for us to dig a little deeper into Theo Osbourne." I conclude, standing from my chair. Reaching into my pocket, I pull out my phone and type a quick message.

"Lennon, over here!" Iris waves at me from across the crowded coffee shop, to a table in the back corner that she's snagged for us.

It's out of the way and provides as much privacy as we can hope to get in public, which serves as the perfect spot for my makeshift interrogation slash friendly catch-up.

"Hey, it's good to see you, Iris." I slide into one of the oversized faux-leather chairs, tufted like the kind you'd find in an old smoking parlor or Richard Gilmore's study. The window beside us is bright, but shaded by a vine-covered wall outside so that neither of us have to squint to see the other. Excellent conditions for a conversation between two deafies.

"You're into chai, right? They make it from scratch here, it's so good." Iris smiles at me and slides a paper cup across the small table between us. She's wearing a striped blouse and jeans that I've seen her in before, her hair braided along one side and neatly kempt. Everything about her is orderly and precise, down to the golden, heart-shaped earrings that match the necklace strung around her neck.

Gratefully, I lean forward and take it.

"So, what's up?" Iris asks, taking a sip of her own drink and crossing one leg over the other.

"I wanted to talk to you about somebody we used to go to

school with." It's a risky move, choosing the less tactful path of blurting out my reason for asking her to grab coffee with me, but hopefully it will pay off. Placating with niceties and bullshit about the weather has never been my speed, and Iris knows me better than to think I'd suddenly find the September sky to be worth commentary. *"You remember Theo Osbourne, right?"*

"Sure. What about him?" she asks, nothing in her facial features raising an alarm within me.

"What do you know about him?" I ask.

"I know he's more interested in football than The Great British Bake Off. He's seen the movie 300 more than a dozen times and can quote it word for word. He'll order a pizza before he attempts to cook anything, because of an incident where he set fire to a Cup Noodles that he was trying to make once. I don't know—what exactly do you want to know?"

"Have you ever known him to keep secrets? Or has he ever given you a bad vibe?"

"No way," Iris shakes her head, immediately dispelling thoughts that he might've let his sister see a darker side of him—a murderous side. *"Not at all, I've never gotten a bad vibe from him. In fact, he was one of the nicer boys in that friend group. Always used to extend invites to me for parties and stuff after you stopped going. For a while, anyway."*

Until she had her mental breakdown and left school,

she means.

"He's never made you feel… unsafe? Or scared to be around him?"

"God, no," she says, both hands wrapped around her cup. *"If anything, Theo is the reason I felt safe enough to stay at Stone Valley after I came back from—"* Iris pauses, the corner of her lip indenting as her teeth dig into it. Clearly she doesn't like to reminisce on those memories. *"He was one of the few kids at school who was actually nice to me. We became actual friends, more than we'd ever been before."*

I nod, a sinking feeling in my chest aching with the guilt of having asked in the first place. This conversation is starting to become one big prying, nosy dig into the cracking foundation of Iris' tragic life. She's been through so much and I don't want to make any of it worse for her. But I needed to ask these things of her because, despite our falling out, she and Theo had become close after Finley and I distanced ourselves from the friend group. In my opinion we'd never belonged. I never thought Iris did either, but I guess that's just one more thing I was wrong about. Turns out she fit in just fine.

"How's school been so far this year? I'm sure it's weird with Theo not being there," I said, trying to ask in a general way rather than using it to poke at the tender suffering

hiding in her hippocampus.

"It's been an adjustment," Iris admits. *"Not all bad, but I definitely keep to myself. Theo still comes around on the weekends, and the house I live in now is closer to his than my old one was."*

"Oh, I didn't realize your family moved."

"Yeah, my mom remarried. Did you know that?" She asks.

I shake my head, because for some reason it feels like information I shouldn't admit to having. I'd heard it through the grapevine, as all rumors circulate with warp speed at Stone Valley, but it was inextricably linked with other rumors; about Iris' health, her disappearance, even her sanity. A lot happened in the year between sightings, and her reappearance in our halls only fed into the rumor mill fire even more.

"She's never been stable, but while I was gone she really took a dive off the deep end. She eloped to the new guy she'd been seeing while I was away. I came home to a house that wasn't mine, with a step-dad and new step-sibling and an annoying yappy dog who wouldn't stop barking at its own shadow."

Honestly, it breaks my heart.

"Anyway, why were you asking about Theo?" Iris asks, head tilted curiously.

"I'm just..." Think fast, Lennon. *"Trying to see if there*

are any red flags that Finley should be aware of. You know, fulfilling my best friend duties of vetting the potential suit-ors. " I fake a laugh, but I can already see Finley coming after me for implying that she would ever willingly date Theo Osbourne.

Iris' eyes light up like Christmas trees, twinkling under the fluorescent bulbs. *"Finley is thinking about going out with Theo? Oh my god, he will completely lose it, he's been in love with her for so long."*

I really shouldn't have used that as my excuse, but now I have no choice but to lean into it and hope the momentum sticks.

"Yeah, well, you know Fin," I laugh again. *"Always changing her mind."*

"True, she has always been a little fickle, hasn't she?"

"Indecisive, sure," I say, not wanting to incite an argument while still defending my best friend. *"But please—don't say anything to Theo, okay?"*

"You got it." Iris pretends to zip her lips shut and throw away the key.

I'd forgotten how great it felt to talk with Iris, our friendship having always been so easy effortless. She understood me, like a kindred sisterhood that remained unspoken. I'd never wanted to leave her behind, but she had been an incidental casualty of cutting ties with my old life. With the fake friends and losers who'd turned on me when Rider committed social homicide and eviscerated me with those photos. It wasn't Iris's fault, but her proximity to Rider had been too much to bear at the time.

It was the kind of pain that I'd never apologized for—it felt too big to mention.

Now, in this cafe, we share a pair of smiles and allow the topics of Theo and Finley to fade away as our conversation continues until the sun almost entirely slips under the horizon.

FOUR DAYS AFTER THE MURDER

Swiping into my messages, I find two unread texts waiting in the group chat from Wade.

Cracked the code!

You'll never guess what I found

I practically sprint over to Brighton Hall, arriving out of breath with aching muscles. Marcus is sitting at a table in the foyer with Finley, waiting for me to arrive so that he can bypass the ID lock and open the door from the inside.

"Took you two long enough," I tease, poking at their undeniable chemistry.

Finley flips me off and Marcus laughs before following after us as we head inside. By all accounts, Brighton is a stark contrast to Thompson. The newly constructed building is less than five years old, with large-paned windows along its façade that allow the morning light to flood in and bathe everything in resplendent, sun-soaked hues. Diagonally tiled floors stretch out across the room and the soles of my sneakers smack against them as we trek to the stairwell in the corner of the room that juts upward, disappearing into the second floor.

The three of us climb in tandem up four flights of stairs, Finley and I trailing after Marcus as he leads the way toward Wade's room. Brighton Hall is unique, in that each of the rooms is actually a suite, housing four students and boasting a furnished living room and shared bathroom.

Moments after Marcus presses the doorbell, Wade pulls open the door and greets us with a warm smile. *"Hey, come on in."*

Stepping through the spacious living room, we pass a trio of gamers gathered on a couch and armchair in front of a television. They're playing a video game involving some sort of zombie apocalypse, and they're so engrossed in it they don't even glance in our direction as we follow Wade back to their bedroom. It's one of two single-occupancy rooms, affording Wade a level of privacy that their roommates in the double room can only dream about. Finley and I take our seats on the bed while Wade slides into their desk chair.

"Tayen's at soccer practice, but I'll catch her up on all of this later," Wade says as they boot up their computer.

"So, what did you find?" Marcus asks, leaning against the wall.

I fidget with the silver ring on my right hand.

"Proof there's more to this than we thought," they reply, turning back to their computer.

The screen powers on and several overlapping windows appear. One of them shows a gallery of photo icons and Wade enlarges it before looking back at us. *"Rider had a bunch of photos in a hidden folder, but it's heavily encrypted and I'm still trying to crack it. There was one photo buried in his camera roll, though."* They select one of the photos and it expands.

"Holy shit." My jaw all but smacks onto the floor.

Finley's brow creases as she nudges me. *"What?"*

The photo is cropped with its focus centered on the bra-covered chest of a faceless girl. If this was in his camera roll, I could only imagine what horrors lie waiting to be discovered in the hidden folder. The longer I study the photo, the more I begin to notice the little details I'd initially overlooked. Fair skin and what looks like strands of copper hair at the edge of the frame. Small, heart-shaped, gold earrings hang from pierced lobes, the ones she never took off. The ones she was wearing when I had coffee with her.

My intestines do a chain of backflips.

"That's Iris," I say.

Fin does a double take. "How do you know?"

"Who's Iris?" Marcus asks.

"Someone we went to high school with," I answer. *"Finley and I were friends with her."*

"Len, how do you know it's Iris?" Finley asks again, her tone saturated with urgency.

"Look at the earrings," I say, pointing at the screen.

The same ones she was wearing the other day, at the coffee shop.

The ones she always wears.

"Oh shit, it is Iris!" Finley exclaims.

And then it all made sense.

Space and time ripple around me and I'm transported back to Stone Valley's halls, bad memories hanging in the air like rotting carcasses in a meat locker. I think about how hard it must've been to be Iris after everything that happened—deserted by her best friend who up and left out of nowhere, then left even further alone once I cut my ties with that whole shallow group. How easy it would've been for Rider to take advantage of her, to worm his way past her defenses and give her the erroneous impression that he cared for her. If Rider did to her what he'd done to me, that would definitely explain why this photo was on his phone.

"Do you think Theo knew?" Finley asks.

I shake my head. *"Not a chance. He was the only one that was nice to Iris. If he knew Rider was treating her like that, he'd have said something for sure."*

"If he found out about what went down between Rider and Iris, he'd want to set Rider straight, right? Make him pay?"

"The timestamp is from a year ago," Wade points out, pulling up the metadata for the photo. *"Do you think Theo would've held his tongue that long?"*

It was possible. No one wanted to take down the king of the high school, but now that he was a nobody freshman, he was vulnerable. It was the perfect time to make a move.

"It's possible," I answer. *"If he knew about this, I don't see him letting it slide. But holding onto something like this for two years? That's a lot of rage."*

It was all starting to fit together now. Every piece was falling into place, but the image it created was heartbreaking. The girl that had been like a little sister to me had fallen prey to the same monster that I had, and I hadn't known. At one point, my finger had rested against the trigger, evidence stacked and ready to prove that he was a disgusting pile of garbage, yet I'd let him walk away out of fear for how it might destroy my life even further. I was scared of what would happen if I opened my mouth and let the dusty skeleton in my closet tumble out. If I'd known that Rider had his sights set on Iris, I never would've left her behind.

At least, I'd like to think I wouldn't have.

"You don't think he's the one who wanted to kill Tayen?" Finley asks.

"What motive would he have to take her out?" Wade asks. *"If Theo wanted Tayen to come forward against Rider, then something had to tip the scales to make her death more worthwhile."*

"Wade has a good point. What good would it do for Theo to kill someone he was planning to use as a pawn in his scheme?" Fin asks.

"I know how we can find out," I say, looking over at her mischievously.

FOUR DAYS AFTER THE MURDER

"Are you sure you have everything?" I ask, running through a mental list of things she might have forgotten as she prepares to go over to Theo's dorm under the guise of a class project.

"Yep, got all of it right here," Fin says as she pats her backpack.

I turn toward Wade. *"What about the live feed?"*

"I've got it configured to my wireless hotspot, so as soon as it's turned on, we'll be good to go," they say.

Turning back to Finley, I ask, *"where are you planning to set it up?"*

"Living room," she answers. *"That way we have a full view of the main living space."*

"Perfect. Wade and I will hang back here and keep an eye on the feed."

"You got it." Fin nods.

She tosses us a two-fingered salute before heading out the door to go meet up with Theo to work on their project. I'm a little worried something bad might happen, but I quickly shove those thoughts aside in an effort to remain optimistic. There's a time for pessimistic realism, but now is not it. Finley knows what she's doing, and if there's anyone I can trust to do this, it's her. Playing into Theo's crush on her is the best shot we've got at sneaking a camera in without getting caught, considering none of us would have a shot at getting invited over there otherwise. If Theo knew what we were really doing, he'd shut this down so fast our heads would spin. And we can't risk that. Not when we're so close to finding the truth.

Wade pulls out the desk chair and sits down, types their password into their laptop, and opens up the video software that's awaiting connection.

"You think she'll get caught?" They ask.

"Doubt it," I reply. *"Fin's always been the best at sneaking around unseen. She can go totally incognito when she needs to, despite that need rarely cropping up."*

On the first day of our freshman year of high school, we'd both had our photos taken for our student identification cards. Hers had turned out fantastically, but mine looked like an entire disaster had occurred on my way to school that morning; from my unruly hair and crooked eyeliner down to the misaligned buttons on my shirt. To be fair, I'd woken up late and Felix had threatened to leave without me, so I didn't have a chance to consult a mirror while I got ready. Doing my eyeliner in the car hadn't helped the matter, either, but it was the least of all the damnable offenses. I'd made it to school just in time to get my ID, but the picture was so bad I considered paying the thirty-five dollar 'lost ID' fee in order to get a new one. Finley, being of relatively sound mind, convinced me to sneak into the office while the staff was gone so she could take a new one for me.

That was the moment I knew we'd be best friends for the rest of our lives. She'd gone above and beyond for me, without a care in the world about what the consequences might be, because she saw something in me that it took me years to recognize for myself. Finley has never let me down, even when I've let her down because I couldn't get out of my own way. Even now, she's going out on a limb for me and planting a covert camera so we can try and catch The Ghost once and for all.

My phone buzzes against my thigh; a message from Fin.

I'm in!

A quick wave gets Wade's attention and I smile as I pass along the message. We spend the next half hour on our phones, sending each other funny videos and laughing about the ridiculous things we come across as we independently scroll through the internet. A cat squeezing through holes of various sizes, a man explaining the scientific complexities of the world with jokes, someone sharing a hilarious personal anecdote about lost luggage, a vulgar chef baking a loaf of specialty bread, clips from cult classic movies and funny tv shows with ensemble casts.

Finally, I get another text.

good to go, check it out

Wade opens the camera and connects to the video feed. Suddenly, we're looking at Finley standing in front of the camera, adjusting it as she hides it behind something in the corner of the living room. She looks around and sits back down on the couch, picking up her notebook and setting it on her lap. Theo is approaching behind her, heading back into the living room from a trip to the bathroom or something. He takes a seat beside Finley and, as they begin to discuss their project, I shift my attention back to Wade.

"How will we know if something happens?" I ask.

"The recorded footage will have a timeline showing when there's been movement. I'll be able to scrub through it to see if there's anything important," Wade explains. *"Plus it'll back up to the cloud, so there's no lost footage problems like what happened during the scavenger hunt."*

It seems like a decent plan, assuming we actually manage to capture anything noteworthy. The signs are half pointing to Theo and half pointing out into the void, and a heavy sigh slips through my parted lips as I lean against the wall and let gravity slide me down to the floor.

"What's up?" Wade asks, shifting their body toward me and quirking an eyebrow.

"Something doesn't feel right," I say.

"What do you mean?"

"I can't put my finger on it…"

"Maybe part of you still wants it to be Rider."

I shake my head.

This feels way too personal to only be about Rider.

"It would make more sense if it was, but it can't be."

"Would it? Like you said before, he's nowhere near clever enough to pull this off. Plus, it's unlikely he would devise a game meant to ruin him."

Brow pleating, I look at them with slight confusion.

"When you say it that way, it makes sense," I admit.

A half-smile grows on Wade's face. *"The truth is inconvenient."*

"Yeah, no kidding," I snort. There's a momentary pause and then I ask, *"Do you think everything will go back to normal after all of this?"*

"Depends on what you consider to be normal," they say, shrugging. *"But in all likelihood, probably not. How could it be after..."*

"I don't want normal. Not really, anyway," I admit. *"But it would be nice to not have to look over my shoulder all the time."*

"So then, what do you want?" Wade asks, thoughtfully.

Thinking about it, I realize there's only one good answer.

"I want to be happy," I say.

"With Tayen?" They eye me carefully, looking for a reaction.

"Look at you, jumping straight to the point."

"Seemed like the best way to do it." Wade chuckles. *"So, how are things between you two?"*

"They're good, I think," I reply, picking at the low-

pile carpet.

"You think?"

"Yeah," I answer, lightly shrugging my shoulders. *"I'm cautiously optimistic."*

"Trading in your nihilism for optimism, huh? Guess it's true, love really does change a person."

"Yeah, yeah, yeah." I wave them off, rolling my eyes and laughing. *"Don't hurt yourself jumping to those conclusions. No one said anything about love."*

Wade laughs and nudges me with their foot. *"For what it's worth, you do seem lighter lately. It's a good look on you, Lennon."* There's a kindness to them that brightens the room.

It makes me want to gush about the other morning and my kiss with Tayen, but I hold it in. The last thing I want to do is jinx myself, challenge the universe to take away this bright spot she's illuminated. Besides, there would be far too many questions and I have too few answers to give.

"Thanks," I say, returning their warm smile. *"Fingers crossed I can hold onto it."*

"You will." Wade says with an assertive nod. *"Gotta have some faith that everything will work out."*

By the time Finley comes back, the credits have just started to roll on Bohemian Rhapsody, the Freddie Mercury biopic starring Rami Malek that we were watching in the living room.

"I'm ready for my parade," she announces, smiling smugly.

"Huh?" I ask. *"Parade for what, installing a camera?"*

"Yes, but also…" Fin digs into her backpack and pulls out a sheet of paper with a list of names scrawled in messy lettering. *"For recruiting Theo to the dark side."*

"What!" I yell, heaving myself over the back of the couch to grab the paper from her hands.

Scanning the page, there's at least a dozen names here including mine, Tayen's, and Iris's. If this is what I think it is, Theo is doing more than joining our side— he's putting his best friend on blast for his crimes against women. With this list of names, we've got something tangible proving that this is a pattern his family's wealth and power has swept under the rug.

"He just willingly handed this over?" I ask.

"I'm a very persuasive person, what can I say." Finley is radiating pride in her accomplishment. *"It didn't take much, all I had to do was ask him if he remembered Iris. It snowballed, and one thing led to another, and I let it slip that I'd heard a few girls talking about how Rider gives them bad vibes. Turns out Theo is actually not as okay with*

his bestie's bullshit as Rider would like everyone to believe."

"You don't say," Wade snarks.

"Eventually we got to talking about what happened to you, Len." Finley nods to me apologetically. *"He said he felt really shitty about the whole thing, so heads up—he might come knocking on your door to apologize or something."* She shrugs. *"Anyway, he offered to write a list of names when I said you were writing a paper about sex and consent on campus and wanted to do some interviews. Apparently the ones with stars by their names are the ones who go here now."*

"Half of these names are starred," I comment, showing Wade the list. One name in particular catches my eye *"Ava Stadtler? Why does that name sound so familiar?"*

"I thought the same thing!" Fin exclaims, dropping into an empty armchair. *"She was in Iris' class at Stone Valley. Turns out, she went to the same creepy Jesus camp, too, but she went months earlier. Came back a month before Iris did, and apparently it did a real number on her."*

"What do you mean?" Wade asks, leaning forward and turning to face Fin.

"Theo said that camp screwed Iris up, that she came back and had to be homeschooled because coming to school was 'too much for her'." Fin's fingers arch into air quotes. *"I don't know what they did to her but, whatever it was, I bet Ava went through the same thing."*

Or worse, given that she was there longer than Iris had been.

Unlike Iris, Ava never came back to school.

Thinking back on what caused her to break, I remember chatter among the halls that something had happened to her. The details never made their way to me—which I was thankful for, at the time—but I do know that she'd pointed the finger at someone and no one believed her. It was a memory I'd blocked out, perhaps because hindsight isn't a friend when you're in the depths of your own despair. Recalling anyone else's pain was unfathomable, unthinkable. But now, clear-headed as I am, the me of the past seems so selfish and self-absorbed.

The more this unravels, the more my past comes back to haunt me.

"She's probably not here," I say, after ringing the doorbell for the third time.

Finley is looking at the crack beneath the door, illuminated with a warm white light on the other side. She must've seen something, because now she's kneeling and holding her phone upside down on the floor in order to peer inside using her camera.

"Not here my ass," Finley growls, looking up at me with a pleated browline. *"I can see footsteps—and she doesn't have a roommate."*

I don't want to know who she flirted with in the housing office to find out that information, so I resist the urge to probe further.

Reaching into her jacket pocket, Fin pulls out a pen and a crumpled receipt from god knows where. She scrawls something hurriedly on the back and shoves it beneath the door. After a few minutes, I turn to leave and Finley pulls me back.

"Hi." We're greeted by a pale girl in a long-sleeved cotton dress, her hair stick-straight and thin, like ironed russet hay. It's greasy at the scalp and tucked behind both of her ears, stopping just below her collarbones—not that you could see them past her modest neckline, that is.

"Hey, Ava," I reply. "We weren't sure you were home."

"I gathered that," she says, partially hiding behind the door while her visible hand nervously toys with the fabric of her dress. *"Can I help you?"* It's not a rude question, but it's curt and tells me she doesn't want company.

That's too bad.

"Can we come in?" I ask. *"We'd like to ask you about*

somebody that you were with at St. Dominic's."

If the subtle twitch I catch is any indication, her memories aren't fond ones.

Finley and I had done a quick Google search before we came over here, because we were dying to know more about the program Iris' parents had sent her to: St. Dominic's Faith Center. From what we'd been able to find on the internet, it was an evangelical facility for troubled youth, designed to 'provide a serene, Christian environment for children aged twelve through eighteen to grow in their faith while also developing respect and discipline using Christ-centered principles.' It was candy-coated sickness in Papyrus font with stock images of kids and teens smiling and running through fields. It looked like they took a bunch of motivational posters and glued them together.

"Sorry, I really don't think that's a good idea," Ava says, as she slowly starts to close the door.

Finley steps forward and uses her hand to prop the door open. Ava is so frail that I can't imagine it took much of Fin's strength to keep it from shutting, either.

"Ava, this is really important," Fin says, attempting to appeal to her humanity. *"We're worried about Iris, and we know you two were at St. Dominic's together so we're hoping you know her better than we do. Will you help us?"*

A few seconds of puppy-dog eyes is all it takes to

wear Ava down until she agrees and ushers us into her room. When most people don't have roommates, they take over the entire space with their own stuff. Not Ava. Half of it is empty—literally right down the middle—and the lack of roommate is glaringly obvious.

Neither Finley nor I know whether to stand or sit, so we just sort of linger awkwardly waiting for the right moment to start rooting around in Ava's brain.

"Why are you worried about Iris?" Ava asks, tucking her dress under herself and sitting gingerly at her desk.

Fin looks back at me and then jumps right in with, *"we think she might be involved in something dangerous."*

Ava's lips pull taut. *"Oh dear... I was afraid that might happen, eventually."*

"What do you mean?" I ask, brows furrowed and begging for a crumb of context.

"She... Well, I—she had a bit of a reputation while we were at St. Dominic's."

I don't dare look away, afraid that losing eye contact with Ava might give her the chance to reconsider telling us whatever is on the tip of her tongue.

"What kind of reputation?" I ask.

Ava's shoulders are pulled inward as she hunches forward, everything about her body language reading as uncomfortable and anxious. I'll be beating myself up later over the guilt I'm harboring for making her relive this part of her past, but right now I don't have time to linger on it. I need to know everything that she knows about Iris and what went on at St. Dominic's.

"All the kids at St. Dominic's had their own challenges," Ava says, reciting the same phrasing as the sanitized website copy that Finley and I read thrice over. *"But Iris..."* She shakes her head. *"Iris had an obsession. She found out what I'd dealt with and started getting close, spending as much time at my side as I would allow. There was a near-constant stream of questions and she never stopped talking about him. It became... too much."* Ava shakes her head.

"Never stopped talking about who, Ava?" I ask.

Ava leans forward and says, *"Rider,"* with a sense of dread varnishing her hands.

Iris must have found out that Rider was the link between them.

"She was the most in need of the Father's individualized support, but the poor girl was just too much for me to handle," Ava adds.

The Father. She must mean Father Carmine, the head of the program. That or God, I guess.

Finley shoots me an are you fucking kidding me glance and I lift my brows.

"Did you notice anything change with her while you were there?" Finley asks.

"Oh, definitely," Ava insists. *"At first, I thought Iris was just lonely."* She gets quiet, her signs shrinking as she pulls her hands back. *"But, eventually, she started lashing out and getting violent. She kept lighting her roommates' beds on fire until they moved her to a single, even though no one could ever figure out how she did it, and she'd sabotage meals when she was on kitchen duty. Bad things started happening to anyone who treated Iris badly, but no one could prove it was her. I saw a darkness in her and I—"* She shudders. *"After that, I stayed out of her way."*

Laying on the communal fourth-floor lounge couch, my head in Tayen's lap, the sense of dread has minimized. It's not gone, but it's shrunk a few sizes like the Grinch's heart.

"Do you want to talk about it?" She asks.

"Not yet."

I want to stay in this moment for as long as I can. Nothing else matters—not the drama, or the photos, or the fact that Theo is actively trying to ruin my life in the name of revenge against the guy that actually ruined my life.

This is it.

Sitting here, with the girl I'm crushing hard for, her

fingers are raking through my hair and making a knotted mess of my curls. But I don't even care. I would take a thousand hair knots if it meant I could stay right here, with her, forever.

Thinking about what Wade said the other day, I wonder if this is what love feels like; if this is the sickly sweet thing that thousands of songs have been written about.

With all of my heart, I want this girl.

Her nails gently scratch at my scalp with each pull of her fingers through my hair. Whatever we're watching on the flat-screen television is none of my concern anymore, because my eyes are closed and I'm fading fast.

Tayen taps my shoulder and I turn to look at her as they flutter back open.

"You're not falling asleep, are you?" She smiles that magical grin and I melt.

"No, no, I'm wide awake." I sit up in a daze. *"Four cappuccinos type of awake, I could drive for Formula One and NASCAR at the same time."*

"That explains the Speed Racer pajama pants," Tayen says with a laugh.

The old me might've sheepishly recoiled at that comment, but I'm oddly relaxed by it. She's seeing the weird little quirks that make me who I am and, for once,

I'm not afraid of being rejected for it. I'm not worried about something as insignificant as my loungewear being the reason the towel gets thrown in. It's oddly freeing.

"*And The Office socks on your feet are doing what, helping with your accounting?*" I tease.

Tayen laughs that infectious, beautiful laugh that pulls at the corners of her mouth and sparkles in her eyes.

"*Okay, fair,*" she says, turning toward me and resting her legs across my thighs.

I lean my head against the back of the couch and let my body sink into it.

"*Ava said that Iris was obsessed with what happened to her,*" I say, biting at the inside of my lip. "*She couldn't let it go.*"

"*You think she should've?*"

I shrug. "*I don't know. Maybe?*"

"*Everyone deals with things in their own time. What Iris went through...*" Tayen's hand reaches for my arm and squeezes it. "*That kind of layered pain would be difficult for anyone to deal with, let alone a sixteen-year-old who hadn't found her place in the world yet.*"

Nodding, my hand snakes around her ankle and rests against her calf. I pick at the edge of her sock, sticking my finger between the fabric and the heat of her skin.

"Something Ava said... I don't know, it worries me."

"What was it?" Tayen asks, brows dipping at the center of her face.

"She said that Iris' personality changed. That she became violent, setting fires and pushing people away to isolate herself. I just can't figure out why."

"Maybe the isolation was her way of protecting herself, of keeping everyone else at bay so that she didn't have to lower her guard. Could ask Fin, but it seems like a textbook trauma response." Tayen shrugs.

"Yeah," I muse, my thumb swiping across the The Office logos that were sporadically placed across her sock.

Tayen's hand rests atop mine and her eyes are wide and soulful.

"You know that what she went through wasn't your fault, right?" she asks.

I shrug.

"I'm serious, Lennon. You were a victim, too. It's not fair for you to carry around the burden of what Iris dealt with."

It's not that I don't believe her. I really, really, want to believe her.

But it does feel like my responsibility.

Iris was my friend and I didn't protect her.

"You have to let go of the idea that this is somehow your

fault," Tayen says. *"But that doesn't mean that you can't help her."*

Our eyes meet and there are tears welling up in mine. They're painful as I hold them back, trying to keep myself from becoming a basket case in front of Tayen. I scoot closer to her on the couch, my arms wrapping around her as my face buries into the oversized Billie Eilish tour shirt she's wearing. It's soft and well-worn and smells like detergent, but past that it smells like home. Like the warm, summer air drifting in through an open window. A deep breath releases from within the hollows of my chest and I fall into her. Over and over and over.

Tayen's arms envelop me and her cheek rests against the top of my head.

This is where I want to stay.

Right here.

Forever.

SIX DAYS AFTER THE MURDER

DEFCON 1! SERIOUSLY! HELP!

Spasms and jitters shake through my body as adrenaline pumps through every vein, a countdown speeding by behind my eyes as I impatiently wait for Finley to haul her ass down here. Sweat gathers at the back of my neck and it starts to make me itch. I'm too aware of every square inch of my body, or all of the things I shouldn't be focusing on. The things that normally don't register as a blip on my radar are agitating me beyond belief. The tag sewn along the inside hem of my shirt, the papercut between my index and middle finger, the seam of my sock rubbing against my toes.

Before I know it, Finley is yanking open the

passenger door and she's looking at me with wide eyes and a downturned mouth.

"What's so urgent you had me Googling the whole DEFCON thing again? I still can't remember whether it starts at one or five," she says, not yet comprehending the seriousness of the situation I've just pulled her into.

Ensuring that no one is close enough to see us, I reach underneath a pile of junk on the floorboards of my backseat. When I sit back up, there's a five-inch blade in my hand. The thin fabric of an old t-shirt is the only thing preventing my fingerprints from touching its handle.

Finley's jaw hits the floor so hard I expect it to shatter.

"What is that!" she exclaims, taking a step back like it's going to bite her.

"Get in," I instruct, putting the knife back where I found it.

Fin doesn't move.

"Now, Finley!"

Like a jolt of electricity has run through her, she snaps into action and climbs in without uttering a word. This has to be the first time she's ever been speechless, and I'd mark it on my calendar if I didn't think she'd strangle me. We peel out of the parking space and off campus as quickly as possible. My gut is screaming at me that this is the knife that killed Bronya, and I don't want to be anywhere near here in case someone comes looking for it.

Fin is closer to the door than she is to me, coiling away and tucking her hands into her lap. Her body language is fearful, but whether it's me or the blood-coated weapon in the back that she's afraid of remains to be seen.

"I have a theory, but if it's true, then shit is going downhill fast," I say, shooting a cautious look at my uncomfortable pal. Her eyes beg me not to continue, but I do anyway. *"That knife? I think it's the one The Ghost used to stab Bronya."*

Fin blinks and shakes her head like I've just said the stupidest thing in the world. *"Bronya died because she was pushed out of a window, Lennon. We both know that. Hell, even the police know it!"*

"At the station, the detective told me she'd been stabbed before she fell. Or before she was pushed, or before whatever the hell happened to her, because at this point everything feels like it could be both the truth and a lie." I'm sure I look just as exasperated as I feel trying to explain all of the thoughts bouncing around inside my skull.

The space between us collapses and Finley relaxes in her seat, even turning toward me a bit as she mulls over my words. She's changing modes, thinking about things like it's an elaborate game of *Clue*—who killed Bronya in the dorm room with a buck knife?

Even then, there's a chance this is a false lead. Perhaps Detective Melendez fed me bad intel as some sort of test, trying to suss out as much information from me as he could without giving up any real information of his own. It's not entirely out of the realm of possibility, but I can't bank on it. I have to assume the information is good. Besides, based on his interview skills, he doesn't exactly seem cunning enough to pull off a double-cross.

"Shit... Seriously?" Fin asks, carefully.

"Yeah."

"Who on our list could be capable of that?"

No. Fucking. Idea.

"If we're right about Tayen being the intended target, then it's likely they executed Bronya because she saw their face. Anyone could've done it if they were panicked enough, right? I mean, look at how many times crimes of passion end up being plans gone awry. My gut tells me whoever it was had to cut their losses, despite the fact that they were using her to get closer to me. She'd done what they needed, so maybe killing her was the lesser of two evils."

"Whoever it is, that's stone cold behavior," Finley adds. *"Straight up psychotic."*

"No kidding." I slowly nod in agreement. *"They could've had a copy of our key and let themselves in,*

catching her by surprise. There was obviously a struggle, but it wouldn't take much to overpower her."

"If it is Iris," Fin starts, going along with my theory for the time being. *"There has to be some way we can prove she's responsible for Bronya's death. Do you think there's a chance we missed a clue in your room?"*

"You mean the room that's blocked off with police tape?"

"C'mon, Veronica Mars, live a little."

I sigh, knowing she's—unfortunately—right.

If we want to find a link between Iris and the planned attack on Tayen that took Bronya's life, we have to return to the scene of the crime.

"Wait," I say, trying to process my thoughts as quickly as they were popping into my head. *"If the cops have Bronya's phone, they'll go through her texts and find all the messages extorting her."* Irritation floods into my body. The last thing we need is the police nosing around and blowing our whole investigation out of the water. *"Do you think Wade can remotely wipe Bronya's phone?"*

"Uh... maybe? That's pretty blatant tampering with an active police investigation, though." Finley tilts her head and shoots me a hesitant glance.

I scoff in return. *"I don't think it would be their first time."*

Thinking about that night after the scavenger hunt, when we combed through the photos left for us to find, the screenshots of Wade's supposed blackmail of a government official seemed fairly innocuous. Sure, we'd all done things we weren't proud of, but Wade actually did seem proud of it—like they'd done a service to the world for taking on this vigilante role. They seemed comfortable breaking the rules when it served their vision of a moral right and wrong, so why would this be any different? Erasing a phone to protect our efforts against The Ghost seemed like it would be right up their alley.

"Or ours," I add. *"Since you want us to contaminate a crime scene."*

"To be fair, that room is already covered with our DNA," Fin says. *"It's not like us being in there is going to raise any flags. You were her roommate, you're probably already on their suspect list."*

That's a frightening thought.

In all of the chaos, I hadn't considered that anyone might think me a suspect.

"On the bright side," she counters, *"you don't really have a motive."*

"Other than having a certain boy who shall not be named in common," I snort.

"Boyfriend, hookup, fling, whatever you want to call him," she says, waving off any minutiae of care. *"Unless the police dig all the way back to high school, I don't think*

they're going to connect those dots."

If they did, they'd find more than they bargained for. Bronya and I had it out when everything went down, just after I'd discovered that Rider had been sharing my private photos with people who were never supposed to see them. I was stupid and furious and so I screamed at her—in front of a crowd of kids—and said that I hoped she'd drop dead for hanging around with someone who treated girls like they were disposable. I'd told her she was worse than he was, and that she deserved to know what it felt like to be caught off guard and stabbed in the back.

I hadn't meant it literally.

"Let's hope they don't," I say, turning down a back alleyway and throwing the car into park behind Off The Record.

There were multiple signs prohibiting my rushed parking job, but what was one more broken law considering how many others we were blatantly ignoring these days. I shut off the car and pulled out my phone to send a message.

A series of light taps against my leg give rise to an upward shift of my eyes.

"Who are you texting?" Fin asks.

"You'll see."

"What the f—put that away!" Felix yells abruptly, interrupting his signing mid-sentence to switch back to English and grab the knife from my hand. Looking around suspiciously, he takes the shirt from around its handle, and covers the entirety of the blade. "Where the hell did you get this?" He hisses, signing the words that he does know, all while his hunter green irises dart between us.

"I found it in my car. Someone must've planted it there," I say as I sign, wishing the sim-commed words could be siphoned out of me in a more confident and articulate way.

Simultaneous Communication is kind of a catch-twenty-two, being that you can't speak both English and ASL at the same time with grammatical accuracy; one of the languages will always suffer, and it's typically always the ASL that falls by the wayside. I've used this as a tool with my family for a long time, trying to encourage them to pick up vocabulary words and transition to conversations solely in ASL, but admittedly it's been doing more harm than good.

Looking at Fin, raised brows and a shake of her head signal that she's not jumping in to explain this one. I found the knife, so I guess it's on me to bring my brother up to speed.

"*What do you mean* planted?" Felix asks, continuing to voice the words as he signs them, leaning hard into English any time he can't remember a sign in ASL.

I can tell he'd been making more of an effort to sign with me since the day I'd given him a hard time in the kitchen, although I'd refrained from bringing it up since then. I'm thankful he's showing up for me in a way that I need—especially when Finley is in the conversational space—but I need to see that this is a consistent change before I give him a gold star.

"*I think it's the same knife the killer used,*" I reply. "*They planted it in my car at some point after Bronya was murdered.*"

One of the only interests my brother and Finley have in common—aside from a deep appreciation of music—is their infatuation with the television show *Brooklyn Nine-Nine*. They each view themselves as Jake Peralta, an overconfident and immature police detective whose charm and wit makes him a lovable standout among the ensemble cast. Based on the many episodes they've each made me sit through, I can safely say neither of them is Jake Peralta. At best, Felix embodies a hipster, childless Terry Jeffords whereas Finley is more-or-less the lovechild of Gina Linetti and Rosa Diaz.

Rolling her eyes, Fin folds her arms across her chest.

There's nothing inherently wrong with Amy, as I've tried to convince Finley, but she's always hated her anyway.

Turning his attention back to me, Felix's eyes narrow.

"So, what, you just found this in your car? You can't drive around with a bloody knife *in your backseat, Len!"* Finding an empty Trader Joe's tote bag on the floor of the car, Felix conceals the weapon within its folds before tucking it under his arm.

I'm oddly relieved he doesn't know how to sign the phrase 'bloody knife'.

"The cops catch you with this? You're done for.*"* Felix ends his sentence with a gesture, pretending to slice across his neck with an extended thumb.

"That's why I need your help," I say reassuringly as I maintain steady eye contact with my brother, willing him to agree without asking any more questions.

I'd been so adamant about not needing his help thus far, that now asking for it felt like a slap in the face to my newly discovered sense of self. My independence was taking a hit here, but it was time for my big brother to step up to the plate like he's been chomping at the bit to do.

A thick, stifling energy boils among us.

Suddenly, Felix sighs and a heavy groan slips out of him as his chin lifts toward the sky. He mumbles something, but I'm not sure what it is. Returning his gaze to me, it's clear he's going to cave.

"Fine," he says through gritted teeth as his open-palmed hand signs the word. *"But if we get arrested, you're never hearing the end of this."*

I won't be hearing anything anyway, but go off, Felix.

Abruptly shutting the car's door, he hands me the tote-covered, shirt-wrapped knife and motions to the back entrance of the record store.

"Wait," Fin interjects, physically blocking our path. *"I can't stay. I've got class in half an hour, so we've gotta get back to campus."*

Shit—class.

"Change of plans," I say, thinking on my feet. Reaching into my pocket, I grab the car keys and toss them to her. This time, I don't sim-com. *"I'm going to skip my afternoon class. You take my car, Felix can give me a ride back after he gets off work."*

"You got it," she says, heading for the driver's seat and firing off her signature salute in my direction. *"Meet up with us at Wade's, okay? We'll be ready and waiting."*

Felix's forehead crinkles and he asks, *"waiting for what?"*

Finley grins in her troublemaker way and signs 'TRAIN GONE', an ASL idiom that means he's missed his opportunity to be part of our little back-and-forth.

I don't say anything more, tossing a nod to Finley as she buckles her seatbelt and puts the car into gear. The Honda pulls out of the alley and out of sight, and I turn to follow in after my brother through the back door of the shop. I expect him to continue pestering me—in fact, I'm bracing for it—but instead I'm met with strange silence as we enter into the air-conditioned space.

He stops in front of me just inside the doorway, at the end of a skinny hallway plastered with old posters, and allows the door to close behind us before uttering a word.

"I thought you said it was just some weird texts? What the hell, Lennon?"

There's a pensive, though appropriately pissed off, look on his face and I'm thoroughly unhappy to see it.

"Yeah, well... Things took a turn."

"Spill," he demands.

Without breaking eye contact, I take a heavy breath and bite at the inside of my lower lip.

"Only if you promise to keep your cool," I say.

"It's the most logical plan."

"Logical?" Felix's face twists incredulously as he organizes a stack of records into their alphabetized bins. He'd been diving so deep into everything, prying with question after question, our conversation had spilled over into his shift. "It sounds like you've got a death wish."

"Tell me how you really feel," I reply sarcastically, picking up an LP he's just put down.

Grabbing it out of my hands, Felix puts it back where it belongs and I scowl, which earns me a scoff and a pair of averted eyes. By the time he turns back to me, there's a look on his face I've seen countless times before. His you're-being-an-idiot look, complete with narrowed eyes and a jaw so tight it might as well be wired shut. The same look that gets flung my way when he thinks I'm being annoying.

Felix pauses his shelving of the merchandise and says, "you gotta be smart about this, Len." He looks around to ensure no one will eavesdrop, then lowers his voice. His hands stiffly sign what words he can as he speaks again. Every third one, give or take. "Are you *forgetting someone* stashed a murder weapon *in your car?* *Someone died* because of all this shit. This isn't some kind of *joke*, or a *game* where you can *change the rules* as you go. *If this Ghost person* really is *responsible* for all of it, then *they're a threat to you and your friends*. This is *not* the kind of *person you want* to underestimate. *You catch my drift?*"

"I get what you're saying, but I've got it handled," I say. "Bronya deserves justice for what happened to her, and so does Tayen."

"So do you," Felix says, a woeful expression flashing across his face.

I know what he's thinking, and I hate it so much I want to screech.

I explained everything that happened with Rider and the photos—how he'd shared them with his friends and practically half the school. The moment I was done, Felix hugged me for longer than he ever had before. Not just seconds, but minutes. So long that I wasn't sure the embrace would ever end, actually. He apologized for not being there to protect me.

"I'm gonna kill him," Felix grumbles, knuckles white.

"No, you're not," I insist.

"I'm gonna drive over there and kick his ass down every flight of stairs I can find," Felix continues, ignoring me entirely. "Then I'm gonna break his legs. How dare that little fucking punk even think about going to the same college as you after what he did."

Time to talk my brother off the ledge.

"Felix, you know I appreciate you, but I need you to simmer down."

"Simmer down? I flew past simmering twenty minutes ago," he huffs.

"I'm serious, chill out. This isn't your battle to fight."

"You're my sister, of course it's my battle," he argues, fueling his own fire.

"Felix!" I raise my voice and everyone turns to look at us—a decision I instantly regret.

Once everyone looks away, I lower my volume and lock eyes with him.

"You know I love you, right?"

Felix's jaw clenches.

"Right?" I ask again, refusing to move on until he agrees.

He sighs and finally says, "yes. And?"

"And I need you to let me handle it. I'm not ashamed of the choices I made. Do I wish I hadn't? Absolutely. But the choices he made afterward, those are on him. I can't live my entire life looking back at that moment."

For too many seconds, he just stares at me.

Then, Felix groans and rolls his eyes.

"Fine," he growls. "I don't like it—and I want that on the record, by the way—but if this is something you need to do for yourself... then you have my support."

"Thank you," I agree. "If it makes you feel any

better, I would pay cash money to watch you beat his ass. Maybe once this is all over."

SEVEN DAYS AFTER THE MURDER

We all gathered to review the hidden camera footage, and that's when we saw it: Finley and Theo in a lip-lock.

"Finley!" I exclaim, my eyes so wide they burn.

Face flush, Fin looks like she's about to barf all over Wade's floor.

"Seriously? You kissed Theo of all people?" I'm flabbergasted. Actually, no, I'm miles past flabbergasted and am straight-up gobsmacked. *"He's a potential murderer!"*

This really doesn't make Tayen's case for Finley's involvement any less valid, and for that I'm furious. She's supposed to be on my side, but instead she's sticking her tongue down Theo's throat. Gross.

"Was!" She corrects. *"He WAS a potential murderer,*

until we crossed him off the suspect list because he gave us the names of the girls."

"That doesn't make it any better," Marcus adds.

"Oh shut up, Marcus!" She yells.

"Why the hell would you kiss him? Did you forget the entire damn plan?" I ask, hoping desperately that she's got some really good reason for why we've got her makeout session on video.

"I got—" Fin's flustered. *"I don't know, I was wrapped up in the moment!"* She throws her hands into the air.

"Wrapped up in a moment?" I ask, incredulously. *"Of all the moments, you chose THAT ONE?"*

A rough hand runs through her hair and she lets out a pent-up sigh.

No one else is saying anything, and it's like I've dropped into a soap opera.

"Fin, what the actual fuck?" I'm defeated.

"I'm sorry," she apologizes. *"I didn't mean for it to happen, it just all went so fast. We were talking about our project and he kept going on about how beautiful I was and how he wished things had been different in high school because he'd always been into me. I folded and I thought I'd ruined everything, but then he gave me that list. I don't know."*

This was my opportunity to know, once and for all.

"Tell me one thing. Were you helping him this whole

time? Were you involved in this shit? Whatever the answer is, I just need to know before I have a mental breakdown." If there was someone else in my life that I couldn't trust, I needed to know. Now.

"What?" Her eyes widen and her head shakes, first in small movements and then larger. *"Oh, my god, Lennon, no! Of course not. I would never do that to you—ever. This was a freak moment that will never be repeated, but it wasn't some elaborate plan to screw you over. I swear on my life and Albert's grave."*

Albert, Finley's dead pet guinea pig, was buried in her backyard and had been known to be her furry soulmate. There was no greater childhood tragedy in our lives than his death, and for her to swear on his grave was not a small feat.

I'm quiet for a minute, but I know that I have to believe her.

"Okay," I nod. *"I believe you that this was a freak accident, and I know it led us to the list and Ava, but I need you to be honest with me next time so that I don't have to find out like that."* My finger points to the laptop where the footage is frozen on a still image of Theo and Finley kissing, with her hands on either side of his face and one of his at her waist.

Fin nods and holds up three fingers. *"Scout's honor."*

"You were never a Scout," I retort.

The rest of the footage is uneventful.

Eventually, everyone goes their separate ways—except for me, because of my determination to find something that resembles a lead.

Lately, I've been preoccupied with thoughts of our shrinking suspect list, and how the only name left is Iris ever since Theo handed over that list of Rider's known victims.

"Do you think it's some crazy revenge plan?" I ask, picking at the ripped knees of my jeans. *"The way Ava was talking about Iris... I don't know, she made it sound like Iris completely lost her mind when she was sent away."*

Wade leans back in their chair. The way they're eyeing me gives me pause, like maybe they're trying to figure out a diplomatic answer out of respect for the friendship I once shared with Iris.

"I don't think anyone can predict the actions of someone who's been through trauma," they say, their face layered with a kind but sullen softness. *"It could've triggered a psychotic break, or compounded her feelings of brokenness. Humans have way too many variables, that's why I've always preferred computers."* A small smile creeps onto their face as they reach up to scratch at their ear. *"Do you actually think she could be The Ghost?"*

"I don't know," I say, heart thumping in my throat. Everything in me wants it to be anyone but her, but I'm

running out of names to cross off. *"Some of the pieces don't fit,"* I admit. *"She's not a student here, so I don't understand how she'd be able to follow us and do everything that The Ghost has done. And honestly... I just—I feel like I've been the worst friend in the world."* My hands lift to my eyes and I rub the almost-tears away before they have a chance to manifest.

I can't cry right now; I refuse.

"I didn't know what she was going through."

It was worse for her, even, because she didn't have a best friend's shoulder to cry on.

"How could you have known? It wasn't all on you, Lennon," Wade says, leaning forward in their chair. *"You can't bear the burden of everyone you've ever known."*

"Can't I?" I laugh through the tears welling up in my eyes.

They chuckle. *"No, but if anyone is going to die trying I'm sure it will be you."*

"I've thought about her a lot, you know? If I could turn back time, I would. I'd have been there for her, made sure that she didn't feel so alone. Maybe then she would've turned out okay, or at least not had to be sent away."

Wade nods, but they're no longer looking at me. They're looking just past me, at something on the other side of me that only they can see. The unwavering steadiness of their gaze is calming, and it reminds me of the way children stare with amazement and wonder when they're seeing something for the first time.

"What are you thinking about?" I ask, resting my chin on my knee and allowing my head to naturally tilt to the side.

"That people are so much more complicated than we think they are," Wade says. *"Just when we think we've got them figured out, it all changes."*

"You're a wise one, Wade Rivera."

"A gift and a curse."

My phone vibrates and it's Finley, asking if I'm ready to sneak into my dorm room to collect evidence—a covert plan she's nicknamed Operation: Midnight Stealth.

"I've gotta go meet up with Fin, but I'll see you tomorrow?"

"Yep," they agree. *"Try to get some sleep, alright?"*

I nod and hug Wade where they sit in their chair, leaving them to continue working through the footage we've been collecting from Rider and Theo's room.

Bee-lining it straight to Finley's room She's waiting for me, dressed in an all black get up that feels over the top in every way I could expect from her. The police didn't know what they were looking for when they combed through our belongings, but Finley and I are keeping our eyes wide open.

Almost tripping over my own feet, I rush through the doorway under the police tape.

The room is more or less how I left it, except for the items that were bagged and removed as evidence. The carpet is stained, black blotches of crusted blood dotting the floor. It feels frigid in here, fresh air from outside blowing in through the broken window. When I'd first entered this room, I thought it could be a new beginning. A fresh start away from the drama of high school. Instead, it's been soured. Tainted by whoever it is that wants to ruin my life for the second time.

I've spent the last week playing out this scene in my mind, trying to figure out how it all could've happened. I've considered that the killer caught her by surprise by letting themselves in and sneaking up on her. Then again, maybe she was expecting them to arrive but was shocked by who turned out to be the mystery blackmailer. All we know for sure is that they came prepared to end a life, even if it wasn't the one they planned to snuff out.

The two of us split up and take opposite sides of the room.

"I had an idea while I was at Wade's," I say, after about ten minutes of looking through bins and shelves in silence with only our phone flashlights providing visibility.

"Yeah?" Fin replies, pausing in the midst of looking

through all of the things Bronya kept atop her dresser.

"What if Theo tried to talk to Iris, got her to open up. From everything she's said, it seems like he's someone she'd trust. Someone she's still in contact with, who wouldn't raise a red flag if he reached out."

"It's worth a shot," Finley agrees. *"Maybe ask her to meet in his room. Then we can get footage of their conversation."*

I nod and smile wickedly at her, hoping she gets where I'm about to go with this before I even have to lift my hands again.

Finley stares at me for two whole seconds and then groans.

"Oh, come on, why do I have to be the one to ask him?" she whines.

"We've already covered this—he's in love with you. You could ask him for a kidney and he'd fill a bathtub with ice and let you harvest it yourself. Besides, you kissed him and I had to watch it. You owe me."

"I hate you. But fine, I'll ask him tomorrow." Casting me a sideways glance, Finley resumes the search of Bronya's side of the room.

Twenty minutes goes by and we've found nothing more than a stray homework assignment I forgot to turn in.

"Jeez, she's got a lot of jewelry," Fin comments, lifting

up the lid of a pink jewelry box and tilting it so I can peer in at its contents.

"I don't even know what I'm looking for," I say, having moved on to looking over the surface of my bed. It's still unmade from the last morning that I climbed out of it, which is a jarring image across from Bronya's stripped mattress. It highlights the whole life and death of it all.

"Something that looks out of place, I guess."

We keep searching, and eventually Fin taps my shoulder.

"Is this yours?" She asks, with something shiny and gold pinned in between her index finger and thumb. *"It was on the floor by Bronya's nightstand, but all of the jewelry in her box is silver."*

"What is that?" I ask, stepping closer to her and holding my phone up to her hand.

She drops it into my palm and I turn it over a few times. It's an earring, missing its backing. It's oddly familiar, but not one I've ever seen Bronya wear—nor is it one of mine. A little golden heart on a post—simple, understated. Definitely not something Bronya would wear, and I didn't own much jewelry.

"It's not mine," I say.

Finley locks eyes with me. *"Could be our killer's."*

"Or it could belong to any of her friends. Not sure this is the smoking gun we need."

"Doesn't Iris wear earrings?" Fin muses.

"Yeah…" What did they look like, though? *I think they're gold, actually.*" My eyes trace the little heart in my hand as I focus on that day I sat across from Iris in the coffee shop. Suddenly, I'm more than sure that this is hers. *"This is Iris' earring,"* I add confidently. I remember one of them glinting at me from the other side of the table, but her hair had obscured the other. If she were missing one, there would've been no way to know for sure.

"Hold onto that, then. If it's hers, it'll end up being something," Fin instructs.

I drop the earring into my pocket for safekeeping and we comb through the rest of the room. Ultimately, we find nothing substantial that raises an alarm. On the contrary, it's all a little too neat and tidy.

How could a killer leave such little evidence behind when we knew they didn't originally plan to kill Bronya? From what I knew about crimes of passion, they were messy and disorganized and prone to mistakes. The famous crimes of Lorena Bobbit, Jodi Arias, and Brynn Hartman—all of these scenes were bloody and gruesome and irrefutable. In comparison, our dorm room was too clean. The cops had been here, sure, but they had even less of an idea what they were looking for. Surely they would've missed something.

They missed the earring, after all.

Unless Iris wanted *me* to find it.

Theo agreed to ask Iris to meet up, but only under the condition that Finley agree to go on a date with him. It was sickening, and I didn't actually think she wanted to, but she agreed nonetheless in order to further our investigation.

Iris responded almost immediately to Theo's invitation, saying that she was in the neighborhood and would be happy to catch up—but not on campus. Instead, she wanted to go to a nearby café, a place called Bean Haven on Van Nuys Boulevard. It wasn't ideal, but we fit Theo with a button spy camera Cameron lent us so we'd have a chance at getting video of her saying something useful. I wouldn't be surprised if she was reluctant to say much in public, but at this rate anything would be better than nothing.

"Just don't touch it, okay?" Finley instructs, adjusting the camera in Theo's shirt in the backseat of my Honda.

He's enjoying it a little too much, but she is all business.

We're parked behind the cafe, out of sight, and Wade connected to the internet without any trouble. For once, it's looking like we might get lucky.

"You remember the plan, right?" I ask.

"Talk to her, get her to relax, and see how she reacts if I bring up what happened to your roommate," Theo says.

I nod. *"And don't be afraid to push her a little. We need her to know we're getting closer, but we don't want her to know exactly how close we are."*

"Right."

"And if you need to, use this." I hand him the earring Finley and I found. *"Tell her you found it somewhere, see if she claims it. If it's hers, then we know she was in my room the night Bronya was killed."*

Nodding affirmatively, Theo pulls open the car door and squeezes through as it shuts behind him. Wade's laptop is open and they're watching the live feed from my passenger seat. I take a few deep breaths to steady my heart rate, closing my eyes for a few brief moments. We're so close but there's still so much that can go wrong.

We follow his movements on Wade's laptop screen, watching as he makes his way around to the front door and to the table that Iris is already sitting at.

"Hey Iris," Theo greets.

"Hey," she says, rising to her feet to give him a hug. *"I was surprised to hear from you, it's been a minute."*

"Yeah. I know. School and everything... but I was

thinking about you. I swore I saw you on campus the other day," he says, with that charming smile he's always got on.

"Oh, yeah, I was actually there for a tour."

That's a little too convenient.

"Really? I thought you'd already decided on Smith."

"I had, but after a little more thought I figured it wouldn't hurt to explore options closer to home."

"Sure, I know how it is."

For as long as I've known her she's never been interested in sticking around here for college. Any mention of post-graduation plans were always focused on her getting out of here as fast as humanly possible. So, why the change of heart now?

I look back at Finley and she's thinking the same thing I am: what the hell was that about? Our eyes find their way back to the camera feed just as the two of them exchange further pleasantries.

"Have you been alright?" I ask.

"Can't complain," Iris smiles. *"Counting down the days until graduation."*

For a moment, I almost forget she's not the girl I've thought she was for so long. The kind, naive girl who used to be one of my best friends. The girl who got straight A's and would've made her mom proud if she'd been around enough to notice. The girl whose isolation and pain attracted the predatory boy who wanted to extinguish her light.

The mask is slipping, though. I can see that she's changed, even if she's damn good at playing the part of the well-adjusted high school senior. If I'm right about who The Ghost is—that it really is Iris plotting against me—then I can't assume I know anything about her anymore.

She's a stranger, now.

"Did you hear about what happened on campus last week?" Theo asks.

"You mean that poor girl who died?" Iris says, her face dropping despite her eyes retaining their sharpness. *"Yes, I did. What a tragedy. Did you know her?"*

"No," Theo answers. *"But she was Lennon Larkin's roommate. You remember her, right?"*

Good, Theo, play it off like you and I haven't seen each other recently.

"Oh, really?" She asks, perking up like he's uttered the magic words.

The eerie plasticity of the face she's wearing makes my skin itch, like a twisted uncanny valley effect that magnifies the strangeness and minimizes anything friendly.

"Yeah, everyone's saying it was pretty grisly," Theo replies.

His hands slide along the thighs of his jeans at the edge of the frame.

"He'd better not blow this," Finley says, lingering in the space between the front seats.

We'd initially planned for Theo to take it slow and ease into the hard questions, but I guess his mouth has other plans. I'd slam my palm straight into my forehead, but there's no use cursing him for being direct. He might be playing the role of the human lie detector, but we're seeing everything he's seeing and I'm happy to hedge my bets with Wade on our side to spot the lies Iris is no doubt going to try to pass off as the truth.

Studying Iris's face, I wait for a tell like it's a high-stakes game of poker.

"That's so awful," Iris croons. *"How's Lennon dealing with all of that?"*

I've got to hand it to her, she's playing this whole innocent act pretty well. Maybe she's even convinced herself that she's standing on the moral high ground. I'd give her a round of applause for her performance, but murderers don't deserve praise.

Theo shrugs. *"Not too well, I'd assume. They still haven't caught the killer."*

I lean towards Wade's computer screen, waiting for a microexpression on Iris's face to reveal itself, but I don't see anything. Not a glimpse of enjoyment, or pride, or even the slightest bit of knowing.

"I'm sure they will," she says with certainty.

"By the way, did you lose an earring while on campus for your tour? I found this..." Theo digs into his pocket and reveals the tiny, golden, heart-shaped earring.

"Oh my gosh, where did you find that?" Iris leans forward, her fingers gently picking up the earring from his palm. Tucking her hair behind her ear, I can finally see her other earlobe—and it's missing an earring. *"I've been looking for this everywhere. Thank you for holding onto it for me, I've been a wreck trying to find it."*

Oh, I bet you have. Losing something the same day you've committed a crime? What a frightening realization that must've been.

"It was on the floor," he says. *"In Lennon's dorm room."*

Theo's struck a nerve, and the veil hiding Iris's true feelings is lifting at the edge. Her sardonic grin fades and what replaces it is something much more sinister and dejected. A formidable darkness clouds her light honey eyes as she leans forward and reaches for the sunglasses sitting in front of her on the table. The harsh lights overhead cast stony shadows across her features and reflect the steely gaze that stares right through the computer screen. It looks like she's staring right into the camera, but there's no way she's seen it.

"Oh, that's right," Iris backpedals. *"I almost forgot that*

I stopped by to visit her while I was on campus."

"That must've been nice," Theo replies.

"It would've been, had she been there. I met her roommate, instead." She shrugs, like Bronya is the least significant part of the story. *"Quite rude, that girl. Not to speak ill of the dead, or anything."*

"I'm sure she'd be thrilled to see you," he says. *"Especially given the circumstances, since her life is pretty chaotic these days."*

We've got her confession that the earring is hers, but it's not enough. If we want to turn over all of the evidence we've got to the police, we need something that unequivocally nails her for all of it. But this conversation was never about getting her to admit to Bronya's murder. It's to show her that we know she's behind it all, and to watch what she does next. Iris has proven herself to be reactionary, which means that she's bound to do something reckless in response to the pressure we're applying.

"I'm sure she would," Iris says, one corner of her mouth tightening. *"Tell her I said hi, will you?"* She looks like she wants to say something else, but the words never come. Instead, she puts her sunglasses on, pushing them into place at the bridge of her nose, and stands up from her chair. *"It was good seeing you, Theo."* Iris smiles. Without another word, she walks away and out the front

door of the café.

Theo stays seated for a minute, but eventually stands and walks back out to meet us at my car. Finley opens the door and he slides in, letting out a heavy sigh.

"She didn't say much of anything," he says, like he's forgotten that we were watching their entire conversation.

But he's wrong.

I look to Wade, hoping their answer to my next question is affirmative. *"Can you hack into Iris's email? I'd be willing to bet that this little conversation scared her into action. If she's communicating with anyone, or planning something, I want to know if she's been talking to anyone."*

Iris has always been a terrible texter—even she's admitted that over the years—but she's obsessive about her email. It's the first thing she checks every morning and the last thing she checks before her head hits the pillow. If there's anything incriminating, it's in her inbox.

"Without a doubt," Wade smirks. *"Send me her email address."*

I'm about to text it to them when Theo's hand grips the back of my arm.

"Lennon," he says. *"I got a weird feeling from Iris. I don't know what you think you know, but you might want to hit pause on whatever detective game you're playing here.*

If she is involved with what happened to your roommate, you need to be careful."

I'm way too caught up in my own thoughts to listen to Theo's warning.

The one bright spot in this whole conversation is it's now beyond obvious that Iris knows something. Not only is she trying to shield her secrets with fabricated niceties, but she's actively avoiding the topic and subtly pointing out that she knows we don't have any evidence of her involvement. I might not be able to prove beyond a reasonable doubt that she's the one who murdered Bronya in the heat of the moment, but I know she knows more than she's letting on.

"We'll get her," I say, looking from Wade to Theo to Finley. *"Secrets don't stay buried for long, right?"*

EIGHT DAYS AFTER THE MURDER

> QUIT DIGGING AND START TALKING.

> YOU'VE GOT 24 HOURS BEFORE EVERYTHING GOES ONLINE.

> AND I MEAN EVERYTHING.

It's the first slew of texts I've received since Theo confronted Iris yesterday, and the two are definitely connected. If she felt the heat from that conversation, it would make sense why she's speeding up the timeline. After all, no one tells you to quit sniffing around unless they think you're getting too close for comfort, too close to finding out what they're hiding in the dark. We're only a few steps away from uncovering the truth and finally getting justice for Bronya.

Deep in my bones, I know we're close.

A photo clip comes in after the messages, and it's of the knife that was planted on the floor of my backseat. It's in full view, but the reflections from the outside of the car's window are useless in identifying the photographer. My breathing gets heavier, deeper, irregular. I knew that this stupid thing would come back to haunt me. I knew it. All I can think of is that Felix had better have destroyed it or gotten rid of it or done something to make it go away. It cannot be traced back to us, or else this is going to be monumentally life-ruining.

EXPOSE RIDER OR I'LL TELL THE POLICE THAT YOU KILLED HER

I shove the phone back into my pocket, unwilling to play a part in Iris' sick little game.

Shifting my attention back to my friends, I take a seat on the floor and cross my legs. Marcus, Wade, Tayen, and Finley are sitting around me in a wonky circle, talking about something in hushed tones that immediately stop the moment I enter the room.

"Don't stop on my account," I say. If they were talking about me, they need to work on their ability to do without tipping me off.

Everyone exchanges looks.

"Is someone going to fill me in?" I ask.

"Well..." Finley starts. *"Theo asked me out on another date."*

I groan. *"Of course he did."*

"See? That's why I didn't want to say anyth—"

"As much as I love talking about Theo, can we focus on Iris?" I ask, exasperated. Lately, I've hardly been sleeping. When I do manage to sleep for a few hours, I dream of death and pain and the looming danger hiding around shadowy corners. Any less sleep and I'd be a barely-functional zombie.

There's too much at risk here.

With only twenty-four hours on the clock, we're running out of time to catch our killer.

To catch Iris.

At my left, Tayen rests her hand on my knee and I take a deep breath.

"Wade, please tell me you were able to break into Iris's email account," I say.

"Yeah, I ran an algorithm to crack the password and it finished up this morning." They flash a confident smirk. *"I think we've got our nail in the coffin."*

Wade is sitting on the floor to my right, computer in their lap, typing and clicking away until they eventually look back up and glance around at each of the faces in our cohort. There's a glint in Wade's eyes, full of excitement and mischief. Whatever they've found could finally get rid of the dark cloud that has been hanging over our heads since this all started.

"Ready?" Wade asks.

We all nod.

They begin to read through a thread of instant messages between Iris and someone else whose email is unc0d3d@gmail.com.

IRIS: They're getting closer to figuring it out

UNCOD3D: What makes you think that?

IRIS: Theo said they found my earring in Lennon's room.

UNCOD3D: Did he say anything about who they think did it?

IRIS: No, I don't think they know

UNCOD3D: What about the texts?

IRIS: He didn't ask me about the texts

IRIS: I think they suspect I sent them

UNCOD3D: Okay.

UNCOD3D: Don't make any sudden moves

UNCOD3D: They might be watching you

IRIS: Okay.

IRIS: Let's meet at Briarwood Park tomorrow night

IRIS: At ten by the gazebo

UNCOD3D: See you then

Wade stops reading and closes the laptop.

We all look around at one another, holding our collective breath as we let the reality of what we've just read sink in. We have undeniable proof, now. Iris is involved and she's not working alone.

"Alright, so we're definitely crashing their party, right?" Marcus asks, breaking the stillness that has settled amongst us.

"Definitely," Fin replies with a readied eagerness.

"Agreed, but first," I chime in, *"we need to figure out a plan for what we're going to do when we get there."*

Walking straight up to them in some kind of a-ha-we've-got-you-now moment isn't an option anywhere other than in an episode of *Scooby-Doo*. Considering we are in serious need of our own Mystery Machine, we're going to have to find another way to pull the mask off our mystery assailant and ensure they don't get away scot-free. The only question remaining is how to get them to admit their culpability and then turn around and use it against them.

And I was going to do it all without an ascot or a fiery sweater-skirt combo.

"The cameras," I sign to myself, looking down while I play a mental game of How Bad Could It Get with myself, contemplating every possible option and all the ways this could play out. *"The cameras!"* I repeat in

exclamation.

"Cameras?" Tayen asks, arching a brow.

Finley, forever on my wavelength, picks up what I'm putting down and her eyes widen as she points at me feverishly. *"The cameras!"* she echoes.

Seeing that Marcus and Tayen haven't caught up, I clarify. *"Like the one Fin put in Theo and Rider's suite. Her brother lent us a whole bunch of them, so we can set some up at the park."*

A brazen half-grin across Wade's face tells me they're in before their words do. *"All we need is a wireless hotspot and this laptop."* They tap the laptop sitting in front of them. *"I'll make sure the entire thing gets recorded in high definition."*

"Guess we need to get there early and set up those cameras, then," I add.

"Time to call for backup?" Fin asks, smirking devilishly.

As I nod, she pulls out her phone and begins excitedly typing out a message to call in reinforcements.

"So, what's the plan then, Lennon?" Tayen asks.

She's looking at me with a supportive smile and those yearning eyes and I hope she never stops. We haven't had much time to talk about what transpired between us the other morning—the way I kissed her as though my life depended on it, or about how badly I want it to happen again. The honeyed sweetness of her lips still lingers on mine. The residual warmth of her hands on my face hasn't yet faded, and even just the thought that it might threatens to splinter my heart into tinder and set it ablaze. There's a magical quality to Tayen I've never felt before, and I'm drawn to it like a moth to a flame.

Looking from one face to the next, I half-expect skepticism or apprehension but instead I find each of them gazing back at me, steadfast and determined. The tenderness of this moment, the lot of them looking to me for a game plan which might lead us to victory, tugs at my heartstrings. I wish there was some way for me to explain to them how much this means. Then, it hits me—they're part of this because they want to be, not because they need to be, and it sends a pang of guilt through my chest. They see this as a cause worth fighting for, regardless of what we're up against, but there are big risks involved. I couldn't save Bronya from her fate. If someone else got hurt over this, I'd never forgive myself.

Instead of dwelling, I managed a resolute smile and quick nod.

"Let's get ready to go to the park," I say.

It's seven o'clock and we're busy at work securing the cameras in each corner of the oversized gazebo at the park. Felix and Cameron have joined us, offering their muscle and extra sets of hands to get this done as quickly as possible so we can find a secluded spot to park and stake out the area. We have no idea which way they'll be facing or if we'll be able to capture the confessions we hope to collect, so Cameron suggests we mount multiple cameras at various viewpoints. The lights mounted around the underside of the wooden structure provide ample light, so we're not too worried.

This is all very Mission Impossible, and I'm Tom Cruising my little heart out.

Without the flying bullets and scaling of buildings, anyway.

"Do you mind handing me the screwdriver?" Cameron asks, balancing atop the highest rung of the stepladder we borrowed from my parents' house on our way to Briarwood Park.

Finley holds up three screwdrivers in one hand and asks, *"which one?"*

He points to a Phillips-head with a navy blue plastic handle and she passes it up to him before tossing the other two back into the open toolbox at her feet. Luckily, Cameron thought to bring the tools from their garage before meeting us at the park. Points to their father for being a handyman and an amateur mechanic when he's home.

As I stand on the opposite side of the large gazebo with Felix, working on the final camera installation, Marcus sits at a nearby table connecting each of them to my laptop and using his phone as a mobile hotspot. Wade and Tayen are back at campus, stuck in a late class, but they promised they'd meet up with us with plenty of time to spare. We've only got one shot at this, and if we're going to make it count, we have to be prepared for anything and everything to go wrong. Starting with our number one suspect alerting his partner that their meet-up was going to be interrupted and taken over.

"Hey, Len," Felix says, bringing the back of his hand against my arm.

I turn toward him, waiting expectantly with raised brows.

"I know I should probably make a point of saying this more often, but..." he starts, wiping his hands along the bottom of his tattered Queen t-shirt. *"I'm proud of you."*

He signs it without speaking, and now it's my turn to be the proud one.

He's finally hearing what I'm saying—actually fucking listening to me—instead of just letting it float in one ear and out the other. I've noticed the recent efforts he's made to at least meet me halfway and attempt to sign as many words as he could manage. I'm sure there's added pressure with Cameron here, since Cam can keep up with our conversations without skipping a beat. There's a symbiosis to having a group of people who can so easily communicate with each other without language barriers, and it's something I never encounter at home. The more time he spends around my friends, the more I think Felix is picking up on that.

Contrary to the way he says it, this isn't the first time he's told me he's proud of me. Not that he goes around randomly bragging and bursting at the seams with pride, but he's not some stoic hardass who refuses to show emotion. As far as older brothers go, Felix has been a pretty great one. Even when he doesn't want to be, I appreciate his willingness to be there for me no matter what kind of trouble I get myself into.

"I know. Thanks, Felix," I respond, without uttering a singular English word.

Felix reaches an arm around me and squeezes me in a sideways hug, clapping his hand against my arm before pulling away.

"Okay, I think we're ready to go," he says to me, signing the words he can, before turning to look back toward Cameron and Finley. "Cam, you guys all set?" he shouts, to which Cameron responds with a thumbs up before climbing down the stepladder and looking up at the work they've done.

"Yeah, I think we're good," Cameron signs.

Finley and I grin as we lock eyes.

"Now all we have to do is wait for them to show up," I conclude.

It's nine thirty-five when Tayen's car pulls up beside us. It looks like she's followed instructions to turn off the headlights as she slows to a crawl, creeping the long way around the back of the park. Our vehicles are luckily both black, indistinguishable from the shadows at this time of night, and we're tucked behind heavily dense trees and shrubbery which will keep us out of sight while we wait in the dark for our suspects to show up. On the dimmest setting, I keep my phone tucked down to minimize the luminosity of my screen.

Everything good to go?

Yeah, I think so.

How are you feeling?

Nervous, honestly

That's fair.

You know you don't have to leave the car, right?

If you don't want to, I mean.

I'm not going to let you face them alone, Lennon

I won't be alone.

You know what I mean

Yeah, I know.

But you don't have to do it.

Let me protect you, okay?

only if you let me protect you, too

As I look up, the faint highlights of Tayen's face reflect in the blackness of the night. There's so much more I want to say to her, but doing it through text is not how I imagine it to go. I close my eyes for a moment, unable to shake the fear she'll walk away, that nothing she feels for me is actually real. After all, it wouldn't be the first time I was fooled when it came to someone else's intentions. Maybe I'm letting the person behind the text messages get in my head, but those mocking words still haven't left my mind since I'd first read them. What if she really does leave once this is all over?

Yeah, yeah, okay.

Did class go alright for you and Wade?

Wade wasn't in class, they said they'd be skipping to join you guys.

Are they not here?

No

What the hell? Where are they?

We're crowded five-deep inside my Civic, the only light a minimal glow from my laptop in Marcus' lap.

All ten of our eyes are glued to the screen, waiting for movement inside the gazebo. It's been since we finished setting up, only a few squirrels and a rogue bird crossing the paths of our cameras.

I look up in time to catch the digital clock on my dash change from nine fifty-nine to ten, and my spine stiffens. Pointing at the clock, I look at each of the dimly lit faces staring back at me in the dark. It's surreal, knowing we're so close to a life-changing moment but not knowing which way the scales are going to tip. Will it end in the justice we all deserve? Or will our voices be drowned out by the ones looking to beat us, sending us back to square one with nothing?

A hand squeezes my shoulder and I turn to look back from my spot in the driver's seat. I can make out the outline of Felix's reassuring features. I feel tapping against my other arm, and Finley is pointing frantically at the laptop screen. Iris is caught on our cameras walking up to the gazebo with her hands in the pockets of her thick knit cardigan. She looks around briefly then takes a seat on top of one of the bench-style picnic tables, arms pulled toward herself to keep in her warmth as she pulls out a phone. The video resolution isn't clear enough to be able to see what she's typing, or to whom she might be sending a message, but we'll find out soon enough.

Our mystery guest is on the way.

"Okay, let's go now," I say, hurriedly.

We climb out of the cars and stealthily move from our concealed spot up to backtrack along the edge of the park so we won't be seen. I shine the dim screen of my phone onto my hands to make sure everyone is paying attention to what I'm about to say.

"Don't turn on any flashlights until we have Iris cornered at the gazebo. Then we can light up the whole place." I say.

EIGHT DAYS AFTER THE MURDER

Everyone's silhouettes nod affirmatively.

Felix, Marcus, and Cameron are our designated brawn—willing to literally get their hands dirty if the moment arises—so they split off from Tayen, Finley, and I as we creep through the brush and stagger behind trees to stay out of sight. Once we're close enough, we dash up toward the exterior of the gazebo while ducking down and spreading out. Surrounding Iris, we move in and space out with lit flashlights in hand, pointed upward to bounce the light against the ceiling of the pavilion. We close ranks around them as their heads swivel, taking in the situation we've cooked up for them.

We ran out of flashlights, so in my hand I hold an electric camping lantern. Iris is visible in the center of our group, but her features are distorted and tenebrous.

She looks around, searching for some sort of exit strategy of which we have assured there are none.

No one is leaving until I say they can.

For once, I'm in control.

"Who were you expecting, Iris?" I ask, keeping a tight grasp on my lantern in case it needs to pull double duty as a weapon.

There is a pause, and for a moment I suspect she's toying with us again. Refusing to play by our rules because we turned everything around on her.

This is not the Iris Whitlock I know—that I once knew, anyway. The light inside her has been extinguished, the put-together façade dropping as she begins to laugh. Her arms cross over her chest and there's a bitter anger at the back of my throat. Throbbing rage builds up behind my forehead, waiting to be released. When had her once-innocent nature been stripped away and replaced with the hellish shell of the person now standing in front of me?

"Lennon," she says, a wickedness marring her features as a crooked smile sits angled on her face. *"I was expecting you, of course."*

That can't be possible.

"You knew we'd show up and foil your plan, huh?" I ask.

"Oh, no," Iris retorts, like it's a simple addition

problem that I can't work out. *"This was the plan."*

"What are you talking about?"

Iris looks through me as hands grab me from behind. They're swift and practiced, wrapping across me and bringing a blade up to my throat. The cold metal edge touches me and holds steady against the skin of my neck. I look down to find a familiar set of rings on the hand clutching the handle of the knife.

"Wade?" I ask, in disemboweling disbelief.

Wade doesn't say a word, their hands kept busy at my throat with the knife.

No one moves, as my friends watch on, realizing we hadn't prepared for this. Their faces are filled with abject horror.

Felix tries to jump into action but Cameron holds him back, shaking his head.

"I wouldn't do that if I were you," Iris warns, after Wade tips her off.

"Wade has been helping you?" I ask, hands shaking as they form the signs.

"Helping me? They've done more than help me," Iris sneers, looking briefly at Wade before settling her gaze back onto me. *"They've been my partner."* She chuckles. *"Guess which one of us took your roommate out of the equation?"*

I'm lost in this space between understanding and not.

The idea that Wade would be helping her is baffling, and the fact that she's puppet-mastering this whole scheme with them the entire time is turning my world inside out. Wade is my friend, they've been helping us get to the bottom of all of this since day one. How could they have been playing us for fools without a second fucking thought?

Finley takes a step forward and Iris holds out an open palm. *"Stay right where you are. Any of you move, and I'll have my darling stepsibling slice Lennon's cute little throat wide open."*

Oh my god.

Her mom's new husband—the one that brought her the sibling and the yappy dog.

Holy shit, how did I miss this?

Did Wade help her kill Bronya?

My mind is racing a million miles an hour and I'm struggling to catch up. Rummaging through the filing cabinets of my mind, I'm frantically sorting through snippets of memories for any inkling of a clue that Wade was part of this all along. Some kind of hint as to why they'd be involved in this and targeting us when we never even knew them before a few weeks ago. Wait...

The instant messages that Wade found in Iris' email.

"You're unc0d3d, aren't you?" I ask, looking up at Wade as best I can without moving too much.

The pieces start fitting together in my head, one after another in rapid succession, and I couldn't slow it down even if I wanted to.

"Bingo! Gold star for you." Iris waves her hands in jeering applause. *"Took you long enough to figure it out, didn't it? I thought you would've been quicker than that,"* she snorts. *"You were always the smart one, after all. Maybe you're losing your edge."*

The eldritch grin on Iris's face makes me want to lurch forward and shake her by the shoulders, but I restrain myself with every ounce of willpower I have. I'm not letting anyone stand in the way of getting the answers we've spent the last few weeks searching for.

"What the hell was the point of all this?" I ask incredulously, the anger in my tone palpable and heavy as my hands move swiftly and forcefully through the air.

"You know exactly what the point was, Lennon," Iris replies, eyes glaring darkly at me. Her tone is cold and harsh, sending a chill straight through me like a vibration. *"You, more than anyone else in the world, know what I went through when Kim left. Then you left, and after what Rider did, I—"* She takes a deep breath to steady herself, that haunting smile back in place once more. *"You're responsible for what happened—to me, to Kim, to Tayen,"* Iris continued. *"You didn't say anything after what he did to you. None of you did. But you were the first. If you had

just spoken up, put a stop to him—but no. You allowed him to keep going, to take advantage of so many others. You need to be responsible for the damage he caused."

"He did it to a lot of girls," Tayen interjects. *"Myself included, but that's not on Lennon."*

"Shut up!" Iris yells.

"Iris, you can't treat people like pawns to fulfill some bitter rage-fueled fantasy of retribution," I counter, attempting to infuse some sense into this before I completely lose my ability to hold back.

"Pawns?" She asks, as if I've insulted her with my insinuation. There's an unsettling, icy laugh that follows. *"You're not some innocent victim here, Lennon."* Iris turns her head to look at Tayen, who is standing to my left. *"Neither are you, princess,"* she says, staring daggers into her. Turning her attention back to me, Iris scoffs. *"Do you realize our conversation that night at Rider's party was the first time you've talked to me in almost two years? Even then, you barely acknowledged my existence."*

"I needed to walk away from all of it. I couldn't just pick and choose pieces of that old life to hold onto, not when it was eating me alive," I defend. *"It's complicated."*

She scoffs. *"So complicated that the only other time I've heard from you was when you asked me for coffee to talk about Theo?"*

I'd thought, sitting across from her in the coffee

shop, that she was happy and excited to catch up with me. That we could find a way back to our friendship and mend the damage that had been done. But that's completely gone now.

We ran in the same circles, had similar friends, spent practically every lunch hour together until everything fell apart after everyone started looking at me differently. Things had become a mess, and I'd distanced myself from everyone but Finley. It was my way of becoming a metaphorical Bubble Boy and shielding myself from everyone and everything that might further hurt me. I insulated myself. Avoided the parties, didn't sit with anyone else at lunch, and limited my exposure to the outside world. The only people I could trust were Fin and my parents, so that's who I hung out with for my last two years of high school.

"I wasn't punishing you, Iris, I was punishing myself. Do you not think I understand what you went through? It happened to me, too."

Maybe it had been selfish of me, cutting her off as I did the rest of them.

"Did you ever stop and think he'd do it again if he wasn't stopped?" Iris asks, wagering a chilling step towards me. *"You know what's so fucked up about you, Lennon? You're so self-absorbed you don't even realize when the people around you are hurting because of the choices you made."*

I don't say a word, but my heart is threatening to hurl itself straight out of my chest.

"We both know what happened between you and Rider," she continues. *"Everyone in school knew."*

It's not clear whether Theo's the one who told her or if she found out through the grapevine, but either way it means Rider gave out every last detail like Halloween candy.

"After what happened to you, you had the chance to show everyone the monster Rider really is, but you didn't." Iris ventures towards me again. *"Instead, you kept your mouth shut and let him do it again and again. To Tayen. To me. To Kimberly."*

There was no one from Stone Valley High who could forget Kimberly Shaw. She and Rider had dated during the spring semester of sophomore year. Back then, he still sort of resembled a person who cared about other people, but the somewhat kind piece of his personality had faded fast. Two months into his relationship with Kimberly, he'd been caught cheating on her. Kimberly had keyed his car after school that day, and he struck back by starting a vicious rumor about her abusing prescription pills. It wasn't true, but it was enough for her ultra-conservative parents to pull her out of school and dump her at a rehabilitation center in Utah. After she left, she never came back. The gossip mill at school spread the rumor she'd been sent to an all-girls boarding school after rehab, but her canceled phone number meant we'd never know for sure.

Kimberly had been Iris's best friend.

Her only friend, other than Finley and I.

It was no wonder she felt abandoned when I walked away.

But none of this makes what she's done okay.

"So you decided to one-up him and commit murder?" I spit back, bitterly.

"It was an accident!" Iris screams, face scrunching as she turns into a child in the midst of a tantrum. *"She wasn't supposed to be there!"* Her hands reach up to the sides of her head and squeeze, like it's pinned between the sides of a vise and causing agonizing pain. *"You screwed up my plan and you're the reason she's dead. All of this is your fault."*

Tayen keeps looking back at me, and I wish more than anything that I could console her. Hold her hand or simply tell her that everything will be fine. What's one more potential lie in the grand scheme of things, anyway.

As if she's forgotten the cherry on top, Iris adds one final note. *"Oh, right! I almost forgot, did you like the little present we left you? The least I could do was bring you a souvenir. You know, something to remember her by."*

The knife in my backseat.

Felix's fists are clenched at his sides and he's whispering something to Cam and Marcus but I can't hear it. All I see are lips moving in the dim light among hushed agreements and furtive nodding.

The weight of it all sinks heavily onto my chest, bullying me into letting it cave in. How easily it could've been any one of us—that it was almost Tayen who would've been gone forever. I knew what Rider did to her had happened after what happened to me, chronologically, but I've never thought about my role in the sequence of events leading up to this moment. I've never considered how my silence may have led to their suffering.

I harden myself and focus back on Iris. *"I can't change the past, Iris. I can't undo the damage he did to you, or Tayen, or anyone."* I make sure not to get hung up when I say Tayen's name, knowing damn well Iris and Wade will take advantage of any information I give them. *"And I'm damn sure not responsible for the choices he made. Him hurting you wasn't my fault."*

"Yes it is!" She argues, hands signing wide and loud. *"Your silence hung me out to dry. All you had to do was say something, anything, and the rest of us wouldn't have suffered. But you didn't care, did you? You always said you'd protect me, but the only person you've ever cared about is yourself."*

Now her anger makes sense.

It's pain that has enveloped her, not hatred.

"Fine. You want me to go to the police and tell them that Rider's a piece of shit? Give them every gory detail about what I went through? You got it. But first, you're telling me why you waited until now to do all of this. It's been two years, Iris! Why didn't you just go to the police yourself if you have the same evidence I do?"

Iris scoffs again and tucks a piece of her long mane behind her ear. *"Who's going to believe me when the rich boy's parents can pay off whoever they need to make it all go away? The only way they'd listen to me was if there were others, so they could establish a pattern."* Her jaw tenses. *"I needed you both in the same place at the same time, didn't I?"* Iris looks between Tayen and I, and I wonder if she's envisioning what we'd look like with sliced throats and broken faces. *"We needed all of you in the same place."*

I hate that I can understand where she's coming from. I was hearing her out right now because of what she'd put into motion, but the pain she's unleashing on the rest of us isn't going to fix the hurt she feels inside.

"You promised you'd always look out for me, Lennon. The night at the bonfire, you told me you'd protect me and make sure I'd be safe," Iris says. *"That you'd never leave."*

The bonfire was last year, right around the start of

my senior year.

That night is crystal clear in my head.

Iris was standing next to Theo and the rest of the friends I'd left behind. She looked upset, though I wasn't sure why, and stalked away down the beach. I followed after her, but she didn't seem to be all that happy to see me. We'd talked and she gave me the cold shoulder at first, but eventually warmed up and said she was hurt that I wasn't hanging out with them anymore. That she felt like I had ditched her. That was the moment I should've known something had changed in her. Looking back on the memory, it's easy to see. The coldness in her body language and the harshness of her words. Something was very wrong, but the Lennon of last year hadn't been looking closely enough—she just didn't want Iris to hate her anymore because she yearned to be absolved of the guilt she felt. It was selfish, pure and simple.

There was no way for me to know what was going to come after that conversation. The pain and the hurt Iris would endure, and the revenge it would lead her to seek against me. Against Tayen. Against Bronya. If I could've gone back in time, I would've kept my promise. I would've asked about what was upsetting her, what had led her to walk down the beach in the first place, why she'd seen my disappearance as ditching when she'd been just as guilty for not reaching out to me after I stopped coming around. The reason why wasn't exactly a secret, after all.

But, alas, memories are imperfect things.

Even this one, as seared into my mind as it is, isn't reliable. Details are blurry and messy, emotions getting in the way far more than we'd like to think. Despite the best of my intentions that night, Iris's recollection could be far different and lend itself to a much darker telling of what happened between us. Of the promise I'd made to protect her.

"And then you walked away," Iris says, nostrils flaring and brows creasing. *"You left me just like everyone else."*

Iris reaches into her pocket and pulls out a gun, small and sleek and crafted of a metal that shines blue in the artificial glow of our flashlights. She steps twice toward me and stops, staring into me as though she's plotting the path of the bullet she plans to launch into my chest.

Tayen's grip on my hand is like a vise, burning with a white-hot rage that matches my own. Or maybe that's my flesh sizzling at the thought of going down like this, at the hands of a girl who'd been my friend long before she became my tormentor.

A girl who turned her anger out onto the world and set it ablaze.

EIGHT DAYS AFTER THE MURDER

Iris stands before me, her expression expectant, waiting for some acknowledgment of the broken promise and the failure she has laid at my feet. I hesitate to break the silence, fingers itching and twitching at my side— but I'd rather pause than equivocate. As I size up Iris, it's obvious she isn't looking to leave here without me answering for the suffering she's long held me responsible for.

The gun in her hands is unwavering, pointed squarely at my chest.

"Nothing I could say is going to make you want to forgive me, Iris," I finally say.

"Forgive you?" she repeats, incredulously and with a bout of sinister laughter. *"Who said anything about forgiving you? This was never about absolving you of your*

sins, Lennon. *Quite the opposite, in fact. You think I'd plan all of this just so you could apologize?*"

I don't say a word.

"*I did this so you'd feel pain. My pain. The knowledge that nothing you do matters because someone else is making your choices for you. Controlling the fate of the worst thing to ever happen to you.*"

Everyone else fades into the background as Iris takes yet another step closer to me. A mere two feet is the only thing standing between us. Threatening to hammer through my chest, my heart pounds rhythmically and blood whooshes in my ears.

"*So why plant the knife in my backseat?*" I blurt out.

"*Finally!*" Iris exclaims, like she's been chomping at the bit to answer this particular question. "*I thought you were never going to ask.*"

"*If you wanted me arrested, you could've told the cops it was there,*" I say. "*Point them to my car where they'd find the knife and haul me off. But you didn't. You put it there just for me to find.*"

Flashing a Cheshire Cat grin, Iris nods. "*I did, indeed.*"

I caution a glance at Finley and then Felix, and both are unnervingly statuesque.

"*What good would you be to me behind bars?*" Iris asks.

A rhetorical question, I'm sure.

"That knife was what I like to call incentive," she adds.

"Incentive for what?" I ask, digging my brows into my eyeline.

"For you to play along," Iris replies, chillingly calm. She's tapped into her villain monologue now. *"Sure, you gave me plenty of ammunition the night of the party at Rider's house, but I could see you still weren't quite properly motivated. That is, until that detective brought you in for questioning about your roommate's... untimely demise."* Iris tilts her head, smiling as if recalling a pleasant memory. *"God, she was a screamer, wasn't she?"*

Felix lowers his eyes, disgust contorting his features and his hands forming into fists.

"Don't," I demand, biting back the ire foaming at the back of my mouth.

"Did I strike a nerve, Lennon?" Iris asks, mocking me. *"You weren't even friends with her. It's not like I killed her,"* she points at Finley, *"or him,"* she points at Marcus, *"or one of them."* She gestures around the rest of our circle at Felix, Cameron, and Tayen. *"In fact, I did you a favor. Now you can shack up with your little girlfriend."*

Flushing, my face burns from both embarrassment and fury.

"If you're expecting a thank you, you can kiss my ass," I say, my jaw clenched.

"A thank you?" Iris laughs. *"A thank you is the least of*

what I want."

"So then, what the fuck do you want?" Finley barks.

Iris turns her head to look back at Finley and then right back to me, ignoring the question.

"You're going to help me get revenge on Rider Abbot, Lennon," Iris says, though I'm not entirely sure whether she's trying to convince me or herself. *"And we're going to end this once and for all."*

I'd looked up the statistics on things like this, back when it first happened. I'd considered reporting Rider, but after realizing how few women were ever believed in situations like these—that they were often filed away in trash bins as 'he said/she said' debacles—I'd tabled the entire idea. I couldn't bear the thought of going to the police and reliving the trauma just to be laughed out of the station. There's dozens of men who get off scot-free without any repercussions, and if they do it becomes a slap on the wrist. There were so many instances of this happening to women like Cheryl Araujo, Emma Mannion, and Dyanie Bermeo. Countless women have been forced to bare their souls only to have the tables turned on them.

Iris's face goes dark—even more than before, which I didn't think was possible—and I notice how creepy her facial expressions can get when just the right button gets pushed. She points the gun at Tayen's chest and my heart drops.

"Iris, we can figure this out, okay? You don't need to hurt anyone else." I need to get her to step away from Tayen, to lower the gun before she does something else she can't take back. *"I have all of it—photos, texts, all the evidence you need to take Rider down. I even have a list of names of all the other girls he hurt. We can end this, right now. Please, just put down the gun."*

Before she can make a choice, a barrage of red and blue lights filter in through the trees and light up the entire park. A team of officers rush in with raised weapons, surrounding us where we stand. They're pointing their guns at us, and the campus police chief is ordering that Wade and Iris lower their weapons.

Iris is staring daggers into me, but obliges and drops her pistol onto the ground before raising her arms and holding them in the air. Wade, who's still holding me against their body, slowly removes the knife from my throat and tosses it aside before letting go of me and raising their hands above their head. The moment they no longer have their hands on me, it's like my legs have stopped working. I drop to my knees so hard I don't think they'll ever work again.

This was almost how it ended for me—staring down the barrel of Iris' gun and waiting for the inevitable flash of light as mine was extinguished. Lifting my eyes to meet Tayen's, I expect some sort of tell or hint that she's the one who tipped off the police. She knew Wade wasn't in class, so she must've figured out that they were double-crossing us.

I always knew she was the smartest of all of us.

Finley races to my side once they've handcuffed Iris and Wade. She hugs me tightly as the others join in, and I'm reminded of the night Bronya died when all I wanted was someone I could trust at my side.

My face buries into her shoulder, and I break down into a puddle of tears.

TWENTY-TWO DAYS AFTER THE MURDER

Sitting across from Wade, inches of bullet-proof glass between us, everything that led us here weighs heavily on my heart. I should hate them, like really fucking hate them, but they also saved my life. They're the reason I'm alive, able to sit across from them in this Department of Corrections visiting area and look into the eyes of someone I thought was my friend.

"It was all a lie, wasn't it?" I ask.

Wade hangs their head, one hand rubbing at their neck. It's no longer clad with rings or holding a knife. There's nothing sinister hiding behind their eyes anymore, either. For the first time, I see Wade for who they are.

"Not all of it," Wade admits. "That conversation we had in my room... that's when it all changed. You aren't who Iris convinced me you were."

I scoff, anger seething within me at the fact that they're trying to play the brainwash card.

"You don't have to believe me."

"Good, because I don't," I bite back.

Moving to stand, Wade flags me down.

"Wait!" They insist.

"What more could you possibly have to say? I'm not interested in listening to you blame Iris for everything."

"I'm the one who told the police about the rendezvous in the park." Wade's eyes lock onto mine. "After everything, I couldn't let Iris ruin both of your lives. The suffering she went through—what you both went through... it wasn't fair." Wade held up both of their hands. "I know I have no business talking about what's fair, but I didn't want you going down because of a grudge Iris was holding onto. Which is why I need to warn you."

Heartbeat speeding up, I'm about ready to slide right out of my chair.

"Warn me?" I crane my neck toward the glass.

Wade nods. "When Iris pulled me in... she wasn't working alone."

It's been two weeks since the night at the park.

The night I almost died and The Ghost was caught.

Since that night, there haven't been any more text messages. No more flyers with my private life plastered across them for everyone to see. No one sneaks into my room anymore while I'm fast asleep, taking pictures of me at my most vulnerable. No secret whisperings about death and murder in the back booths at The Brew. No threats. No fear. Nothing hangs over our heads as we wait for the next bad thing to happen. No more secrets getting out.

We're safe now.

Iris was arrested and charged with a laundry list of crimes, the foremost of which was Bronya's murder. Her lawyer is asserting that she's not-guilty for reasons of insanity, claiming that she wasn't in her right mind due to emotional and psychological trauma. She's headed to trial sometime soon, where she'll be tried as an adult and hopefully be locked away for a very, very long time.

As it turns out, Iris and Wade had really put in a lot of effort to make their scheme work. Bronya and I being roommates wasn't a coincidence, for one thing. It turns out Kimberly Shaw's mother is the Director of Housing and is in charge of all residence hall assignments in the housing office. Iris took advantage of her friendship with Kim—and Kim's undying hatred for Rider. Another victim of the same stupid, spoiled boy. It leaves me questioning just how many lives he has ruined—how many girls we still don't know about.

Visiting Wade was eye-opening. I'd learned that they'd not only turned themselves and Iris in, but also that Iris had another partner somewhere that we didn't know about. I wanted to believe that Wade told me for a reason, but if the events of the last few weeks have taught me anything it's that I can't trust them. They lied to me for weeks and I can't simply take their words at face value. Maybe one day I'll know the truth.

Speaking of, Rider's got plenty of his own problems these days, thanks to the truth.

I followed through on what I said to Iris about coming forward and reporting what happened between Rider and I. Told my whole story and, for the first time, I felt like I could actually breathe. Along with my and Tayen's testimony, another three victims have been uncovered. Not all of them have agreed to testify, but most have. There is substantial evidence showing that Rider's family paid off each of those five victims to keep them quiet, so that won't help his defense.

In light of all of that, Rider was arrested, charged, and is currently sitting in jail awaiting his court date. The judge assessed him as a flight risk because of his family's money and connections, which I personally find to be a hilarious turn of events, so he's currently being remanded without bail. I have a feeling he won't earn much of a sentence, as rich kids rarely do, but it still feels good to know that he's being held accountable for his part in what happened to Bronya and Iris. Even if he wasn't actually the one who killed her, what he did contributed to the psychotic break that led her to do what she did.

As for me and Tayen?

Things have never been better.

We're going out on our first official date this weekend, and the butterflies have made a permanent home in the pit of my stomach. I'd say I hope I never lose this feeling, but through all of this, I've realized if I want good things to happen to me, then I have to will them into being.

No more Lennon the Downer. For the foreseeable future, I'm spending my hopes on more adventures with my family, my best friends, and my girl by my side—because they're the ones that matter.

Before I forget, I guess I should add the other good news I've received in the wake of all of this: I received an email this morning from Emery Choi, the editor at The Courier. Y'know, the one I was pretty sure wanted to choke me out every time she saw me? In fact, I had myself entirely convinced I wasn't going to get the reporter position no matter how great my article had been. Something about the way she looked at me made me certain I'd lost my chance as soon as I'd nearly turned her into a hood ornament. Fortunately, as it turns out, I was wrong. You're looking—metaphorically—at the newest staff reporter of The Clerc Courier! I'll be kicking off my first week with the paper at the start of next month, and I can't wait to write a new story for myself.

The keys click under my fingers as I type, finally coming to a stop as I hit the final punctuation mark. The therapist I've started seeing in the wake of everything that's happened has been encouraging me to write down my thoughts, even if it's just for my eyes only. Originally, I'd thought it was a dumb idea, but the journalist in me decided it wasn't the worst thing in the world to get in some more practice writing articles about murderers and creepy college kids. So far, I have to admit, it's been cathartic. This was my latest post in my private online blog, which I've aptly titled 'The Clerc Chronicles'. A way for me to remind myself about the things in life which matter the most—both the memories and the people.

I close my laptop and rise from my chair, picking up my phone from atop the desk where I'd left it when I started writing. There's a message waiting for me.

I'M WATCHING YOU

I glance back at the sender, and it's from an unknown number.

ACKNOWLEDGEMENTS

This project was a labor of love that took several years to complete and publish. I waffled for a long time on exactly what I wanted to do with this book, but at the end of the day I am incredibly proud of it and I hope that you enjoyed the ride.

First and foremost, I have to thank my mom. She was the first person who saw the early pages of this work, back when it didn't have a name and the opening chapters were more poetic than plot-centric. Her support from the first page gave me confidence in my ability to complete this novel and share it with the world.

Second, the rest of my family deserves thanks for their endless support, as well. Michelle, I'll forever be proud to call myself your kid and to have you standing in my corner. My grandmother and my aunt both read early drafts of this work and were my ecstatic champions. My dad and my siblings were also integral to many conversations about this book and the work I was putting into it on a daily basis.

Thirdly, I'd like to thank my friends. You all know

who you are, but there are a few whom I shared bits and pieces with and whose feedback was crucial to the success of this work—as well as the close friends I made during my time at Gallaudet University that inspired parts of this novel. In no particular order, I'd like to thank Denisse Barria, Marlee Brambila, Ryan McCrary, Colleen (Hart) Firl, Jake Weidner, Cody Spruill, Jake Poole, Weston Broache, and Gail Brooks.

I also want to thank my writing community friends that I've made over the last two years and change that I've been working on this novel. My critique partner and longtime writing friend, Jessica Fowler, deserves a heap of thanks that I'll never adequately be able to bestow upon her—she's got a book coming out soon, as well, so please go check it out and give her work some love! My other writing partners and friends, who supported me through revisions and feedback and endless Discord conversations (also in no particular order) include Darelle Cowley, Sophia Plavalaguna, and Olivia Riesling. I couldn't have finished this without the help of each of you.

This work was a labor of love and I hope you found the same joy in it that I had in my soul when I wrote it. Every page is full of queer love, feminist rage, and glimpses into the lives of college students who view their deafness as an integral part of them, while not being all of who they are. I hope this work opens new eyes to the Deaf Community, encourages young adults entering college to embrace their differences, and shows that you can find family even at the most unexpected times.

Last, but most certainly not least, I want to thank my incredible partner, Giavanna. You've believed in me so much, at times even more than I believed in myself. Your faith in my work and unending encouragement mean the world to me. I love you so much, Geeg.

Thank you all for your support, and to all those who were part of this process but whose names didn't make it into these few final pages. To all of the readers who have traveled these pages with me, I am eternally grateful for every ounce of time and effort you have poured into this adventure with me. Know that I couldn't have done this without you.

Thank You For Your Support & Best Wishes,

J. D. Mills

SURVIVOR RESOURCES

If you, or someone you know, has been a survivor of sexual assault, sexual misconduct, or other related situation, there are resources out there that can help.

The National Sexual Assault Hotline
1.800.656.HOPE (4673)

The Rape, Abuse, & Incest National Network (RAINN)
https://www.rainn.org/get-help

The RAINN Database of State Laws
https://apps.rainn.org/policy/

National Sexual Violence Resource Center (NSVRC)
Visit https://www.nsvrc.org

NSRV's Directory of Organizations
https://www.nsvrc.org/organizations

RELIANCE's Directory of Local Programs
https://www.raliance.org/rape-crisis-centers/

Centers for Disease Control & Prevention (CDC)
https://www.cdc.gov/violenceprevention/sexualviolence/resources.html

ABOUT THE
AUTHOR

J. D. Mills is a Hard of Hearing, queer, Star Wars loving book nerd who currently resides in the Silver State. They graduated from Gallaudet University, '19 and G-'21, with a BA in Deaf Studies and an MA in International Development. They love all things horror and thriller, is a proud supporter of the #DeafShelf, and *SECRETS DON'T STAY BURIED* is their debut novel.

You can learn more about their work by visiting:
https://www.jdmillswrites.com/

* 9 7 9 8 9 9 9 1 6 6 6 7 4 9 *